SEVEN DIRTY SECRETS

PRAISE FOR NATALIE D. RICHARDS

"An intense psychological mystery. [This] novel has the feel of a high-stakes poker game in which every player has something to hide, and the cards are held until the very end."

—*Publishers Weekly* on *Six Months Later*

"A page-turning thriller that will keep readers guessing until the very end."

—School Library Journal on *Five Total Strangers*

"A twisty thrill ride that will leave you breathless."

—April Henry, *New York Times* bestselling author of *Girl, Stolen* on *Five Total Strangers*

"Full of drama and suspicion."

—*Kirkus Reviews* on *One Was Lost*

"A gripping whodunit with a challenging ethical dilemma at its center."

—*Publishers Weekly* on *Gone Too Far*

"Brimming with suspense and intrigue… A thrilling, romantic, all-around captivating read!"

—Megan Miranda, *New York Times* bestselling author of *All the Missing Girls* on *My Secret to Tell*

"*My Secret to Tell* is as addictive as it is unpredictable."

—Natasha Preston, #1 *New York Times* bestselling author of *The Cellar* and *The Lost* on *My Secret to Tell*

"A taut, compelling mystery and a compassionate realistic fiction novel all in one."

—*Kirkus Reviews* on *What You Hide*

SEVEN DIRTY SECRETS

ALSO BY NATALIE D. RICHARDS

Six Months Later

Gone Too Far

My Secret to Tell

One Was Lost

We All Fall Down

What You Hide

Five Total Strangers

SEVEN DIRTY SECRETS

NATALIE D. RICHARDS

Cover and internal design © 2021 by Sourcebooks
Cover design by Kerri Resnick
Cover images © Abigail Miles/Arcangel; Yurlick/Shutterstock
Internal design by Danielle McNaughton/Sourcebooks

Published by Sourcebooks Fire, an imprint of Sourcebooks
P.O. Box 4410, Naperville, Illinois 60567-4410
(630) 961-3900
sourcebooks.com

Library of Congress Cataloging-in-Publication data is on file with the publisher.

Printed and bound in the United States of America.
WOZ 10 9 8 7 6 5 4

For Ian, Adrienne, and Lydia.

How did I get so lucky to have

the three of you in my world?

SEVEN DIRTY SECRETS

I know seven secrets.

One caused the fall.

One did nothing.

One saw it all.

One didn't care.

One used their head.

One played the hero.

One was left for dead.

ONE

I WAKE WITH A DEAD MAN'S SCREAMS ECHOING IN MY ears, but that's nothing new. Declan has stalked my dreams for the last three hundred and sixty-three days. I know I earned those nightmares fair and square, but couldn't I have a break on my birthday?

I grab my phone and scan my unread texts—a smattering of happy birthdays and good wishes that make my stomach twist. I'm eighteen today, but this day is more than that now. I guess in some part, it belongs to Declan too.

I grab a pair of yoga pants and a buttery-soft T-shirt from Connor's high school physics club. Might not be much of a birthday, but I sure don't plan to spend all of it in the house. Inside the bathroom, I turn the water up as hot as I can stand it.

When I'm squeaky clean and smelling like a sugar cookie—thank you, Hope, for constantly passing along the pricey toiletries you don't like—I pull the shower curtain open and freeze.

There's a present on my bathroom sink.

A small white box with a green satin bow sits at the edge of the counter, near my toothbrush and clothes. My hair drips onto the tile floor, and goose bumps rise on my arms.

This was not here before. I search my memory, trying to revisit every moment of my shower. Did I hear anything? A door? Footsteps? No. If I'd heard anything I would have called out or looked. But I definitely did not put my clothes two inches from a gift box without noticing. Someone put this in here…while I was *showering*.

My parents gave me a card with forty bucks before they left yesterday, Bennett is already on the road, and Connor isn't big on wrapping and ribbons. So there's only one explanation for a mystery birthday gift appearing in my bathroom.

Hope.

I grin and quickly pull on my clothes and run a towel over my hair. No chance am I touching that box. My best friend Hope is the ultimate prankster. But while she's good at setting the elaborate traps, I'm good at sabotaging her efforts.

I grab a can of Connor's cheap shaving cream from under the sink and open the door a crack. I hear a lawn mower outside. The tick-tick-tick of the cat clock over our kitchen table. I don't buy the silence. Hope would wait until I open the box and scream at whatever creepy-ass thing she stuffed inside. Bugs maybe. I hate bugs.

Hearing nothing, I push the bathroom door wide and slip into the hall. The box of horrors stays exactly where it sits, thank you very much.

My toes stick to the laminate floor as I sneak into the empty living room and the kitchen table buried under piles of old mail and an assortment of bolts and parts from whatever car Dad worked on last. Hope must be waiting in my room with a shit-eating grin and a bag of Doritos. Or rice cakes—God forbid she eat anything a normal person would consider junk food. Either way, I've got her.

The only thing better than a perfectly executed prank is nailing the prankster before they get to enjoy your suffering. I enter my parents' bedroom in ninja mode, stepping over the pile of dirty jeans in front of the dresser and hopping onto their bed. The window beside it overlooks the driveway, so I can climb out, run to the street, and coat every single window of Hope's car in shaving cream while she waits and wonders why my shower is taking so long.

But when I push the curtain open and unlatch the window, I realize the car isn't there. Not on the street or in the driveway or anywhere else. A couple of kids play on the sidewalk. The guy with the lawn mower I heard is pushing it through the tiny patch of overgrown yard between his front stoop and our street.

I jump off the bed and check the other window to see farther down the block, but Hope's car isn't there either. She's not here.

"Weird," I say.

It's not like Hope to miss out on my reaction, and I'd know because we pull a lot of pranks. We live to stump each other with puzzles, mystery parties, and escape rooms, so we're always scheming a new gimmick or angle to our tricks. Her not being here has to be part of the prank.

I think.

Still, it's unusual. My hair drips onto the carpet. I press my toes onto a droplet that landed next to an old stain. Brownish, so maybe whiskey. Mom's wine stains always turn pink.

The air conditioner kicks off, and the silence is even heavier now. I walk back to the bathroom and brush out my hair, keeping an eye on the gift. I try to convince myself I do not see a black spindly spider leg poking out of the lid.

Or millipedes. I shudder. If Hope put millipedes in this box, I will kill her. I try to think of other possibilities, but I can't push out the idea of those walking-eyelashes nightmares that creep into our house every spring and fall.

I grab my phone from where I left it on the back of the sink and clear a missed call from an unknown number before I text her.

Me: Is it a bug thing? Because if it's a bug thing, I'm throwing it away.

Her response is immediate. Um. What?

Me: Look, you got me. Happy birthday to me. I'm as freaked as can be. But I'm not opening it.

Hope: Opening what?

I stare at my phone and then the box. My phone again. The shiny green bow. Can Hope even tie a bow? That girl is all thumbs. Another message buzzes in.

Hope: Cleo?

And then. Are you okay?

An icy tentacle slithers up my spine. I turn to face the open bathroom door. Suddenly, my house feels different. I hear a warning in the silence. I see a threat in the shadow that stretches across the hallway.

Someone was inside my house—inside my *bathroom*.

And I have no idea who.

TWO

I TEXT BENNETT FAST. DID YOU LEAVE ME A BIRTHDAY present?

Bennett: No. Sorry. I suck.

Another response buzzes in on my conversation with Hope.

Hope: What's going on?

Bennett: Am I in trouble?

I ignore Hope and text Bennett:

Me: No, not trouble. Unless you're pulling my leg and trying to keep my present a surprise.

Bennett: No. I could lie and say I have it all wrapped on my dresser, but I should tell you now, since it's our first birthday as a couple. I'm crap with presents.

Me: No big deal. Don't stress it. Seriously.

My phone buzzes with another message.

Hope: Did somebody leave you something?

Bennett: I do know what I'm getting you. So, points for that, right?

Me: Total points. This is weird though. Someone left me a box. Like a present.

Bennett: Did you open it? What is it? Maybe there's a card.

Hope: Hello?

Hope: Are you going to leave me hanging? What is it?

I narrow my eyes at Hope's text message. She's got some serious rapid-fire texting going on. Unusual. Unless she's desperate for my reaction to something. I frown at the message. It was her. It had to be her. If it wasn't, she wouldn't be going on with these quick, persistent texts. Also, if it wasn't her, then I have to face the reality that a complete stranger was in my house, and that's too scary to contemplate.

I text Bennett: Never mind. It's Hope. Wish me luck.

Bennett: Thoughts and prayers. I'll text you at the next stop.

I square my shoulders and put my phone down. Time to open the box.

It's fine. Completely fine. If it's millipedes, I will throw it into the bathtub...and light the house on fire on my way out.

I untie the ribbon from the box and tap it experimentally, jerking my fingers back. I don't hear anything moving. So not crickets or bees. I don't think those damn millipedes make noise though. I shrink back as far as I can from my own fingers as I gingerly pry off the lid. I jump away the second it's loose, but nothing moves.

No bugs.

I inch closer to the open box and spot a single slip of paper nestled on red velvet backing.

Find your partner in crime

And follow the clues.

No one else can know.

Happy hunting, birthday girl.

I run the tip of my finger along the slip of paper. It's cool. Smooth. There's nothing on the back.

My phone buzzes again, and when I check it, I see Hope's name. My *partner in crime*. I pull up the message.

Hope: Here with birthday goodies. You coming out? Or should I come in?

Five seconds later, I fling the front door open and storm into the yard, holding out the white box. Hope catches sight of me and looks up from the driver's seat of her car. Her pale ponytail is high and bone straight. Her thin lips purse as a furrow forms between her brows. She's holding a large iridescent gift bag with absurd amounts of tissue paper poking out of the top.

She pushes open the car door and steps out. "What's going on? You look upset."

"I'm freaked. So, tell me right now, is this you?" I wave the box.

Hope lifts her gift bag, and come to think of it, I can't ever remember receiving a wrapped present from her. It's always gift bags. She puts her other hand up in surrender. "This is your present from me."

"Look at my eyes," I say. "If this is one of your stunts, boo-yah you're the winner and now you need to tell me that it's just a prank and I can calm down."

Hope shakes her head slowly. "I swear to you."

And that's enough. Because Hope wouldn't look me in the eye and lie to me. She's the one person in my life I truly believe. Which means this box…

I shiver. "When I got out of the shower, this was sitting on the sink."

"On your bathroom sink?" She's already gathering the facts.

I nod, and stare at my house like I've never seen it. The cracked stoop. The faded plastic awnings providing a sliver of shade over the two front windows. It's small and white and a little ugly, but it's never been frightening to me. Now I can't stop staring at the dark windows. I can't stop wondering if someone is in there right now.

Watching us.

"Are you sure this wasn't here when you got in the shower? Your parents didn't leave it for you? Or Connor? It *is* your birthday, Cleo."

She waggles the bag again and I open it, pulling out a perfectly folded gray hoodie. The logo on the front is a human fingerprint with an Edmond Locard quote. "Every contact leaves a trace."

I hug her. "I love it. It's perfect. Thank you."

"I'm glad. Searching for gifts for a future forensic scientist leaves you open for some seriously creepy targeted ads. Now, let's get back to this mystery gift."

I show her the note, and a crease puckers the flesh between her brows.

"It was just sitting there," I say. "I pulled back the shower curtain and bam."

"It was left on the bathroom sink, correct?" Sometimes talking to Hope is like being interviewed.

"Yes. While I was *showering*." I shiver again, imagining it. Someone standing there. Listening to me. Watching me through the curtain. I shake my head to push the thought away. "I didn't hear a thing, no one was home, and the front door was still locked."

"What about Bennett?" she asks. "Would he know about the spare key?"

"I don't think so. Besides, he's driving his grandma on an antiquing excursion. He didn't do it."

"Connor?"

"No chance." Once upon a time, my birthday would have been a big deal to my brother. Last year he planned an entire whitewater rafting trip for me and my friends.

But with the way that turned out, I'm not expecting any grand birthday surprises this year.

"Are you sure? You two are close."

"We were close. Past tense." My throat feels suddenly thick. "After what happened in West Virginia…"

Hope nods and finishes for me. "I know it was awful, and I'm sure today is hard, but it still could be Connor. He knows you like a good mystery. Heck, everyone knows."

"I guess. Maybe I should check with him."

I text him to ask:

Me: Did you leave me a birthday present?

His response is what I expected.

Connor: Not me, but happy birthday. Have fun!

Is this the same brother who made me chocolate chip pancakes on my birthday when he was eight? The same guy who helped me when I couldn't write my sevens? He was my hero. And now…

I sigh and show the message to Hope, who looks at my house, worry falling over her features. "Any chance it's your parents?"

"Definitely not. They're on Dad's job site in Virginia. They left yesterday."

Dad works giant cranes, so he follows the work. He's out of town for months at a time. When we were little, that meant Mom was alone a lot with me and Connor. Now, she goes with him more often than not. For Connor's junior and senior years, it was kind of fun. Me and him against the world. But then Connor went to college. Other than the stint with Declan and the times my dad is in between contracts, I'm alone a lot.

Hope doesn't take her eyes from my house. "First things first. Tell me who you think would leave this in your bathroom while you're showering, because honestly, that feels…"

"Terrifying," I say. Hope doesn't argue.

My mind conjures images of fingers curling around my bathroom door frame. Then placing the gift—just so—on the edge of my sink. Who the hell would want to scare me like this, on my birthday of all days?

My mind supplies an easy answer—Declan. But Declan is long gone. I know that better than anyone.

"Do you have any neighbors who are overly friendly?" she asks. "Does anyone make you uncomfortable?"

I shrug, because that applies to lots of folks around here. This isn't the land of PTAs and picket fences. Break-ins and street fights are common, so most of us are a little on edge.

I follow Hope's gaze back to my house and try to imagine myself striding up the sidewalk and pulling the front door open. In the end, I can't shake the idea that someone is in there right now. Watching me through my own windows. Just waiting for me to come back inside.

Yeah, there's no way I'm going back in that house.

I pull out my phone and unlock the screen.

"Are you calling your parents?" Hope asks.

I laugh. My parents hardly ever answer their phones and are never helpful when they do.

"The police," I say. "I'm calling the police."

THREE

IT TAKES TWENTY MINUTES FOR SOMEONE TO SHOW UP. The officer who arrives is probably in his thirties with a close-cropped beard and deeply tan skin. He takes his time getting out of the car as Hope and I wait in the yard.

He approaches and extends a hand. "Hi, I'm Officer Ramirez. Is one of you Cleo?"

"That's me," I say.

"You called because someone was in your house?"

"I was in the shower and when I got out there was a gift on the sink. I thought it was her," I gesture at Hope, "but it's not. My parents are out of town, so I don't know who it could be."

He asks for the box and if he can come inside. He's super polite. Some cops aren't like this. They roll up with attitude dripping off them like the guy beating his wife next door is a terrible inconvenience to their day. But he's different.

"Was the door locked?" he asks.

"Definitely. I'm pretty paranoid about it."

"Smart thinking," he says, but when he examines the door, he shakes his head. "It doesn't look like the lock was tampered with. Is there a spare key?"

I show him the box taped to the wall behind the bushes. The key is inside, like always.

He shakes his head. "Keeping a spare isn't always a great idea."

"Yeah, but my brother lost his," I say. "He needs it when he comes around."

"Maybe try to get him a new copy."

We go inside and Officer Ramirez does a quick scan of what he can see from the front door. I wince at the general state of everything. My parents are complete slobs, and every time they leave town I have to spend a day sorting, scrubbing, and organizing before the house looks livable again. I haven't had time to do that yet, so there are piles of mail, empty water cups, a heap of shoes by the door. Everything in here makes me cringe. The kitchen, dining, and living rooms are on one half, with a wall and hallway behind them that lead to four small bedrooms. Our single bathroom sits at the end of the hall across from the closet that holds our washer and dryer.

Officer Ramirez checks the kitchen and dining room, using his flashlight to look under the table. He doesn't say a word about the stacks of crap, but I feel my cheeks burn as he looks around the cluttered table and the shelf in the corner crammed with cookbooks and extra rolls of paper towels and spray paint. Hope's house never looks like this. Her house has clean counters and gleaming floors, and it always smells faintly of lemon drops. I think I've been trying to re-create that kind of space since my first sleepover at Hope's.

"I'm sorry about the mess," I say. "I promise, my room is better."

He checks the windows in the living room and finds one unlocked, but it squeaks and gets stuck when it's about ten inches open. He dismisses that idea and locks it once it's shut.

"Are the bedrooms back that way?" he asks.

I gesture and then follow him into my parents' room, where he checks the window above their bed. "This one is unlatched."

"That was me." My cheeks are really burning now. "I was planning to put shaving cream on her windows because I thought *she* was playing a joke on me." I point at Hope.

"I am a prankster," Hope admits.

"I thought she gave me spiders in a box for my birthday."

"Okay," he says. "What made you think it *wasn't* a prank?"

"Uh, she told me she didn't do it."

He barely gives her a cursory glance before accepting that story. From her baby-blue sweatshirt to her white sneakers, Hope just looks wholesome. Especially next to me in a stained shirt and ratty yoga pants. Hope wants to structure programs that help people lead better lives. I want to analyze body fluid samples and gunpowder residue in a forensics lab when those people inevitably crack up and commit heinous crimes.

Officer Ramirez moves to my room, right next to my parents'.

It's barely large enough to hold my single bed, a nightstand, and a desk at the end. My dresser is crammed into the tiny closet, and there are storage cubes I found at a thrift store tacked to my wall.

But small or not, it is calm. Neat. My own tiny version of Hope's house. My things are tucked away in the cubes, socks in a basket in a larger one. Nail polish and makeup in a smaller one. My desk has my school-provided laptop and a coaster, and my nightstand holds a lamp and a clock.

Of course, Officer Ramirez focuses on the shelf of books above my bed. Mostly true crime and forensic science, with titles I definitely don't want a police officer associating with me. Like *Interpretation of Bloodstain Evidence at Crime Scenes* and *The Anatomy of Evil.*

"You're right," Officer Ramirez says, glancing under my bed and in my closet. "This is very tidy." My window is too small for any normal-sized person to fit through, so he doesn't bother. But he does nod at my bookshelf. "You have an interest in criminalistics?"

"I do." And then it hits me that it's not just an interest anymore. I have *plans*. I blurt out, "I'm actually going to Michigan State for forensic science."

He gives me a nod that feels approving and heads back to the hall, because it's time to look at the other rooms. My heart speeds up at the idea of opening Declan's door. I don't want to look inside that room. I don't even want to think about it—especially not now.

He stops at Connor's door and pushes it open. A mix of old coffee and boy soap fills the hallway. My brother usually stays with friends in an off-campus apartment now, but his room still smells the way the bathroom would smell after he showered. Officer Ramirez walks around framed academic awards and a book of legislative code. Despite the prestige of the room's accessories, it's an absolute pit, the floor a foot deep in heaps of shoes, papers, and discarded clothes. Connor had better grades than me and twice as many friends, but I don't even know if there's carpet underneath the mess on his floor.

Officer Ramirez doesn't seem moved. He ignores the crowd of empty water cups on his nightstand and toes away a pile of shoes to check the closet and bed. Then he closes the door and my stomach clenches tight when he turns to the last bedroom. Declan's room. Oh, God.

"Wait." My heart is in my throat now. I try to swallow it down, but it feels stuck there.

He turns to look at me, and his expression sharpens with interest. "Is something wrong?"

I breathe out hard. I don't know what to say. But I know the idea of him opening that door makes my stomach slosh miserably.

"Whose bedroom is this?" Officer Ramirez asks. The easygoing officer is gone now. I see the authority figure in him instead, the probing questions, the unflinching stare.

"Cleo?" he asks.

"It was her ex-boyfriend's room," Hope says. "Declan."

"Your boyfriend lived with you?" he asks me.

I don't even know what to say. I know this is weird. He wasn't my boyfriend when he moved in. He was just Connor's friend. A guy in a tough spot.

A liar.

"Cleo." Officer Ramirez's voice makes it clear he expects a response this time. "Is someone in the room now?" His hand drifts toward his gun, and my eyes go hot.

I'd be terrified of that hand drift if Connor was here. Connor wouldn't have even called the police. He'd remind me that as a white girl I better remember that his being a Black man in a poor-ass neighborhood makes calling the police dicey. But my brother isn't here, and I'm scared, and I just need to answer him.

"He was my brother's friend. He needed help. We got together after he'd been here a while."

"He's gone now." Hope's voice is tentative. I close my eyes because if I look at her, if I see all that compassion and goodness right now—I'll break to pieces.

"Gone?" Officer Ramirez asks.

I swallow hard. "Dead. He drowned on a rafting trip last year."

In two days, it will be exactly one year ago.

"I'm sorry," he says. "So he lived with you before that? In this room?"

I nod. "My mom and dad let him stay here when Connor asked. He had a…troubled home."

"That's very kind of them."

I shrug and fight the urge to scoff. I don't want to tell them that I know almost nothing about Declan's home life or family except that his parents were in rehab a lot. And I sure the hell don't want to explain that my parents only let him stay here because he paid rent.

"I'm sorry for your loss," Officer Ramirez says. My *loss*. Before I blurt out a wildly inappropriate laugh, he goes on. "Is it okay if I take a look? I'll be careful not to disturb anything."

No one goes in Declan's room. I know that sounds cheesy, but it's true. Maybe it just feels weird or tainted now. It has to be that, because I don't think Mom or Dad are that broken up about what happened to the kid who rented their room for a while. It's not like he had the place decked out with sentimental items, and most of it was gone before West Virginia, because he'd moved out when we broke up. We were supposed to be over.

And we were until I lost my mind and decided to hand out second chances.

"Cleo?" Hope asks.

Her soft question jars me back to the present and I nod. "Sure."

He opens the door and I hold my breath when he flips on the overhead light. I know every inch of this room. After Declan died, I stood in the doorway every night for two months, trying to find some evidence or clue that would explain why it all happened. Who he really was.

But there weren't answers in there then, and I don't see any now. There's a Corvette poster on the wall. The red pen by the desk lamp. The black sock balled under the left side of the bed. A bookshelf with a few unread paperbacks—probably not his. A corkboard, mostly empty and sporting tons of holes from pushpins.

Despite my dread, there's nothing here, and Officer Ramirez moves on. He checks the bathroom, the laundry room, and the back door. We gather in the living room again, and he scratches the back of his neck.

"Well, there are four unlocked windows in the house, so someone could have gotten inside," the officer says. "But I don't see any signs of forced entry or theft. Was there anything else in the box?"

"No. Just the note." It *is* just a note. And now that I look at it, in itself, it doesn't look overly threatening.

I don't like receiving any invitations while I'm naked behind a flimsy vinyl shower curtain, but maybe this isn't from a serial killer in waiting.

He reads it again and frowns. "Is it possible this is a family member or a friend? Someone who might think you'd like a mystery like this?"

I turn my head and meet Hope's eyes. We smirk.

"Yeah," I say. "There are plenty of people who know I like mysteries."

"Scavenger hunts, escape rooms, mystery parties," Hope adds. "All the dorky stuff. We've been obsessed since we were kids."

I shake my head. "She's right, but that's just us. Not our friends. Definitely not my family."

"But people know this—people who might want to pull a prank on you?"

Hope and I share another look. I consider it. Because Hope was right about what she said to the officer; we're fans of all things mystery. And we're the worst people on earth to watch a murder movie with because we always figure out who did it.

"I can't imagine who," I say, "but I can't be a hundred percent sure it's not someone I know."

Now that I'm thinking about it, there are a few people who'd get a kick out of pulling one over on me.

Bennett: my boyfriend of three months who definitely has a good enough sense of humor to plan some sort of ridiculous birthday scavenger hunt.

Valerie: the third leg of our friendship stool who's been a lot less in the picture since the nightmare at the river. She might try to pull a big to-do to get things back to normal. But she's also a competitive gymnast who literally spends five hours a day training.

Which leaves my brother Connor. We haven't been the same since the trip, but he's creative, brilliant, and an expert planner, so he could absolutely pull this off.

"Do you feel like you're in danger or that someone might want to hurt you?" Ramirez asks.

The roar of the river echoes in my memory, the taste of blood sharp and coppery in my mouth. But that was a long time ago. Declan is dead and gone, and he's not coming back.

"No," I say. "No one wants to hurt me."

Not anymore.

"It *could* be a birthday thing," Hope admits. "Her boyfriend is very clever."

"I'm sorry." I feel a little stupid now. Maybe I jumped to conclusions, not just because of where the box was left but because my birthday makes me think of Declan. And thoughts of Declan still scare me to death.

"I should have thought this through before I called," I say.

He gives me a somber look. "If there is a stranger in your home, you're in danger. Calling us is the only good option, okay?"

I nod and he hands me a card with the number to the police department. The nonemergency line, I guess. His name is handwritten in the lower right-hand corner. Officer Miguel Ramirez.

"Check it out with your friends," he says. "Maybe it's going to be a lot of fun and a great story, but if anything fishy or strange turns up or even if you have a bad feeling—give us a call."

We both thank him and watch through the living room window as he settles back into his car. He's probably radioing back to the station right now, telling them about the hysterical girls who freaked out over a little prank. Because that's what this is. It has to be. I sigh as he pulls out of the driveway.

"So, who are you thinking?" she asks. "Is Valerie a possibility?"

"Maybe," I say. "She used to make a big deal about birthdays, but isn't she busy?"

"Yeah, she trains a lot," Hope says. "But she always said she wanted to do something like this with us."

I shrug. "Feels more like Bennett, except he's with his grandma."

She frowns. "Jack's creative enough, but I don't see Jack even remembering your birthday."

"I'm going to go with no," I say with a laugh. I hadn't even considered him. Jack is Hope's on-again off-again boyfriend. Artist. Gorgeous. Sort of a jerk. They've been together for three years, interrupted by probably twelve breakups. Jack belongs in an industrial loft in New York, drinking weird tea and walking around barefoot in paint-stained jeans. Hope, on the other hand, looks like she stepped out of a Vineyard Vines catalog.

Weird couple. And he's definitely not a big fan of me. No way he's creeping around my bathroom.

"I'll text Valerie," Hope says. She pats her jeans and frowns. "Shoot, I'll be right back. I left my phone in the car."

The screen door bangs shut behind her, leaving me standing in the living room with the cat clock ticking. We've never even owned a cat. But then, Mom also owns some weird-ass little kid statues called Precious Moments. Ironically, we don't have those here either.

I pull out my phone to text Bennett, my eyes catching on the four open bedroom doors down the hallway. I linger on Declan's door, and think of him chasing me down this hallway. The screaming. The nail file. The blood.

I walk quickly to his door and pull it shut. And I close down all those memories too, because there is no point in looking back on any of that.

The front door opens, and Hope calls my name.

"What is it?"

"Someone is definitely playing a birthday game." Hope holds up a white box with a green satin ribbon. Exactly like the one I found in my bathroom. "I found this in my car."

She reads the card inside like a movie announcer.

Someone saw, someone knows.
At the Service Door, that's where it goes.
Near the deer water in the city's heart.
Isn't that where everything starts?

"Okay," I say, swallowing against my suddenly dry throat. "So that's it?"

Hope turns the card over and frowns. "No, there's something on the back."

"What does it say?"

"Whoever this is, they're good," she says, shaking her head. She gives me a mischievous smile and reads in that same announcer voice. "*You have until Monday at 2:00. Tick tock.*"

FOUR

49 HOURS LEFT

"THIS CLUE IS KIND OF CHEESY," HOPE SAYS. "CHEESY and Bennett are old friends, right?"

"Definitely. I'm going to call him and push him a little harder."

"It also sounds like every escape room competition we've ever done. They sell this kind of thing, you know."

"Scavenger hunts?"

"Yep. People will pay top dollar."

My laugh comes easy now that I'm no longer worried a psychopath is waiting in my closet. "No one's paying top dollar in my world," I say. "Trust me."

"Let's see if we can't figure this out. If I try Valerie, do you want to try Bennett?"

She starts firing off texts, and I try to call Bennett, who is still listed in my phone as Bennett Florida because he moved here from Florida to live with his grandma. He doesn't really talk about why, and I don't really ask. I'm a girl who can appreciate weird family things you don't want to discuss.

Bennett doesn't answer, so I fire him a text.

Me: Interested in more news on the creeper-in-my-bathroom birthday story?

Predictably, my phone rings.

"Hey," I say. "Are you in an antique mall?"

"I'm waiting for her to finish up in the gift shop of an Amish restaurant," he says.

"Wow. That's something."

"Well, it gives me time to hear all about whoever's sneaking into my girlfriend's shower."

"Technically, they only came into the bathroom, not the actual shower."

"Well, in that case I guess it's all good."

I laugh. There are three reasons I'm dating Bennett. One, he always makes me laugh. Two, he has great shoulders, and I have a thing for shoulders. And three, he doesn't drink or do drugs. Not ever.

I met Bennett on a bench beside the running path at Southland Park at the end of December. I was running preseason track drills. He was…well, brooding, I guess. The Southland running loop is only a mile, so when I'm training, I run it four or five times before I'm done for the day. Usually it's empty, but one day Bennett was just sitting there, not moving. Every single lap, he was still there, arms crossed, vacant expression, and a frequent shiver that told me he was miserably cold.

Finally, I asked him if he was okay, and he asked—point blank, no preamble or introduction or anything—if I had strong opinions about the merits of the Browns and Bengals football programs, because as a recent Florida transplant, he didn't want to choose wrong. I laughed and told him in Columbus the only team that matters is the Buckeyes, and he promptly made a joke about creepy guys on park benches who ask pretty women random football questions. The next day I asked him to take a walk with me. The day after that, he showed up in an OSU Buckeyes T-shirt. I asked him out immediately.

"So, tell me about this present," he says. "How worried should I be? On a scale from you-have-a-weird-friend to there's-a-serial-killer-in-your-neighborhood."

"I think we can rule out serial killer. The box had a note inviting me to a scavenger hunt."

"Hope. You said so yourself."

"It's not Hope."

I can almost hear him shake his head. "It's *obviously* Hope. You guys do crap like this all the time. You tell me her poker face is legendary."

"It's not her. She thinks it's Valerie. I think it's you."

"I wish," he says. "It's a cool idea."

I sigh. "Maybe it is Valerie."

"Does she ever actually leave the gym?"

"Sometimes to sleep, I think."

"You know her better," he says. "I've only met her a couple of times, but I always picture her hanging upside down from the uneven bars."

"Like a bat? I'll be sure to pass that along."

"Not concerned," he says. "She likes me."

"Everybody likes you." I wrinkle my nose. "I don't know about Valerie. We're not that close."

We were once, I think. But now every time I look at her, I think of her sitting by Aiden at the campfire in West Virginia. Her arm around his shaking shoulders. Her eyes watching all of us with suspicion.

"What about one of your mystery club people?" he asks.

I laugh. "What, a club consisting of me and Hope?"

"Why not?" he asks. "So, what do you think it's about?"

I think of the clue again. *Someone saw, someone knows.* Is that what it's about? The smell of the river. Mud under my nails. The tang of copper on my lips. I shiver and push the images away, forcing a jaunty tone.

"The point is to drive me slowly crazy trying to figure out who's behind it," I say. "You can see why I suspect you."

"I certainly can. Alas, I'm not this smart." There's a binging like a car door is opening. "I gotta go. But do me a favor."

"What's that?"

"Make sure it's someone you can trust before you go following a lunatic's step-by-step instructions. And if you ignore all of that because you're you—"

"Hey, now."

"Truth hurts and all," he says. "Just text me if some weird clues lead you into a dark forest at night. And for God's sake keep your phone charged. Don't be the person who dies because you can't make a phone call."

"I'll be smart. Remember, I actually am hot shit."

"I know," Bennett sighs. "The hottest."

I'm laughing when we disconnect, and everything feels lighter and better. Hope is waiting for me, perched on the arm of our ancient green sofa, chewing her lip and staring vacantly at her phone.

"I can't reach Valerie," she says. "Or Jack either."

"Read me the clue again," I say.

She pulls out the card and reads it again.

"The city's heart is maybe downtown, right?" I ask.

"Makes sense. Not sure what deer water is." She frowns. "I hope it doesn't mean deer pee."

"Is it the river?" I ask. My voice wobbles because I desperately, *desperately* want it to be something else.

I can still smell the damp and rot of the river in West Virginia. Sometimes at night, I can even still hear him scream.

"It *is* the river," Hope says, her face lit up even as my heart falls. "Do you remember that deer statue on the bridge?"

"The one we see at the art festival?"

"Yes, the one on two legs!"

I've always thought that thing was ridiculous. Deer probably cause eighty thousand car wrecks a year in Ohio, so it feels a little tongue in cheek. But this one is particularly over the top, leaning wistfully over the railing to gaze at the city.

"Good thought," I say, "but what about the service door? There are buildings everywhere."

She taps another search into her phone and after a few moments of browsing and reading, stretches three fingers toward me. "There are three of the statues, and two are installed near COSI. COSI has to have service doors."

COSI is our science museum, and it's cool, but I don't remember any weird metal deer lingering about. That said, if Hope says they're there, they're there. She doesn't make mistakes when it comes to research. I grab her keys off the coffee table and toss them to her. She catches them automatically.

We're halfway to the car when I hear the rumble of a motorcycle. I feel a chill roll up my back as I pause, the passenger door to Hope's car half open. A black motorcycle pulls up the driveway, and then off into the grass so it won't block us in.

The driver guns the engine a few times before shutting it off. He's not wearing a helmet, and his hair is a mess of dark curls. His chin has a dimple, and his dark eyes crinkle at the corners just like mine. And when he smiles at us it's like looking at my own reflection. A scruffy, male, Black version of my reflection.

"Connor," I say, and it hits me that this is the first time I've seen him in a month.

"Hey. Happy birthday."

I thank him, feeling awkward. Out of the corner of my eye I notice Hope has rotated toward him, her whole body suddenly tensed and alert. A soft expression falls over her face when Connor meets her eyes. I don't understand the look they exchange, but it feels like a static charge.

Hope twists her hands and launches into a chattery explanation of the clue we received, the scavenger hunt in general, and our theories on who might be behind it. She seems kind of jumpy and nervous, but if I think about it, Hope's been like that around Connor for a while.

If it wasn't Hope, it wouldn't surprise me. Most of the girls I went to school with were jittery around Connor. Two years older and definitely not hurting in the looks department, my brother gets more than his share of attention. Plus he was a solid running back, in the NHS, and blah, blah, blah. It's ever-so-much fun being his younger sister.

Unlike Hope, Connor is not twitchy. He is still and attentive. Maybe *too* attentive. His eyes follow the swing of her ponytail, and a muscle in his jaw jumps when she crosses her arms.

She finally finishes her scavenger hunt recap, and her cheeks go faintly pink. "So, how have you been?"

Her tone is School Office Hope, prim and professional. But the way she's standing… I don't know. She looks like she wants to step toward him. Am I imagining this?

"Not bad," he answers her. "Busy. It's the season. I've got exams coming up."

"Are you still working at Greenscapes?" I ask, noticing he is wearing one of the battered landscaping shirts I remember from last year.

He looks at me, and the shields go up. "No. I've got an internship with the state prosecutor."

"You got the internship," Hope says.

Connor lights up. Just absolutely blooms. "Yeah, I did."

My heart cracks seeing him like this. Happy. How long has it been since he looked happy around me?

"I knew it." Hope beams. "I told you you'd get it."

"I know, I know," he says. "Thank you."

"Wow, the state prosecutor? That's really cool." And really unexpected. I knew absolutely zero about this. But Hope did, which makes me feel like I'm living in the Twilight Zone. Did they become buddies and I somehow missed it?

Connor notices my confusion. "Yeah, Hope helped me out. I ran into her at Starbucks, and she agreed to take a look at my application essay."

"I didn't even know," I say, though that last part makes sense. Hope is a writing tutor and editor of the school paper.

He shrugs. "Didn't figure it would matter. Didn't really think I had a shot."

"I did," Hope says softly.

"Well, congratulations. Not that I'm surprised," I say, and I mean it. Unlike me, Connor did not have trouble landing college offers and merit awards galore. With a 3.9 unweighted GPA, a 33 on his ACT, and proven athletic talent, it seemed like half the colleges in the state were offering him something.

"Thanks," he says, but he has that same guarded look he's worn around me for a year. "So, what are you two going to do next?"

I shrug. "Check the deer statue on the river downtown. See if we can figure it out."

"Right. Cool." He lingers by the side of the car, stretching his arms high overhead in a yawn. I'm one million percent sure this yawn is just an excuse to make sure Hope gets a look at his abs. Ugh, I love him, but he's kind of gross. He nods at her. "You going with?"

Hope turns the color of a tomato. "I think so."

It occurs to me that Connor has just shown up out of nowhere. With no explanation. And he's mighty interested in this scavenger hunt.

"Did you leave the gift on my sink?" I ask. "Is this you?"

"What?" He laughs.

I narrow my eyes. "Don't mess with me."

"I don't have time to plan a little birthday parade for you, Cleo."

His cool expression stings like a slap. Because he *did* plan a birthday parade for me once. I was eight. He was ten. Mom had gotten me a doll even though I hated dolls, but Connor had made my birthday amazing. He lined up every stuffed animal we owned, creating an elaborate parade route through our living room.

Once upon a time, Nana called us two peas in a pod. We used to pretend we were twins, which is a little ridiculous. Our mom is white and his dad is Black, but we still look related. Same expressions. Same dimpled chin and long fingers. Even when we got over the twins phase, we were inseparable.

But everything between us changed when he found me in the woods in West Virginia. He told me to breathe and washed the blood and filth from my hands. Connor took care of me that day, but he never asked me how Declan ended up in that river. Not once.

Looking at him now, a terrible thought prickles in my mind.

Maybe he didn't ask because he already knew.

FIVE

49 HOURS LEFT

I SWALLOW DOWN THE LUMP OF GUILT IN MY THROAT, AND refocus on our scavenger hunt. Which brings me right back to the suspicious timing of Connor's visit.

"So, why are you here?" I ask him.

"Clothes." He toes a giant crack in our driveway instead of looking at me.

Probably because he knows I wouldn't buy that line of shit if someone printed it in a textbook. Connor is not here for clothes. First off, Connor barely wears clothes. Or shirts, anyway. He's always pulling them off, doing that ridiculous I'm-not-flexing-flex in front of girls. And when he does decide to wear a shirt, he pulls it out of the pool of wrinkled cast-offs carpeting his bedroom floor.

In contrast, Hope is the kind of girl who plans her outfits for the week on Sunday. Her sneakers look brand new for a *year*.

Nothing's going to happen between the two of them, even if they are making weird googly eyes at each other.

"Well, wish us luck figuring this out," I say, trying to get us on our way.

"You don't need luck, you'll solve it," he says.

Hope looks up at him through her lashes, and they exchange a breathy goodbye. Last year, I thought maybe there was something going on with them, but after West Virginia, our whole group fell apart. I haven't seen them together since. Ugh. It's all a bit weird. When I was little, I used to tell Connor I'd make him marry one of my friends because he was so handsome. And he is.

But I was just young and stupid. I wouldn't let any of my friends marry into this family. Hell, I don't want to be in it myself. And I won't be. With this scholarship I'll be in Michigan, sitting on park benches and learning in beautiful brick buildings.

I'm *going* to get out of this place, just like Connor did.

Hope drives us downtown, and we don't say much on the way. I'm working out whether or not I should ask her about Connor.

She's pulling into a parking meter when I finally can't hold it in another minute. "You can't seriously think Connor is hot."

"What are you talking about?" she says, all mock outrage, but the spots of pink high in her cheeks tell me I am dead on the money.

I palm my face. "Oh my God, you do. When did this start? Was it last year? That New Year's party he picked us up from?"

"I was with Jack last year," she says.

"Please. You're on and off that roller coaster every ten minutes. It's like background noise to…well, apparently to this creepy attraction to my brother. Hope, you've seen Connor's room. Hot guys do not have rooms like that."

"It's not like that!" She looks down, and I can see that her grip on the steering wheel is tight, her knuckles pale and tense. I swallow hard, a new feeling forming in my gut. It's one thing for her to think my brother is cute, but is this more than a crush? Is this…a real thing?

"Did something actually happen between you two?" My voice is calmer. Quieter.

"Cleo, I really don't want to talk about this."

I feel faintly ill. "You don't want to talk about what?"

She doesn't say anything. Doesn't look at me. Scooters whiz past on the sidewalk. A horn honks. I let out a weird, stuttering laugh, but I don't say anything, and finally my silence gets to her because we don't have secrets.

At least, Hope doesn't.

"It isn't… Whatever it was, it's over," she says. "And trust me, it was barely anything to begin with."

"It *wasn't* barely anything, or you wouldn't be sitting here squirming like a weirdo. What happened? And why didn't you tell me?"

"We talked some," she says. "There was a single kiss. It happened once, so please calm down."

"Why couldn't you tell me? I thought we told each other

everything." Hypocrisy rings in every one of these words, but I squash it flat.

"This was different."

"Because you were making out with my brother? That's what makes it different?"

"There wasn't a good way to tell you."

"Why? Why couldn't you tell me?"

"Because it happened on the rafting trip." She looks down, her voice going very soft. "It happened right before..."

Before Declan drowned.

There is a special kind of quiet—still and heavy—that falls when there are no words left. But what would either of us add? Seven of us went on that trip, but only six came back. Not the kind of memory anyone wants to revisit, right?

Sometimes I wonder why I ever agreed to go. I'm terrified of water. Always have been. When Declan and I first started flirting, I took him to a pool party downtown. I just wanted to look cute in a bikini, but I don't swim—*can't* swim—and I had no intention of getting anywhere near the water. Declan tossed me in, like some of the guys were doing, and Hope and Valerie had to haul me out.

It was so humiliating. But somehow, six months later, Connor and Hope convinced me that a rafting trip would be different. That I might conquer my fear of water at last.

Didn't quite work out like that. Declan and Aiden spent the trip wasted, and Declan was such a belligerent nightmare that the river guide took us to shore and informed us we'd lost rafting privileges. Two days after my birthday, we were left to camp overnight and wait for a specially arranged pickup in the morning.

But Declan wouldn't get picked up.

He'd never make it home at all.

Someone saw, someone knows.

I shiver. My eyes drift to the river at the edge of the park, only barely visible here, a green-brown stripe, curved and manicured and perfectly controlled. Nothing like the river where Declan died.

But still…

"It's weird, right," I say softly. "That I got a scavenger hunt for my birthday. And it's bringing us back to a river. I mean, not the same river, but…"

Hope nods, but she seems lost in her own head. "Maybe it's about how bad your birthday was last year. Maybe this is an attempt to look toward the future." Then she smiles, and I can tell she's aiming to change the subject. "Speaking of the future, when are you supposed to get the official notice on that scholarship?"

The forensics scholarship—I still can't believe it's mine. As soon as I'd seen Organization of Women in Criminal Science on my phone screen, I knew. I just knew I'd gotten it.

Ever since my first college fair freshman year, I've desperately wanted the real college experience. I've spent an embarrassing number of hours virtually touring the Michigan State campus, imagining myself sitting on every bench, walking every path. My parents told me community college was just fine for a girl like me, but I wanted more. So, I applied for what felt like six hundred scholarships. I got turned down for all of them—except this one.

"It's all over but the background check," I say. "They said they should be finishing that up in the next couple of weeks and then…"

Hope's grin is almost as huge as mine. "And then you're off to Michigan State to fight crime and be a hero and all that."

"Well, yeah. As soon as the background check is clear."

"Well." Hope grins. "I guess you can be glad you didn't get caught back in eighth grade when you replaced all of Mr. Osborn's pencils with pink highlighters."

I laugh, and my phone buzzes in my lap, an unfamiliar number flashing on the screen. Probably spam. I hit ignore and follow Hope out of the car. It's a breezy spring day with cottony clouds marching across a cobalt sky and people zipping by on scooters and bikes. The Scioto Mile is a pristine stretch of winding bike paths and park benches overlooking the river. Today the water ripples under the bridge. The Columbus skyline, small but lovely, rises sharply on the horizon.

Hope and I jog to the first deer statue, waiting for someone to finish taking a picture before we approach.

"This seems like a risky place to leave a clue," I say. "It wouldn't last two seconds before some tourist stole it."

The tourists move on and we step forward, circling the statue like if we look hard enough, a white box with a green bow will miraculously appear. It doesn't. So, we jog across the bridge, toward COSI. It's a swooping, modern behemoth situated at the top of wide stairs that lead from the museum patio all the way down to the river walk.

The second deer statue is reclined in the grass, belly up and frankly a little disturbing in its repose. No gift there, so we move to the one on the stairs. We take a seat on either side of the buck who's seated overlooking the river.

There isn't another white box.

"Maybe we were wrong," Hope says, reading the clue again. "Maybe we solved it incorrectly. It could also be a joke and we're on a wild-goose chase."

"Maybe," I say. "Seems like a lot of trouble for what would be a pretty pathetic prank."

"True."

"Still, it feels off. Maybe this isn't the right place."

I stand up and start picking my way down to the path along the river again. Hope follows, shuffling a few steps behind me. I'm trying to feel my way to the solution, but Hope is all about the data analysis. She's back on her phone, looking for facts—analyzing possible solutions. But there's another element to things like this. Every puzzle or mystery has a theme. A tone. That's what I'm trying to determine.

I pause at the edge of the river sidewalk, staring at the opposite shore. Joggers move along the paths, and behind them, rolling green lawns slope up to Marconi Street. The Capitol is a couple of blocks from here, but most of Columbus's government buildings are on the other side of the street. Marconi marks the boundary between city buildings and the Scioto Mile.

I pause. *The Scioto Mile.*

"Hope, I don't think it's the statues. I think there's something about deer and the Scioto. I remember it from social studies."

After a brief pause and another search, Hope looks up from her phone, her eyes bright with excitement. "You're right. Scioto is derived from a Wyandot word for *deer*."

A frisson of excitement runs up my spine, and I nod across the river. "A lot of service doors on those buildings, I bet."

Hope's grin matches mine. "Let's go!"

She breaks into a jog toward the bridge and I follow, trying to match her pace. We slow as we approach Marconi, spotting the stone lions that stand sentry at the entrance to the police station.

"Should we check there?" Hope asks. "Maybe there's a service door? Or because the police protect and serve?"

"I don't know," I say. "I don't see anything." There are plenty of police cars out front and officers heading in and out, so I don't feel comfortable lurking around the steps. I can't imagine planting a clue here would be easy.

"Valerie just texted," Hope says, checking her phone. "She says we can stop over if we want."

I narrow my eyes as we walk back toward the car. "She invited us over?"

She shrugs. "She used to invite us all the time. We just haven't gone lately."

"Yeah, but she hasn't asked in…a while."

Cute the way we're phrasing it. Like it's been an indeterminate amount of time that had nothing to do with Declan drowning. Declan was Aiden's best friend and Aiden…didn't take it well. Frankly, neither of them did, which seemed weird for Valerie. As her brother's friend, she tolerated Declan, but she definitely wasn't inviting us out for double dates.

Not that he would have gone for it if she did. Declan didn't really do dates. Or most of the other things normal boyfriends are supposed to do.

But he sure did plenty of things they shouldn't.

We start walking again, checking the doors on the U.S. District Court. The riverside park sprawls out beside it, sporting plaques and memorials for reasons I couldn't list if you paid me. There's a service door on the side of the district court, so we check it out. A loading dock, a double door, and some nondescript landscaping but no box.

"Onward then," Hope says, calm and deliberate.

I plow my hands into my hair. "What are we missing? Nobody would expect us to check every service door along the Scioto River."

"I have no idea," Hope says. "If it's someone who didn't think it through, it's possible."

But whoever planned this *did* think it through. They waited until I was in the shower. Wrapped the clues with pretty green bows. They even timed putting Hope's clue in her car. This wasn't thrown together.

"Let's check city hall," Hope says. "That could be considered the city's heart, right?"

"Right," I say, but my body tenses, a wordless resistance stamped onto my bones. Declan kissed me there for the first time. It's hard to think of it now, how badly I'd wanted him to do it. How I'd looked at his scarred knuckles and hard eyes, my whole heart begging him to let me in.

Funny that five months later, I'd watch a river drag him away.

Someone saw. Someone knows.

Dread is building low in my stomach. I think I know where we'll find the next clue. I take the lead when we get there without explaining, but Hope doesn't seem to mind. She follows me up the stairs onto the plaza that overlooks the river. The door I'm thinking of is on the opposite side of the plaza, but I slow my pace near the metal tables and chairs that dot the terrace.

It's breezier here. Cooler. In the park, someone is throwing a Frisbee. Four red kayaks make their way down the middle of the river. I can almost feel myself back there with him. I wanted to kiss Declan so badly I couldn't even eat the Frosty we'd bought at Wendy's. I left it untouched beside the empty paper bag from the restaurant.

Declan held up my hands and laughed at my shaking fingers. My face caught fire, and I was sure my chest would cave in. But then he kissed me. His hands felt *so* gentle on my shoulders. It made it easy to ignore how cruel his laugh sounded.

I wish I hadn't ignored it though.

"You okay?" Hope asks.

"I'm good."

City hall is breathtaking. It's one of those old limestone constructions, made back when people cared about the way things looked, every inch carved and polished and just...beautiful. I spot the large door on the northwest corner, and my heart stutters as I read the word above it.

Hope gasps. "Service."

I nod, glad she's seen it and I don't have to squeeze my voice out of my too-tight throat. The seven letters are carved into the frame, a single-word nod to a government of and for the people: SERVICE.

I don't see a gift, but then I spot the crumpled Wendy's bag under a shrub beside the door. Images flash through my mind. A chickadee finding lost crumbs. My untouched Frosty, sweating on the table. Declan's ruthless laugh and gentle hands. The pieces of my memory coalesce into a single focal point—a crumpled fast-food bag.

I square my shoulders and reach for it.

"Cleo, don't!" Hope cringes. "You have no idea what's in that bag."

"Please. Have you seen my house? I'm impervious to filth." I'm forcing mirth into my tone, but I'm shaking. Something's in that bag. It's not heavy, but I can feel the bulk.

"Just be careful," she says.

I unroll the top, and there it is. My next breath catches. A box, slim and white and tied with a neat green bow sits inside. I pull it out, half triumphant, half terrified. The last clue told me someone was watching.

What will this one say?

"Well done," Hope says.

"Thank you."

"It still could have been a dismembered finger," she says.

"Wow, you took that to a dark place," I say, my voice still perky and bright. I don't want her to see that I'm scared. "That's usually my role."

I untie the ribbon carefully and pull out the thick white slip of paper inside. The note is typed, like the others.

Ninjas, birds, and towers
And some that take a fall.
If you don't win this hunt,
I swear I'll tell them all.

Tell them all? What the hell does that mean? My heart is racing, and I need to chill. This is stupid. No one was there—no one saw what I did.

They don't even know what he did to me.

Hope makes a scoffing sound and thrusts her phone underneath my nose.

"Okay, this is dumb, but did you text this picture to Jack?"

"What? I don't even know if I have Jack's number. Here, read this." I thrust the paper at her.

Hope rolls her eyes. "I thought so, but he's being dramatic."

I pull her phone closer and look at the picture she's referring to. The hairs on the back of my neck prickle. It's us—Connor, Declan, me, Jack, Hope, Valerie, and Aiden. We're surrounded by backpacks and rolled up sleeping bags. We are squashed together, wide smiles and squinty eyes, our arms flung around each other's necks, our cheeks flushed with excitement. Declan has me on his shoulders—I had argued about it, but he didn't listen, and I desperately wanted to avoid a fight. Hope has Jack on her left, but Connor close on her right side. And there's Aiden and Valerie, tucked on either side of Declan. Declan's got one arm around my leg and the other slung around Aiden's neck.

We look happy. We look like a good memory waiting to happen. Which is the opposite of what we were about to become.

Seeing the photo is weird enough, but it's been photo-shopped. Scrolling white font in the blue sky above our heads reads: SOMEONE WAS WATCHING.

Blood roars behind my ears. "Who sent this?" I ask, and I feel breathless and shaky. This can't be happening now unless it has something to do with the scavenger hunt.

"No idea," she says. "It's an unfamiliar number."

"Did they say anything?" I ask. "Was there a text?"

I look at the picture again. My eyes look away in the

photograph. I was right to be afraid, but now I'm afraid for a different reason. What is going on and who is doing it? Who was watching that day at the river? And what the hell do they want from me?

This picture showing up now, a year after Declan died, feels ominous at best. At worst it feels like a setup, and if it is, I'm the one who's going to take the fall.

Hope taps a quick message on her phone and a few seconds later looks up. "Valerie just got the same text. She said Aiden did too."

And then a text comes in from Connor. I ignore the all-too-familiar photo he sends and go straight to his text.

Connor: What the hell is this about?

The ground tilts beneath me, and I reach out to steady myself. I don't know what's happening here, but this isn't just a birthday gift.

This is blackmail.

SIX

47 HOURS LEFT

MY HEART CAN'T FIND A STEADY RHYTHM. I LOOK AT Hope, who's scanning her phone with a frown.

I'm going to have to tell her what I've hidden from her for all these months. Hope, who's never stolen so much as a pack of gum. Hope, who's never cheated on a math test. I don't know if she'll ever look me in the eye again.

"I have to talk to you," I say.

"What is it?" She's still focused on her phone.

"I need to talk to you about what happened in West Virginia."

Hope puts her phone away and looks at me, steady and true. "Cleo, I know what happened. It's okay."

I shake my head, feeling my knees go limp. "No, you don't. Not really. I didn't tell you the truth."

Hope's face goes very pale. "What do you mean?"

"I was there when Declan fell. I was—" I break off, my words chopping themselves into bits, my breath faltering around a rush of heat in my eyes and a sudden thickness in my throat. I'm going to cry. "We were fighting. It was bad. God, it was so bad, Hope."

"Slow down." She touches my arms, leads me to one of the metal chairs, and all but pushes me down. "Just breathe. Breathe."

I almost break down at those words, the same words Connor used by the river. My whole body is a shuddering mess. Tears spill down my cheeks, and I'm gasping for each breath. "We fought. Declan and me. He found me in the woods after I was walking with Valerie. He was angry—"

Hands around my throat. My knees hitting the ground. Blood on my tongue.

"It was awful." I'm sobbing now, choking out every word. "It was the worst fight. The worst—" I suck in a sharp breath and force the words out. "I was—he was in the water."

"He fell in."

I gulp in more air and my tears have left my vision smeary. I've said more than I want and not nearly enough, but I have to finish. Whatever fire pushed these words out is dying now. I am spent.

"No, we were fighting. It's my fault. I—he drowned because of me." I can't catch my breath through my sobs. "I saw and ran. I just left him, and they know."

"What do you mean?"

"Someone was watching. Look at the picture they sent everyone. Think about the clue."

Hope pulls a folded napkin out of her back pocket and hands it over. I blow my nose and feel my breathing hitch over and over.

"Cleo..." She touches my hand, her pale eyebrows pulled together. "No one saw anything or they would have said something. And even if they did see something, so what? You had every right to walk away. If he attacked you—"

A bitter laugh erupts from me, cutting her off.

I shake my head, but she squeezes my arm. "I'm serious. It isn't a crime to walk away. That river was dangerous, and you can't swim. Once he fell in, there was nothing you could do. You're not a criminal."

"It was more than that. And it doesn't even matter."

"Yes, it does. I can help you. If anything comes of it, we'll explain. It might not be pretty—"

"It will be more than not pretty." And then I freeze, because I suddenly realize what it *will* be. What it could cost. "Oh my God, Hope, this could ruin me."

"How?"

"Don't you remember why I got this scholarship? I wasn't the first choice!"

"I know they found something on the first person's background check," she says patiently. "But who knows what that is? They could have been charged with a felony."

"And so could I!" I argue, shaking the clue. "What if whoever is planning this does what they're threatening here and tells the police?"

"What is there to tell? You had to defend yourself. There's an explanation."

How can I blame her for digging in her heels like this? In Hope's world, explanations work. Teachers line up to listen to Hope. Adults trust her. Maybe it's some mystic combination of the right clothes and grades and zip code, or maybe it's just Hope. People instinctively believe her.

But that's not how it works in my world. If this comes out, no one will believe me until I prove it. And by then it will be too late. This scholarship will be someone else's.

"Look," I say, trying to explain. "Forget the police, what if they tell my school? Put it on social media! In a few days, this could be everywhere, right when they're looking at my background."

"Okay..." she says, and I can tell she's trying to formulate an argument, but it's not coming. Because deep down she's listening to me.

I clench and unclench my fists. "How many times have they warned us that we need to be careful about what's online because of college applications? How many horror stories have we heard of places like Harvard rescinding invitations because of insensitive jokes or threatening content? If I'm involved in the investigation of someone drowning—"

"I get it." Hope's face has gone perfectly white. She has the softest smattering of freckles on her cheeks, but now they are stark against the paleness of her skin. Her mouth thins, and she shifts but stays quiet. Because she knows I'm right.

This could destroy me.

"Every single day in that house I'm surrounded by his memory," I say, my voice thick. "I feel like he's haunting me. That scholarship is my one way out. A chance to start over."

"I know," she says.

I sag, my guilt now heavy and palpable in the light of my confession. Whatever Declan did to me, I had my own choices to make. Could I have chosen another way? A way that left him alive?

"Maybe I shouldn't have that," I say softly. "Maybe I shouldn't get the chance to start new."

"No." Hope is firm and clear. She pushes into my space, pulling an arm around my shoulders and squeezing me in a brief, tight hug. "Do not for one second pretend he didn't put you through hell. I saw you in that kitchen, Cleo. You could have…"

She doesn't finish and I don't either. I squeeze her back and try to push out another memory, one of pain exploding behind my eyes, my ears. My hair slick and sticky with blood. I don't want to think of any of these things. I don't want to go back.

"I don't know what to do," I confess.

Hope pauses for one moment. I can feel that she's a little shaky now and breathing faster. But she's still here and I am so grateful. When she drops her arms and squares her shoulders, I know she's made up her mind about something.

"We're going to finish it," she says.

"Finish it," I repeat.

"The scavenger hunt." She picks up the card. "The last part reads: *If you don't win this hunt, I swear I'll tell them all.* So that's what we have to do. We have to win it."

I shake my head. "I don't know what they want from me. I don't know where this will take us or if it's dangerous."

There's a long pause and I can see the resolution building in her expression. Her voice is low and deliberate when she speaks. "All that time with Declan I didn't do anything," she says, shaking her head. "I'm not leaving you alone in dangerous situations anymore."

"I don't know."

"Well it's a good thing I didn't ask." She bumps her shoulder into mine and smiles. "Besides, I don't think it's going be dangerous. What we do is up to you, but you know this is probably theater. That's what scavenger hunts are. Nobody would plan elaborate rhyming riddles if they just wanted to attack you in a dark alley."

It's a reasonable point. What's not clear is the goal. To scare me? To ruin me? To get something out of me? Whatever it is, I'm not ready to take the chance of having my name smeared through the mud and possibly losing my one shot out of my parents' house.

"I want to keep going," I say.

"Me too," she says. "We will win this thing. First things first, let's go see if we can figure out who's behind it. I think we need to talk to Valerie."

"You figure Valerie knows something?"

"I think Valerie might have planned it. Think about it."

It's not the craziest thing. Valerie has made elaborate plans in the past. She used to give us birthday gifts in hand-designed wrapping paper with origami bows. I remember a pirate-inspired Halloween party freshman year when she turned her entire backyard into a pirate ship. But…

"Valerie has barely talked to us since West Virginia."

"Exactly. I'm wondering if there might be a reason for that." Hope nods at me and we head back toward the car.

Valerie lives just north of me, but it's a better neighborhood. We lived on the same street when we were all little. Hope and her mom lived in a duplex two doors down from my house. Valerie, Aiden, and their parents lived across the street. Hope, me, and Valerie did sidewalk chalk and rode our bikes back and forth to each other's houses. Aiden mostly kept to himself, but sometimes Connor would teach him stuff. How to ride a bike. How to make us girls miserable.

When we were in the fourth grade, though, Hope's mom married Glen, and they moved to Bexley, five blocks over and a world away. Aiden and Valerie are still in the neighborhood, but in a bigger house on a safer street. None of that mattered to us though. We were always friends.

Until Declan drowned. He wasn't even part of us, but him dying… It was a baseball of a tragedy hitting the glass window of our circle of friends. We splintered to pieces.

When we pull up to the Drummond house on Oak Street, Hope and I tense, looking at the porch. She doesn't say anything, just sits there with some crappy alternative music playing on the radio and the engine humming softly. I chew my thumbnail and look out at the large porch with wicker furniture and a variety of advocacy flags lined down the door frame.

"We don't have to do this," Hope says, but then Valerie opens the door, waving energetically from behind the glass.

I give Hope a rueful grin and we get out.

Valerie is exactly what you'd expect out of a medal-winning gymnast. She's short and powerfully built with an explosion of auburn curls always knotted at the nape of her neck. In direct contrast to her broad shoulders and calloused hands is her face, which is pixie delicate—pointed chin, wide eyes, and a small mouth. She waves us in, scooping Hope into a hug. After the briefest pause, she hugs me too.

It's a tight, short squeeze that leaves me unsettled.

"Happy birthday, Cleo!"

"Thank you."

"I didn't get you anything, but maybe we can order sushi for lunch? My treat."

"No, no, I just ate," I lie. "It's just good to see you."

"It's been too long. How are you both? How are Jack and Bennett?"

"Fine, I think," Hope says. "Jack and I aren't together."

"Again?" Valerie asks.

I laugh and cover it with a cough when Hope glares. "Bennett's good."

Valerie moves us into the living room where we shift into our standard places on the wraparound couch. Valerie sits in the far corner. I perch on the edge nearest the door. And Hope sits in the exact center of a cushion one seat away from me.

Sunlight filters in through the large windows that overlook the porch, and Valerie tucks her legs underneath her, looking catlike. "So, tell me everything! What's this mystery gift Hope says you got?"

"We thought maybe you already knew about it," I say.

"Me?" Valerie looks perplexed, but that doesn't mean much. Valerie wears that look often, sometimes when she's genuinely clueless and sometimes when she'd really like you to think so. "No. But if I can get presents, I'm in."

We laugh, but it feels strained. Is it strained? Is she forcing all this chipper attitude?

God, I'm getting paranoid.

"I don't know if these are really gifts," I say. "It's a little weird. It feels like someone's messing with me."

"Who's messing with you?"

My heart clenches at the sound of Aiden's voice. It takes me right back to that night in West Virginia. Valerie sat beside him, and he was so wasted and hollow-eyed she practically had to hold him up while we waited for help to arrive. I've never seen a person look as lost as Aiden looked that night. Which is why I force myself to push every bit of warmth I can muster into my smile when I turn.

"Aiden." He looks at me and smiles back. He looks tired, but to be fair, he's looked tired since Declan drowned. "It's been a long time. How are you?"

"I'm okay." He pushes a hand through his hair. Dark with a reddish cast, like his sister's, but with softer waves instead of curls. He's always been pretty, with high cheekbones and the same angular face that's more striking than dainty on him. But Aiden is serious and a little sad, and I think he was half in love with my boyfriend.

"How's college?" Hope asks. "Are you working too?"

"School's good. I'm tutoring where Valerie teaches gymnastics," he says.

"That's great!" Hope says.

"So great!" I mirror.

The room goes quiet, and my phone buzzes in my pocket. I pull it out, but it's not a number I know. I reject the call and clear my throat. "So, do you like it?"

He shrugs, hair sliding into his hazel eyes. "It's cool."

"You're a great tutor," Hope says. "Remember when you helped Cleo in math?"

"You totally saved me," I say.

He tilts his head. "I think it was just once. You were just having trouble with polynomials, right?"

I nod and Hope and I look at each other, a silent agreement to ease up a few notches on the super supportive schtick. It's pretty clear we're laying it on too thick.

"Get this, Aiden, Cleo got a scavenger hunt for her birthday," Valerie says. "Only she doesn't know who it's from. I think it's the mystery person who sent us that photo."

For a second I'm confused, but then I remember. The photo of the seven of us. The one sent to everyone but me and Hope.

"Maybe," I say. "That part felt a little insensitive."

"I thought so too," Valerie says brightly. I can't read her. Does she think one of us sent the photo? Is she trying to say something I can't figure out?

I look at Hope, who looks equally confused. She holds up the clue box with a smile. "So, there are clues in each one."

Aiden's brow furrows and he leans back against the wall. "What does it say?"

I wave my hand, trying to look blasé about the whole thing. "Just a weird riddle. We have to solve it to find the location of the next clue."

"But you don't know who's behind it?" Aiden asks. "Isn't that a little disturbing?"

"Scavenger hunts always have a mysterious element," Hope says, and I'm grateful she's not giving away too much about the ties to West Virginia. "That's part of the fun."

"I think this one has us looking for a place with ninjas and birds. And someone taking a fall."

Valerie claps her hands and I'm sure she's going to confess, but she just bounces on her couch cushion. "Let's figure it out!"

Aiden takes the box, and before I can flinch or say or do anything, he lifts the lid and reads the whole clue out loud.

Ninjas, birds, and towers
And some that take a fall.
If you don't win this hunt,
I swear I'll tell them all.

Aiden looks at me and his eyes are suddenly clear and sharp. "Tell them what?"

I feel my mouth go dry. I stutter out a laugh, but it's like a movie with the sound running half a second off. "No idea."

I can't decipher Aiden's expression. And then he hands me back the box, and his face shutters.

"I don't understand the ninja thing," Hope says. "Maybe one of the trampoline parks?"

"They have ninja classes, but I don't think they have towers," I say.

"No birds either," Hope adds. "They're all inside, aren't they?"

"As far as I know."

"A costume shop?" Valerie tries.

I shake my head, still rattled by Aiden's reaction. "Too obscure. I don't even know where I'd find one in April."

"It's Audubon," Aiden says. He sounds absolutely certain. "The climbing wall at Audubon Park."

"Huh," I say, but I yank my phone out of my pocket, because

I don't want to look at him anymore. Or anyone for that matter. Because I think Aiden is right, and I don't know how he figured it out.

Chills race up my arms as memories from that climbing wall assail me. The red scratchy blanket we sat on. The stars shockingly bright so close to the city. I remember lying back watching Declan climb and fall over and over.

We swore it would always be our secret night. Only ours. No one should know about our trip to that climbing wall.

But someone does.

SEVEN

46 HOURS LEFT

FORTY FEET IS HIGHER THAN I THOUGHT.

Hope tilts her head, looking up at the wall. "Valerie said this was supposed to be an easy climb."

"Valerie spends five hours a day doing back handsprings on a two-by-four, so I don't trust her judgment."

Hope chews her lip and toes the weird, padded gravel covering the area beneath the climbing wall. "This feels cushioned, but the signs say you need a harness."

"That's because a lot of people fall. I bet if we sprayed it down with luminol, there'd be a sea of blood residue."

"Sometimes you scare me," Hope says. "Do you collect the hair out of my brushes?"

"I'll never tell." I grimace at the handholds, imagining all the sweaty palms that have gripped these bad boys. "It's kind of icky."

"We have sanitizer in the car."

She's right. And frankly, I'm stalling. I know damn well the clue is up here because this scavenger hunt isn't about winning a prize. It's about Declan and me.

I glance over at the grassy area nearby. The picnic was Declan's idea. Sneaking out of the house. Catching the bus and getting off just south of German Village. My heart was thumping that night, when we approached the barrier blocking the park driveway. I felt like any moment a helicopter would appear overhead, casting a spotlight on my criminal behavior. But Declan just took my hand and dragged me around the side of the gate.

It's as quiet now as it was that night. Thick, dark clouds have rolled in, pushing all the spring warmth away.

"Cleo, is that the box?"

I look up at where she's pointing, and my heart clenches. Of course. It's at the top of the highest section, wedged underneath one of the hardware loops. Declan climbed it that night. To be fair, he climbed the lower wall and walked along the top while I half laughed, half begged him to come down.

He fell from the top of the short wall once, and I rushed for him in terror. He was flushed with excitement, pupils blown wide as he reached for me. I thought he couldn't tell I was scared that night. Now I wonder if maybe he liked my fear.

"Okay, who would be able to climb this?" Hope asks. "Because whoever planned this hunt can climb a forty-foot wall *and* silently creep into your bathroom while you're showering."

Connor.

Bennett.

Valerie.

Declan.

The last name brings a wave of ice up the nape of my neck. It's stupid. Declan is gone. I know that; I saw the current drag him away. It's not him. Not possible.

But who else would know about the Wendy's I couldn't touch? Who else would bring me to this place, where we ate and laughed? Who would want to drag me back to the worst day of my life? I can only think of one person, no matter how impossible it seems.

"I don't know," I say, and I remind myself that there is currently one way to find out. I need to win this damn thing. "Let's think on it after I climb up this wall and get this stupid clue."

"I really think we should get a harness first," she says, brow furrowed. "Did you see the signs?"

They're hard to miss. CLIMB AT YOUR OWN RISK and HARNESSES REQUIRED FOR THE MIDDLE PANELS signs are prominently positioned to make it clear that what I'm about to do is definitely not okay.

Still, I shrug. "I'll be fine. No one's even here, and I *want* that clue."

She laughs. "Where was all this competitive spirit in cross-country?"

"Cross-country wasn't going to get me out of my house and

onto a beautiful campus." I force my mind back to my goal—the crisscrossing sidewalks and towering buildings. "I don't want to lose that scholarship. I already picked my favorite bench, you know."

"The one you showed me by the stairs?"

"That one," I say, feeling stronger. If I think about my future, if I think about what this could cost me, it will make me brave enough to keep going. I force some humor into my tone. "If I fall, I'm going to need you to switch your major so you can fulfill my forensic dreams."

"I'll just add a third. I'm already committed to economics and sociology. If I add a third, I'll work on economic strategies and trade training programs for disenfranchised women, *and* I'll spend my weekends as a freelance crime scene investigator."

"You were born for Vassar," I say, but it's no secret how proud I am. I think I screamed more than she did when she saw the decision online. "You probably *could* do a triple major."

"Not really." She shrugs. "I got lucky with Vassar."

"You worked your ass off. Luck had nothing to do with it. But let's hope luck is involved now so I don't die up here."

"Try to stay alive," she says.

"I'll do my best." Then I look up at the wall and clap my hands together. "It can't be any harder than climbing a tree, right?"

Twenty seconds later, I decide it's harder than climbing a tree. I make it ten feet up before I lose my grip and have to hang and drop back to the padded ground. I remember Declan sprawled out like me, his elbow bleeding and his laugh ringing out.

I shiver and try again, my sneakers slipping on the rounded nubs of the grips. I'd need suckers on my hands and feet to hold on to these things. Another fall. I land on my butt with an oomph. The picture of grace. The third attempt I make it almost twenty feet, and my arms are shaking when my foot slips. I hang, my legs pinwheeling like I'm a cartoon character.

"Cleo!"

I find a grip with one foot and then the other. I press my whole body flat against the climbing wall and close my eyes. Breathe in. Breathe out. The wind gusts, slithering around the nape of my neck. I turn my head, leaving my cheek flat to the lab-created sandstone. I'm fine. This is all fine.

"Are you okay?" she asks.

"Yeah. I just need a minute."

I slow my breathing and open my eyes. There are picnic tables and an empty parking lot. Behind that, the walking trail—a gray line curving along the river—holds a single, brave soul in a hooded sweatshirt. They're not moving.

I think they're watching me, or at least looking in this direction. I feel small and exposed clinging to this wall, struggling to move or breathe. I hope it's not a ranger watching me climb without a harness. Do rangers wear hoodies?

"Cleo?"

"I'm okay," I say, regrouping. I search for the box and find it, a sliver of white sticking out of the gray.

I can get there. I'm probably only ten feet from being able

to grab that box, and ten feet is not going to stand between me and Michigan State. I take a deep breath and climb. Right hand. Right foot. Left hand. Left foot. Right foot again, and I pause, searching for my balance. My hands are slick on the knobs. And the wind feels stronger—a sibilant rush of cold that makes my eyes water.

A raindrop splatters my forehead and arm and my chest goes tight. I look up, squinting at the thick layer of clouds overhead. It was sunny earlier, but Ohio's infamous for its weather tricks, and it definitely looks like rain.

I swallow hard. I'm barely hanging on to these perfectly dry grips. If they get wet, I'm in trouble. As if on cue, the rain falls harder, cold drops splashing in quick succession into my hair and jacket. I need to move.

I reach, my fingertips graze the edge of the white cardboard. The box shifts, a tendril of green ribbon unfurling. I reach again, stretching up on the balls of my feet. I pry the box loose, but it tumbles down toward Hope.

My toes lose grip. My foot slips, shoe squeaking in protest, and then my leg is dangling loose. Hope sucks in a sharp breath and I look down. She's right underneath me, hands at her throat, rain slicking her ponytail. She looks *so* far away. My head swims, and a terrible loop of nausea curls through my middle. If I fall right now, that padding will not help.

I should be harnessed on this wall. I am too far up and I am out of strength. Out of grip. My hands are slipping, my fingers cramped and aching. I drag my loose leg up and over and hold on as tightly as I can. My fingers are going to give. I need to get down.

Right now.

"Cleo, please…"

Please don't fall. That's the part she doesn't say. And there's real fear in her voice, because if I fall from here, some part of me will break. Probably lots of parts of me.

My foot finds a grip, but it's too far to the right. My legs are stretched too wide. I don't have much strength, but I have to descend. I move my stronger hand down and try to reposition my feet. I'm shaking. Every movement is a jolt to my joints and a fresh stab of fear through my veins.

I make it down another rung of the handholds, and take a second to breathe and rest my legs. I'm beginning to tremble, real panic setting in. I look across the jogging trail and spot the same person in the hoodie.

They still haven't moved.

The hairs on my arms stand up, and my body tenses. That person *is* watching me. They're just standing there staring. Every thump of my pulse is yelling one word. *Danger. Danger. Danger.* I have to get down. Right now.

But I am afraid to drag my eyes away from that dark figure.

"Are you stuck?"

Hope's voice jars me back to the present. I look to the holds. Remind myself to go. I am clumsy and stilted but I do it. My left shoe squeaks on the rubbery grip, my thumb snags on an awkward outcropping. I manage to descend another three feet and I'm okay. I've got this. I have it.

And then I fall.

My body bumps the wall twice, busting my lip and then—bam! I land hard. I let my joints crumple and flop gracelessly to my side on the padded ground. The side of my hand is scraped and bleeding. My blood's here too now, mingling with all the rest.

"Are you okay?"

I groan and test my ankles. Knees. Elbows. I taste old pennies, and for one second I am back by the river, my face in the dirt. Hands around my throat. My vision swimming.

No.

I force myself to my feet and brush off my legs with shaking hands.

"Are you okay?" Hope repeats.

I nod, panting to catch my breath, and I look to the path. I search for that person who was watching me, but they're gone.

Hope has the clue, and she hands it over. We run to the car, dripping and shivering. She turns on the defrost, and I pull the edge of the soggy ribbon to untie the bow. There's another note inside, but I don't read it. I barely see it. All I can see is the braided brown coil of leather underneath it. I pull it out, and my chest rises so sharply, I feel like I've swallowed balloons.

"What is that?" Hope asks.

"A bracelet," I say, barely getting the word out.

It could be coincidence. I bought it at a gift shop, it's not unique. It could belong to anyone. But none of those things convince me—none of them makes me forget tying the leather straps on Declan's wrist.

"Why is there a bracelet in there?" Hope asks. "Does it have something to do with the clue?"

I run my thumb along the leather braid like I'll find some tiny imperfection and remember—yes, this is it. This is the bracelet my boyfriend wore. But it can't be his. Declan's bracelet is at the bottom of a river. And this one was put in this box for one reason—to mess with my head.

"Do you see any connection?" she asks, reminding me I haven't answered.

"I don't know," I tell her. I don't know why I'm lying. Maybe because if I speak it, I'm afraid it will become true.

I read the clue, typed and sterile like the other three:

Don't tell another soul.
You know I'm watching you.
Past Bellows, Pierce, Demuth.
Find the starry dress that's blue.

My phone buzzes again in my pocket, the insistent rhythm of an incoming call. I pull it out, hoping it's Bennett, but it's not. I've seen this number before though. I check the details to see it's the same unfamiliar number from earlier. From a few earlier calls.

I frown. Whoever this is, they're getting mighty insistent about talking to me.

My finger hovers over the Block Caller option, but then the ringing stops and the voicemail icon appears. Six seconds long. I try to pull it up, but my phone buzzes again with an incoming text.

It's a photograph. A picture of Hope's car, taken from across a residential street. Hope has her keys in hand, and I'm getting out of the passenger side of the car. I spot the edge of a rainbow flag in the background, and I recognize the faded black sweatshirt I'm wearing right now.

"What is it?" Hope asks.

My voice is trapped in the fist-sized lump in my throat. I can't speak. I can barely hold the phone, I'm shaking so hard.

"Cleo, what is it?" she asks.

I turn the phone to show her what I've seen. It's a picture of us at Valerie's house. Someone took this picture today.

EIGHT

45 HOURS LEFT

I'M SHAKING AND COLD AND SO SCARED, I THINK I MIGHT be sick. No one I know would do this to me. No one except the monster who slammed me into walls. Threw me into my own kitchen cabinet. Choked me at the edge of the river. A terrible fear rises like smoke in my mind.

Did Declan somehow survive?

Unlike me, Hope seems strangely calm about this development.

"Are these towns? Bellows, Pierce, Demuth?" she asks. She uses a towel from the back seat to dry off her hair, then offers me one. She always keeps them in her car in case of mid-run downpours.

"Hope, there is a picture of us," I say, barely breathing. "That picture is from *today*."

Hope narrows her eyes at me. "Tell me what's the most clichéd thing that happens in an escape room?"

"Getting stuck in a small space," I say automatically, "or the lights going out."

"Right. The lights go out or the walls close in, and they do that because humans are naturally afraid of the dark and of being trapped. Half of the reason we have won so many of them is because we recognize the fear tactics."

She's right. Closed spaces. Darkness. Feeling like someone is watching you. They're all tactics that mystery game makers use. Is that what this is? Is it really just a game, however cruel? I cling to the idea, to Hope's unshakable trust in the logic.

"You think this is a fear tactic," I say.

"I'd bet money on it," she says. "Think about it. What would freak us out more?"

My dead boyfriend's bracelet showing up in a box. Of course, I don't tell her that. I want to believe her, so I nod.

"So, do you think those names are towns?" she asks.

"Bellows, Pierce, and Demuth? They're artists. Or at least Demuth and Pierce are, so I assume Bellows is too. They're all at the Columbus Museum of Art."

"How did you know?"

"My painting class in freshman year. Ms. Bishop was big on talking about artists we could see here," I say. And then, because my freshman art class isn't why I know we're headed to the art museum, I admit, "Declan and I went there too."

It's where I bought him a leather bracelet—just like the one I found in the box.

"So, we're going to the art museum," Hope says.

"I think so."

"Jack works in the gift shop, you know."

"I do," I say, "but Jack didn't do this."

"I know," she says, but her brow is puckered with worry. Who could blame her? Fear tactic or not, whoever set this up is following us around, making sure we see it through. And that's just the part Hope knows about.

Hope doesn't know the details. That the first clue was picked up where Declan and I kissed. And the last clue was where we had a secret late-night picnic. And this one is set in the art museum we visited.

"It's disturbing," Hope says quietly. "I mean someone taking pictures of us."

"Definitely disturbing," I say, and then I turn to her. "Hope, you don't have to do this."

"You don't either. Let me ask you something. Do you really think this will stop them from telling?"

"I honestly don't know," I admit. "But I don't know what choice I have."

"You could come to Vassar with me. I'll sneak you into classes."

"To Vassar?" I laugh. "Hope, that's practically an Ivy League school. They'd sniff me out in a minute."

"No, they wouldn't," she says, but she's wrong. I am not Vassar material. Not even close. Her application process was *intense.*

Competitive doesn't even begin to cover it. Which makes me think…

"Maybe you really *shouldn't* keep doing this with me," I say. "If even a whiff of this came back on you… If there was even an inkling on social media that you were involved, I'd never forgive myself."

There is a long pause when she stares at the rain collecting on the windshield and I stare at her soggy, but sleek ponytail. I pick at the chipped nail polish on my thumbnail and wait her out.

"No," she says quietly. And then again, with that classic Hope confidence. "No. They aren't doing this just to take you down. It's not logical to put in this much work if the point is just to cause you harm. I think it's possible they don't have anything but a suspicion, and they're hoping to stir the pot or get information."

"Maybe. Or given the creepy picture of us, maybe they're stalking me."

"Then we keep going and find out what we're up against."

"And what if they don't have anything?" I ask.

"Then we figure that out, and you don't spend the rest of your life wondering if this is going to surface someday. Either way, winning this is the best way to figure out who this is, what they want, and what we need to do."

I meet her eyes and see the same steady determination that got her to eighth fastest in the state in cross-country.

"Okay, we keep going," I say.

Before I know it, we're at the doors of the art museum. Hope tenses as we walk inside, but I don't do the dumb friend thing of asking if she's ready for this. That's the expected question to a friend who's about to see an ex, and I offered it up after the first couple of breakups in the never-ending saga of Hope and Jack.

For the record, I was good at it. Like morning talk show host good. I touched her arm and tilted my head and used that very gentle voice that is about as comfortable to me as chewing broken glass. By breakup three, it was pretty clear I was going to need a degree in psychology if I wanted to be of any help to their weird-ass relationship.

Instead, I have a few basic rules when it comes to them.

First, Hope is always prepared, so I'm only there to support whatever plan she's carrying out. Second, no matter how much drama there is, somehow Jack and Hope always end up back together. He's literally the boy next door, and the son of the worship leader of the Baptist church her mom visits now and then. They have next to nothing in common, but that's never mattered before. This isn't my first rodeo, and I know how they all end.

Still, I honestly cannot understand why she puts up with all the drama.

And then we turn the corner to the gift shop and I remember—she puts up with it because Jack is *gorgeous*.

I mean, look. I love Bennett. He's got killer shoulders and a beautiful smile and better hair than mine. But Jack? He's like a supermodel.

He's tall and lean with a square jaw, full lips, and warm brown skin that makes me think of islands and sunshine. And his eyes? His eyes are such a striking pale green that you'd think he wore contacts. He actually does, but Hope swears they aren't colored.

Jack isn't just hot or cute or even sexy. He's the kind of stunning that makes people stop midsentence to watch him walk past. He'd be perfect, except that he's an artsy snob and sort of a prick.

He's behind the gift shop counter now, folding a hideous scarf. He's in jeans and a Columbus Museum of Art T-shirt with a blue smudge of paint on the sleeve, but on him, it's haute couture fashion.

"Hey, Jack," Hope says.

He looks up, and then sees me. "Did she send it?"

"No. It's lovely to see you too," I mutter. He nods at me, either ignoring or completely missing the healthy layer of sarcasm floating over my words.

Lucky for Jack, Hope handles assholes like a pro. "Believe it or not, we're on a scavenger hunt. Tell me about the photo."

He shrugs. "There's nothing to tell. I don't know the number. I sent you a screen shot from the studio right when I got it."

Jack has a studio above his parents' garage. One foot inside and you'll forget you're in Bexley, because it is nothing but angsty music, modern art, and exposed brick.

Hope starts filling him in on the gifts and the birthday scavenger thing, and I am relieved beyond words when Bennett calls. I slip into a remote corner in the shop by a display of colorful rocks.

"Have I ever told you how glad I am you aren't Jack?" I ask in greeting.

"It would be unbearable to be with someone so attractive."

"So, how's the trip?" I ask.

"Meandering, but good," he says. I hear the faint murmur of voices behind him. It sounds busy.

"What exciting stops are next for you?"

"A yarn store, if you can believe that. How's your scavenger hunt going? Are you running from a creeper in the woods or anything?"

"No, but someone's taking pictures of us."

"Wait…what?" There's less humor in his tone now. More concern. "Pictures of you…"

"And Hope," I say with a sigh. "I think it's part of the atmosphere of it or whatever."

"Cleo, that's not cool," Bennett says. He sounds worried. "Do you think you're in some kind of danger? What is this about?"

"No, it's fine," I lie. I'm not about to visit the Ghost of Relationship Past with my new boyfriend who thinks I'm funny and smart and *normal*. And who might lose all of those good opinions if he learns the truth about me and Declan. God, is Bennett one more thing I stand to lose if I don't win this hunt?

"I think it's just somebody trying to mess with my head," I say. "It's a childish game."

"Then you're quitting?" he asks.

"No, I'm going to see it through. Can't have this jackass thinking I quit that easy."

"So much badass in such a little package," he says with a laugh. Then he makes a regretful sound. "I'm sorry, I have to go. But I promise I will be the properly doting boyfriend and you can tell me all about your badassery when I return."

Hope is still talking to Jack about the hunt when I hang up. It feels like a waste. Jack showed zero interest and even less talent in these kinds of things. We talked him into an escape room once—a double date with me and Bennett—and he spent the entire hour complaining about the room being too hot. Not his thing, to say the least.

But this could go on all day, so I interrupt. "Jack, do you have any paintings of a blue dress?" He wrinkles his brow, and I gesture vaguely toward the museum. "Or blue clothing?"

"There's the imperial dragon robe," he says. "It's in Textiles."

"Perfect! Thank you. I'm going to go look. You guys hang out." I start backing toward the entrance, my eyes catching on a display case of leather bracelets. It was the first thing Declan had really stopped to look at in the museum, and I immediately bought one for him. He didn't say much about it, but he wore it every day after.

Every day until he died.

I touch my pocket, where I stuffed the coiled loop of leather. It's just a bracelet. One of thousands that are floating around on random strangers' wrists.

I move on. The Columbus Museum of Art isn't very big. I didn't know that until the eighth grade, when our whole class went to Washington, DC, and I saw the Smithsonian art museums. I wasn't going to be able to go, but Hope's mom, Mrs. Deb, paid my way. CMOA is much smaller in comparison, but still, the light just *glows* in the galleries. And I love the way my footsteps sound on the wood floor.

I don't know much about art—the decor in our house consists of a few framed black and white landscape photos and a collection of cutesy cross-stitch circles with sayings like "Hang in There!" and "Be a One of a Kind!"—but I can get lost in some of these paintings. There are landscapes that look so real I can imagine the way the grass might tickle my feet. And there are abstract paintings that make me feel things I don't understand. I doubt any forensics in the world could explain art. Hope maybe could. That girl can explain anything.

I don't let myself get swept up this time, though. I walk through the halls and across the courtyard, down to the textiles area. The dragon robe is easy to find. Laid out beautifully in a well-lit case, it's definitely dress-like and undeniably blue. I can't imagine anything in here fitting the clue better, but I don't see a gift.

I check every inch of the room, careful to keep my respectful museum distance, before pulling the clue out of my pocket to reread it. I'm definitely looking for a blue dress, but this isn't the right one.

Fine. Fortunately, I am *not* at the Smithsonian. If I have to scour this place room by room, I can probably do it in an hour. How many blue dresses can exist in a Midwest art museum?

Actually? More than you'd think.

I've made my way through five galleries, and I've found four dresses, five if the grayish blue blob with a boob in the Picasso counts as a dress. You never know. Not that it matters, because I'm pretty sure a white gift box is going to look obvious around here.

For all I know the robe was the blue dress and some other museum visitor took the clue and now they're running around Columbus on my scavenger hunt. It's quiet though, maybe because most people don't realize the museum stays open late one Saturday a month. I saw a group of art students sketching near some of those old paintings of food that make no sense to me at all. And one old couple arguing over how to hold the map.

I turn a corner and move through two more galleries but find nothing. I get caught up staring at a textured piece on the wall. Out of the corner of my eye I spot someone in a dark sweatshirt heading away from me toward the stairs, but otherwise this whole area seems empty, unless you count the vacant-eyed security guard who looks utterly uninterested in my presence.

I check out a few more statues—nothing blue, and everyone is naked, so no dresses either—before slipping into the alcove near the stairs.

I freeze the second I'm inside. The room is dark and small with an enormous midnight-blue figure towering in the center of a platform. The only light in the room glows up the bottom of an umbrella-like skirt, then filters through small holes in the dress. Every dot seems to change the pinpricks of light, sending constellations traveling across the statue's skirt.

The whole dress is lit up like a starry night sky. And then I see the gift, tipped up on its side and tucked under the edge of the platform. My skin tingles at the sight. This couldn't have been here long. Someone would have taken it to the staff. Or just snatched it. This had to be left recently.

And then I remember the person in a sweatshirt walking up the stairs. A dark, hooded sweatshirt. I think of the lonely figure on the jogging trail—the one who watched me fall.

Is it the same person? Is that who's doing this to me?

My stomach jumps to my throat and I snag the box, bounding out of the room. I whirl toward the stairs, but there's no one in sight. I fly up the steps like a woman on fire. Nothing.

I rack my brain for details, but my mind is empty. Short, tall, male, female—my memory supplies absolutely nothing but a dark hoodie marching away. It is a good thing I'm interested in forensics and not detective work, because I'm not cut out for suspect identification.

I zip through a few more galleries, white box still in hand as I make my way back toward the gift shop. I could have been wrong. Spring in Ohio is a sea of dark hoodies, but something tells me this particular hoodie is the same. And the person wearing it is the person who planned this hunt.

I was only one second behind them. But one second is late enough.

I deflate after a while, leaning my back against an empty corridor wall. After a minute or two to sulk, I find stairs to the main floor and start climbing. I pause just before the top, spotting Hope's blond ponytail and the animated swing of her arms. She's talking to someone. Maybe arguing. I hear Jack's voice.

"You know why."

"I didn't say anything, Jack."

"Then what's this picture about?"

"Who knows," Hope says. "It could have something to do with the anniversary. Declan died a year ago, you know."

"How could I forget? Still think you're both crazy to go on some whacked-out scavenger hunt. You know it's got something to do with him."

"Do you know something?" Hope asks.

Jack just laughs. "Hell no. I barely knew Declan, but I'm going to go out on a limb and say he didn't keep good company. Maybe some old friend of his is pissed and wants revenge."

"What for?" she asks. "There isn't anything to avenge."

"Let's not pretend shit didn't go down in West Virginia."

My body goes cold, the hairs on the back of my arm standing up.

"We talked about this." Hope's voice is a steely hiss now. "All of us."

"You talked all of us into it, more like," he says. "But don't worry. I have my own business to worry about. I say you're the one who won't keep her mouth shut."

Hope sighs. "I don't tell her everything, you know."

I stiffen at the words, feeling my palm go damp on the white box. Am I the *her* in that sentence? I search my mind, coming up completely blank on anyone else that could fit the bill. Part of me wants to burst into the hall, to confront her right then and here, but I don't. I slip back down a few steps, my throat dry and heart beating fast.

I always thought I was the one who kept secrets.

Looks like I was wrong.

NINE

44 HOURS LEFT

WE'RE IN THE CAR, BOX ON MY LAP AND HOPE DRIVING down Broad Street, and I honestly don't know what to say. Do I start by telling her I did a little eavesdropping in the stairwell? Do I wait and ask Connor what the hell she might be talking about? Does it even matter? Because I know *exactly* how that trip ended.

"Read the clue again," she says, answering my question for me.

I blink, looking down at the clue on my lap.

You want the future, not the past,
But your dreams and lies are blind.
Look for an old capital neighbor,
A doctor's gift, a citizen's find.

"This is ridiculous," she says. "I don't know what any of that means. Dreams and lies could mean anything. And is the old capital neighbor an actual person?"

"I don't know," I admit, but I'm still distracted.

I turn the bracelet over and over in my fingers and watch her out of the corner of my eye. I don't know how to be strategic with Hope. She's my living, breathing sounding board—the place where all my zany ideas shake off their ridiculousness and land, stronger than they'd been in my head. She's steady, and that steadiness always brings me back to earth.

Except now she's something else. She's the girl who's hiding things from me. Connor. This thing with Jack. Something that went down that I don't know about. Then again, maybe I shouldn't go digging in the backyard for bones when I know damn well there's a Declan-shaped skeleton in my closet.

"So, what's up with you and Jack?" I ask.

She shrugs. "Nothing. The usual."

"You guys seemed sort of tense when I ran into you," I say.

I made a real production of barging in on their conversation. After I spotted them, I tiptoed back down the stairwell and then stomped back up, making a stage-worthy entrance. They both sprang apart like I'd caught them half naked.

"Well, Jack is Jack." Hope looks at me. "We're not back together, if that's what you're asking."

"Is something going on?" I ask. "He hasn't been around much."

"Who has?"

No one, that's who. Not since we stood around a campfire waiting for Search and Rescue teams to find Declan. Or not find him, as it turned out. They drained the dams, but it took a while, and they weren't sure it was fast enough. Sometimes, that's the thing that keeps me up at night, thinking of his body, rolling and churning. Knocked against rocks. Dragged under logs in the rapids.

Hope pulls up to a red light and looks over, her mouth pursed thoughtfully. "I don't get this one."

"Me either," I admit. "This clue makes zero sense."

"Okay, let's talk about what the first locations have in common," Hope says. "They're public."

"They're also significant to me and Declan," I say, feeling my neck go hot. "And I lied about that bracelet. I bought one just like it for him. All of this stuff is about us."

Her eyes narrow. "How many people know about that bracelet?"

"I'm not sure," I say. "But Monday is the anniversary of his death. That's my deadline, you know. For this hunt."

"I know," she says, turning into my neighborhood. "Do you think the deadline has something to do with school being out on Monday?"

I arch a brow. "I doubt our school's schedule factored into this hunt." And then I take a bracing breath, because the possibility skirting at the edges of my mind feels too ridiculous to name. But

I do it, all the same. "I know this sounds unhinged, but do you think there's any chance he survived? That he's coming back now to make me pay?"

Hope pulls into my driveway and turns off the ignition. I'm not sure what she's thinking.

"Declan could not have survived that river," she says plainly. Her conviction on this is absolute. "But even if he did, does this feel like his style? Declan didn't do subtle and clever. Can you think of any reason that this is the way he'd come after you? After a year of silence, no less."

Her argument is strong, but she waits for my rebuttal. I can't offer one, so I stay quiet. My ears hum with the sudden silence in the car. Hope doesn't look at me or ask me why I don't answer. She waits me out.

"He knew I loved scavenger hunts," I offer lamely.

"I don't remember Declan caring very much about the things you loved."

My eyes go hot. I think I might cry, and I don't know if it's shame or guilt or some mix of the two, but Hope must read my discomfort, because she sighs.

"I don't know what this person wants from you, but I'm pretty sure it isn't good. Anyone who wants justice for Declan's death is screwed up. He wasn't some helpless victim. He assaulted you. Multiple times."

"I know that."

"He should have gone to jail."

"Probably," I admit. "But did he deserve to die?"

"I don't think it matters what I think he deserved. He *did* die."

"Because of me," I say.

"You can't swim, Cleo. What were you going to do? Jump in and hope someone saved you both?"

"I didn't even try. I didn't even *tell* anyone," I say. "What does that make me?"

"Safe," she says sharply. And then she presses her thin lips together, composing herself. "It makes you safe."

It stuns me, and I take a breath to steady myself. I can't blame her for not caring that Declan died. Hope never expected to see him again, because that was the deal. When she drove me to the hospital with a wad of paper towels pressed to the back of my gashed-open head, she agreed to stay quiet.

As long as he stayed away for good.

But he didn't stay away, and that part is one hundred percent on me. Three weeks after Declan put me in the hospital, I bought his shit, dried his tears, and quietly added him to the rafting roster. Because he begged and cried and, God, why did I believe him? Why was I *that* girl?

"I'll never be able to tell you how sorry I am about bringing him on the trip," I say, "but I also don't think I'll ever forgive myself for being part of what happened to him. Do you understand?"

"I do understand. And I also understand that he put fourteen stitches in the back of your head, and, dead or alive, I'll never forgive him for that."

Our conversation grinds to a halt. Hope tells me it's getting late, which isn't really true, but she needs time. Maybe we both do. It isn't a fight—we don't really do fights. But we are both experts at quiet when we don't see eye to eye.

I head inside the house and toe off my shoes, tossing my house key on the counter. My eyes drag to the cabinet door I hit. The scar on the back of my head tingles. I force myself to turn away and head to the living room. But then I freeze, my eyes on a sliver of light pouring across the dark hallway.

The light is coming from Declan's open door.

The hairs on the back of my neck and arms prickle as I stare. Nothing is moving. There is no sound. I force myself to inch forward, because there has to be an explanation. Maybe I left the light on and the door open. Or maybe it was Connor when he was here.

Except it wasn't. I didn't turn the light on, and Connor wouldn't touch anything. He wouldn't even open the door. And I remember pulling it shut clear as day.

I stay perfectly still at the foot of the hallway, listening. It's as quiet as it was earlier when I found the gift on my sink. The cat clock in the kitchen. The chatter of kids on the street—older kids this time, but still someone with a lawn mower. Everything is the same as this morning. Except I'm not grinning and tiptoeing through the house looking for Hope now.

I'm trembling.

Stop. Just stop.

I clasp my hands, twisting my fingers to keep them still.

"Hello?" My voice is strange and startling in the quiet. But there is no answer. No noise. Just my own insanity that forces the next word out in a whisper. "Declan?"

It's just two syllables, but I feel sick. Sweat beads on my forehead. I have to calm down. Declan is not in this house. It is a light in a bedroom, nothing more.

Unless whoever broke into my house before is here again.

Unless Declan climbed back out of that river and is coming for me.

My body tenses. I'm on high alert, my focus narrowing on the rectangle of light on the hallway floor, yellow and motionless. I step into the kitchen and slowly slide a carving knife out of the block. I do not take my eyes from that spot of light. My heart thumps in my temples. In my fingertips.

I pull out my phone with my free hand, punch in 911, but I don't press Send. I need to be sure this time. So, I scan the room trying to channel every crime scene documentary I've ever watched. Every forensics textbook I've read. If someone was here, this whole building is a crime scene. There will be evidence, clues that will add up to the story of what's happening. I just need to look for them. And at the same time, I need to be ready for a maniac to burst out of any room.

My hand is slick with sweat on the handle of the knife, but I wait for long minutes, my ears straining for any change. Outside the lawn mower eventually stops, and then the silence is absolute.

Nothing moves. Nothing shifts. My father's backup work boots are still heaped near the door. Mom's sweatshirts bulge from the overstuffed coat closet. The same mess clutters every surface, cans and tools and books crowding the shelves. An empty Mountain Dew can sits on the kitchen counter, and the skin on my arms prickles. That's new.

But it's also probably Connor. Connor believes Mountain Dew is a food group. Plus, he's allergic to throwing things away.

I take a steadying breath and keep looking. There is no broken glass in the kitchen or the living room. The pillows on the couch are as I left them. The book I'd been reading is still on the coffee table, my place marked and waiting.

So, not much here, then.

I lick my dry lips and inch slowly down the hall, placing every step with care. I don't want to make a sound. Don't want to even breathe. The quiet feels heavy—thick like the sky when a summer storm is coming. I keep moving slowly until I can see inside the open door, and then the foot of Declan's old bed, the comforter still smooth.

No one is here. I would hear them now, I'm sure of it.

But someone *was* here. Someone who locked the door and covered their tracks, except for this one single light.

I square my shoulders. I push the door wide open in one big bang. No one jumps out. Nothing changes. The room appears, brightly lit and completely empty. I catalog everything slowly, making sure it's the same. The black sock. The poster on the wall. The books on the shelf. The red pen—

I stop, my skin turned to ice.

The red pen is not where it should be. I saw it when Officer Ramirez was here, and I would have noticed if it moved, because it has stayed exactly where it sat for a full year.

I step inside, moving swiftly to the desk. A fine film of dust covers the surface, except for a narrow clean line on the left side. The line where the pen sat before. A shudder rolls through me, and I resist the urge to whirl around. No one is behind me. No one is here at all. I would have seen or heard something by now.

But someone was here. I know this without a doubt. Whoever it is can get in and out as they please. I am not safe in this house.

Even though the thought freaks me out, I force myself back to procedural mode. A guiding principle of forensics is ruling out the obvious. Connor was definitely here at some point. He could have moved this pen. Unlikely or not, I have to rule it out.

I pull out my phone:

Me: Have you been in Declan's room?

There's no reply for ten seconds. Twenty. Thirty.

Me: Answer me.

Connor: Why would I go in there?

Me: Just answer me.

Connor: No. And it's not his damn room. He was there for seven months.

Me: Can you think of anybody who would?

Connor: Why?

Connor: What's up?

Connor: What the hell is going on?

I don't know how to explain the pen thing, especially over text, so I change course.

Me: The door was open and the light was on. I know I closed if after the police officer left.

Connor: Wait—what the hell are you talking about? You had a cop in the house?!

I wince, feeling bad. What if Connor had come home twenty minutes earlier when Officer Ramirez was still there? I feel sick at the thought.

Me: I'm sorry, I forgot to tell you. That box was put in my bathroom while I was showering. I was freaked out. I thought maybe someone was in the house.

Connor: What'd the cops find? Why the hell didn't you tell me all this?

Me: Nothing. He looked around the house, but we closed Declan's door.

Connor: But nothing's missing now, right? No broken lock? Busted window?

The spare key. I rush to the front door and slip outside, finding the lockbox and the key inside quickly.

Me: No.

Connor: Then the cop left the light on and the door open and you don't remember it. Calm down.

Me: I'm taking the spare key inside.

Connor: That's cool. I found mine in my room.

No idea how he could find anything in his room, but I'm grateful that I won't have a key outside anymore. I double-check the door locks and stalk back to the living room, annoyed.

But after I sit and calm down for a while, I realize Connor's right. I could be remembering it wrong. The pen could have rolled or maybe he moved it? It feels wrong, but witnesses get things wrong all the time. Memory is *not* as reliable as we like to believe.

I sit down and pull up my phone, trying to figure out who to call. What to do. I notice the voicemail icon at the top of the screen.

This is the number that has called me repeatedly. On a hunch, I check my texts, looking for the photo of Hope and I getting out of her car earlier. The chills are back, chasing each other up my sides as I verify the number at the top. They're the same.

Whoever texted that picture left me a voicemail. Or an accidental voicemail. It's only six seconds, but it could be enough to tell me who's behind this. I push Play.

Fast drums and a whining guitar. Distant like someone's holding the phone up to the car radio. And then a voice. Garbled in the background. I can't quite make it out.

I turn up the volume and put my phone on speaker before I play it again. The music again. Instruments first and then a fast indistinct murmur of lyrics.

And then a voice. Two words.

"You ready?"

My heart drops to my stomach. My knees. The voicemail ends.

I could have heard it wrong. I *had* to have heard it wrong. It's two words. It could be anybody. Background noise. A host at a restaurant offering to seat somebody, for God's sake.

I pull it back to the beginning, my thumb shaky on my phone screen now. I turn my volume up as far as it will go. Press Play.

The drums and guitar fly, tinny and distant. The vocals kick in and I know this—there's something horribly familiar about this song. And then there it is again.

"You ready?"

Chills slither up my back. I pull the voicemail back three seconds. Play it again.

"You ready?"

Again.

"You ready?"

I stop the voicemail and swallow hard, my heart hammering behind my ribs. It's him.

I'd bet a million dollars the voice in that message belongs to Declan.

TEN

42 HOURS LEFT

MY SKIN IS ABSOLUTELY CRAWLING WHEN I FINALLY PUT my phone down. I pick it right back up, though. I don't get it. It's not possible. Is it somehow part of the scavenger hunt? A good impression of Declan that my stress-addled mind is transforming?

I don't know. I need to call Hope. My fingers move on autopilot to dial her, but then I remember our conversation in the car. Our weirdness. I don't even know why it's weird—she's my best friend. Of course she doesn't think I hold an ounce of blame in this situation. But she's wrong. And I can't deal with that right now, so I call Bennett.

To my surprise he answers on the second ring and starts talking before I can say hello. "Why do you think gum and toothpaste only come in mint and cinnamon flavors?"

For a second, I freeze, because I didn't think this through. Bennett is great, but I can't talk to him about the horror show I lived through a year ago. Bennett is normal. And I am desperate for a dose of that right now.

"Cleo?" he prompts. "Toothpaste answers?"

"Because dogs would eat it if it tasted like bacon?"

"Sound theory," he says. Wherever he is, it's loud. "So, what's up?"

"Oh, nothing much," I say, the lie making my voice squeak. I can hear a soft woman's voice in the background. I recognize it at once. "How's your grandma?"

"Exciting." He isn't biting. "Why aren't you telling me about the hunt? Did you already solve the whole thing?"

"Not yet," I said. "It's fine. Not much to tell."

"This from a woman who spent half of our first date doing an oral compare-and-contrast report on murder mystery parties versus escape rooms."

"Hey, you were the one who asked me out again."

"Guilty as charged," he says. And then, because he is good and gentle, he adds, "Everything okay, though? I don't want to be the weird, overprotective boyfriend, but I'm a little worried."

"Yeah, it's kind of weird. It's just... I don't know. It's a little creepy that I still don't know who's behind this or what I'm after. The first clue was in my *bathroom*."

"Definitely creepy, but the police came and checked it out, right?"

"Yes," I say, totally forgetting I texted him about that earlier.

"Which makes me think it's someone who can get into the

house whenever they want. Could someone have gotten Connor or your parents to put it there? To go along with it?"

"I don't know."

"Didn't you tell me that Connor once ate a worm for a dollar as a kid?" he says.

"Point taken," I say, holding my light tone. But this is way beyond a worm. This is a trip down blackmail lane.

Maybe Connor knows more than he's letting on, but I can't see him doing this. He's my brother. He's been my hero my whole life.

"Look," Bennett says. "You're smart. You're strong. I know you could solve this, but you know you can walk away if you're not feeling it, right?"

"I guess," I say, except no, I really can't. Someone is watching me. Someone is threatening to drag this filthy skeleton out of my closet. Someone is maybe trying to ruin my future because I ran out of good choices at the edge of a river.

I sigh. "Can we talk about something different?"

"Sure, yeah," he says. "Uh, why don't you tell me about your plan for surviving Michigan winters, because frankly, I don't think you know what you're getting into with all of that lake effect action."

"Well, we can't all have the balmy winters at Vanderbilt on our list of options," I say.

His laugh is weak and I frown, wondering if I've struck a nerve. But then he goes on. "I kid, but I know you can handle

Michigan. You're going to do more than handle it. When you get there, I think the whole world is going to feel bigger and brighter."

"Yeah," I say, ignoring the lump forming in my throat. I've never wanted anything the way I want Michigan State. I took the online tour so many times, I thought their IT department would contact me for harassment. I've been through every building. Every map. Every section of the website over and over, just dreaming of the chance to be somewhere else. Somewhere far away from the girl I've been and the things I've done.

"Of course, you're going to kill any brightness with all the talk of blood spatter and serial killers, but to each their own."

"You're one to talk. My boyfriend, the future biochemist. What even *is* that, Bennett?"

"You want to stare at murder scenes. I want to cure cancer. We all have our calling."

I laugh for real, and he keeps it going, keeping me on the phone for half an hour, until I can put away the thought of the voicemail and the scavenger hunt and every scary, awful thing. I keep the knife nearby, and I bolt the chain above the dead bolt, but I also calm down enough to make a frozen pizza and eat half of it while I watch TV.

Mom texts me sometime around ten. She's usually good for a couple of these when Dad and her are living at a work site. A few occasional texts usually fulfill her parental need to know I'm alive.

I ignore the message for twenty minutes or so, until she sends it again. The same exact message, a copy-and-paste job.

Mom: How was your birthday, kiddo? Did Connor stop by?

This time, I answer.

Me: He stopped for clothes, but nothing big.

Mom: Typical. Anything else going on? Did Hope get you anything good?

Me: Yes. A forensics sweatshirt. I love it.

Mom: Good deal. Happy birthday!

I drop my phone on the table and give the clue one more look.

You want the future, not the past.
But your dreams and lies are blind.
Look for an old capital neighbor.
A doctor's gift, a citizen's find.

Everything else has tied back to me and Declan, but I can't think of a place we've been that matches this clue. The emergency room where I was treated? Something near the capitol building? Nothing jumps out so I put it back down and turn on the TV. Hopefully by tomorrow, Hope and I will be back to normal, and we'll figure it out.

I plug in my phone and change into one of Connor's old Greenscapes T-shirts. I stole it, but in my defense, he has a million of them. Plus, since he's going to be some hotshot attorney wearing business suits, I may run out of big-brother T-shirts to steal at some point.

The fan is on, and the TV is playing reruns of some decades-old sitcom. My brain is a low static hum. I know I should move to bed, but there are more exits in the living room, and some part of me is still a bit unnerved. The carving knife sits safely on the coffee table in front of me, and as my eyes grow heavy, I look at it, reassuring myself that it's there. That I'm safe. When I feel myself drifting to sleep, I don't even try to stop it.

I toss and turn on the lumpy couch, damp with sweat, my neck growing stiff. And then I sit up, suddenly wide awake and surprised by the brightness suffusing the room. It must be morning. Late morning. I take a breath and smell cigarettes and pine trees. *Declan.*

"What are you doing?"

My pulse quickens at the sound of his voice. My phone is in my hands, and I don't remember grabbing it, but I answer him. "I'm texting Daniel. My lab partner."

"Right. Your *lab partner.*"

He says it like it's a dirty word, and I swallow hard, tasting a mix of anger and fear. "Yeah. Remember how I told you I'd actually like to graduate from high school?"

"You think you're so smart," he says. "Is your *lab partner* smart too? Going to college on Mommy and Daddy's dime?"

"Why can't you drop this?" I ask, finally looking up. Declan is in the doorway, sunlight leaving shadows under his hooded eyes, his shoulders broad enough to block out light from the window. Declan's blond hair is tousled. Greasy. I see the bandage on his pale hand, and my heart clenches with guilt.

He hasn't slept. And he's on something, and suddenly I'm very, very tired.

"It's ten o'clock in the morning, Declan."

"Daniel, right?" he asks. "That's what you said. *Daniel.*"

"Is this what you've been doing all night?" I ask. "You've been out getting messed up?"

A whisper of panic beats faster than my heart. I get up and move closer, though my body goes stiff with dread. Voices scream through my mind, so loud I can almost hear them. They command me to get out. To run. To never look back.

But I am moving underwater, and I can't stop myself. I'm in the kitchen now, yelling in quick staccato bursts, the light smeary in the windows. He is so beautiful, and I hate him for it, those razor-sharp cheekbones and that too-soft mouth that even now makes me think of kissing him and God, this is messed up.

Even I know this is *so* messed up.

"You're sleeping with him, aren't you?" Declan asks.

"What?"

"Daniel. You're sleeping with that little shit because you think he's better. You think he's got something I don't."

"You don't even know what you're talking—"

"Don't you lie to me, you little bitch!"

And I hear myself saying it. I see my hands, palms up, washing my hands of this whole ordeal. "You know what? I'm done with this. You've got to go."

"Where the hell am I supposed to go, Cleo?" he screams.

"That's not my problem."

"You made it your problem! You're the one who makes me crazy like this."

"I haven't done anything!" I'm right in his face now, and I should know better. God, I should know, but I don't learn. I never learn. "You're the problem!"

"What did you say?"

"I said you're the problem!" I scream. "And I want you out of my house!"

I jab my finger, going to point, but he misreads me—thinks I'm aiming to hit him. He jerks his head back and cracks it on the frame of the door.

"Declan!" My voice is different now, frightened. "I'm sorry. Are you hurt?"

I reach, but he jerks. "Don't you fucking touch me!"

I move in, insistent and worried, and he shoves me off. I pause, rattled, and then he strikes, one wide hand popping me hard in the center of the stomach. It's one push, but he's got eight inches and eighty pounds on me. And I fly. Feet sliding, body tumbling back. My head smacks—I hear it more than I feel it at first, but the pain comes. A great, wet bloom of it wrenching a cry out of my throat. I'm on the linoleum staring at the dirty alcove under the cabinets. I see a twist tie. An old cap from a milk carton. Declan's shoes.

"Get up," he says, and I blink, my vision blurry and dark at the edges. His boot nudges into my arm, and my stomach roils. I almost vomit. He steps back quickly.

"Shit!" His voice is different now, like mine was earlier. High and worried. "You're bleeding."

I hear him grab for something on the counter. Swearing. I roll to my side, dizzy and intensely nauseous. Something warm and slick oozes out of me. Coats the back of my hair. The pain rolls in heavy beats—a rhythm that churns my stomach and matches my heart.

I see paper towels. See a blur of jeans and black T-shirt in front of me, and I push, terrified.

"No! Get off!" My voice is breathy. Shaking.

"Cleo, you're bleeding. Shit, you're really bleeding."

I claw at the streamers of paper towels falling over me, and my head is swimming. I can barely sit up, but I hear him. I can hear Declan sobbing. Sorry. So sorry. He's begging. Touching my face. My stomach roils, and I kick blindly. My hand plants into the floor—slips on my own blood. I push him away. Scream. Finally, I threaten him. With the police. A gun we do not own. Anything to make him leave.

And then he does. He's gone. I move, my stomach heaving. I scoop a wad of paper towels and press them hard to the back of my head.

My hair is soaked—shirt too. It's bad. I feel that now—feel that the blood was worse than I thought. This is all so much worse than I thought.

Need my phone. I have to find my phone. I do, but my vision is too hazy to make out the screen. Hope. I tell my phone to call her and it buzzes.

It should be ringing, but the screen is dark and it's just buzzing. Insistent. I press the glass again, smearing blood across the screen, but it only buzzes again. Again. I'm losing too much blood. I have to get help, but my phone just buzzes and buzzes and—

I wake up with a lurch, my arm stretched out, reaching for something I can't see. My heart is running wild in my chest, my breath coming in quick, shaky bursts. I touch the back of my head—test the scar with my fingertips, but my hair is clean and dry and Declan is dead and gone.

My phone buzzes on the coffee table, and I swipe my hand over my face before grabbing it. I squint to focus on the notifications screen. Three text messages are waiting.

The first is Hope.

Hope: I need to talk to you. Text me when you're up.

Me: I'm up.

Hope: I'll be there in ten.

Me: What's up?

Hope: We'll talk when I get there.

Weird. Hope is a serial texter and notorious for spilling the beans of any serious conversation ahead of time, so this isn't typical.

The other message is the number that called me. This time, it's a text with a single image attached. I stretch the picture on my phone because I don't quite understand. It's a little unfocused, and there are dark lines at the top and bottom of the photo, like it was taken through a frame. And then the shapes and shadows coalesce in my brain and I get it.

The photo was taken through a window. I can see the edge of a coffee table, a marked book beside a remote. And I can see two sock-clad feet on the cushions. A slim arm dangling off the edge of the couch, the fingers splayed.

My fingers.

Chills roll up my arms and legs, and I stand up, my stomach balled tight as I double-check the image. I'm not seeing it wrong. It's a picture of my living room—of me asleep on the couch. I turn to stare at the window where the picture was taken. The blinds are lifted, leaving six inches of bare, dark glass. Plenty for someone outside to get a clear shot. My skin goes cold. Someone stood in my yard and took a picture of me sleeping. While I was trapped in my nightmare with Declan, someone was watching me through that window.

Are they still out there?

I pivot between rage and terror. Rage wins. I pull up the keyboard to fire off a quick message and see the text message I had missed before. The one accompanying the image.

Unknown: Are you giving up?

Me: Who do you think you are?

Unknown: Does this mean you're giving up?

Me: It means I'm going to call the police.

Unknown: That didn't work very well the first time.

Me: I don't think they'll like someone peeking through my windows.

Unknown: I think we both know they'll be more interested in what you did at the river.

Me: What do you want from me?

Unknown: Solve the clues.

Me: And what if I don't?

Unknown: Ask Hope what happens if you don't. You have until tomorrow at 2:00.

My heart thumps once. And again. Whoever this is, they know what happened. They know what I did, and I don't know what they want.

ELEVEN

32 HOURS LEFT

IT'S 5:35 AM WHEN HOPE ARRIVES ON MY DOORSTEP. Early for anyone else on the planet, but Hope voluntarily gets up at 4:30 every school morning to get an extra run in.

"Hey," I say.

"Hey."

She doesn't come in, so it's clear she has more to say. She smooths her pale peach T-shirt and checks her ponytail, though not a hair is out of place. She's nervous. And I haven't shown her the photo that was taken of me from outside my living room window, so I don't think it's going to get better soon.

"I'm going to come right out with this," Hope says. "I got a text."

Oh God, please tell me someone wasn't taking photos of Hope sleeping too.

"What is it?" I ask.

She steps inside then, closing the door behind her. She pulls up her phone screen and turns it so that I can see it. "Just look."

It's a video. Hard to see at first, but I can make out trees and movement at the edge of a river. "I can't really tell what I'm looking at."

"Start it again. It took me a second."

I play it a second time, and the shadows and shapes come together. There are trees. Movement. Water. This was taken at the river in West Virginia. My gut drops like I'm in a car going over a hill too fast.

The video is taken from overhead, almost from across the river, but above. It's from the bridge. The focus is a figure at the edge of the shore. I rewind it and watch the motion. Someone is close to the water, shuffling feet, searching, then picking up something from the ground. Is it me? Or Declan?

But it's neither of us.

It's Connor.

I can't move. I've studied videos like the one I'm watching. I know what this is. He's cleaning up the scene of the crime. It's like my whole system stops, my every cell frozen in shock, because I understand what's happening. I rewind it again, and I watch my brother sweep away footsteps. Find my hair tie. He's checking for evidence.

I know what people will see in this video, and I know what they'll think. Poor abused sister. Enraged brother. The math adds up, even if the facts don't. Connor will look like he's covering up his crime, but he's not. He's covering up mine.

"Hope, Connor didn't..." I swallow. "He would never. He wasn't there. He found me after."

"I know," she says. "But I don't know if it matters what we think or know about this. This is incriminating."

I feel sick. Hope meets my eyes and understanding passes between us, solid and terrible. "He's my brother. He didn't do anything but show me kindness."

"Cleo, it's the kind of video... He just got that internship and he's doing *so* well."

I shake my head, resolved. "We have to find the next clue. Right now. I can't take the chance of anyone else seeing that."

"Agreed," she says.

"I need to show you some things."

I share the photo and texts, and her pale face whitens further.

"We need to be careful with this person," she says.

"Yeah, and I need to play you something," I say.

I set my phone to speaker and play the short voicemail, Declan's barking out the two words once. After the end, she frowns, looking confused. "Okay. Someone pocket dialed you?"

"Listen. Listen to the voice at the end."

She does as I asked when I play it a second and even third time. At the end of the fourth time she shrugs her shoulders. "I don't get it."

"Do you recognize the song?"

"Yeah, it's Green Day, right?"

I don't tell her it's Declan's favorite. I don't want to feed her clues or build a case. I want her to evaluate this on her own, because this is why witnesses are never as reliable as evidence. Our perspectives and memories and interpretation are all subjective.

I play it two more times, and Hope listens carefully, but no realization dawns in her eyes. She doesn't even look like her attention is piqued by the voice.

"I thought the voice sounded familiar," I say with a sigh. "It's from the same number that sent the photos of you and me earlier. And me sleeping tonight."

She frowns. "It sounds like a pocket dial. But I wish we could figure out that background noise. If we knew where this was recorded, it could tell us something." Her eyes light up. "Wait, did you search to see when that number first called you?"

"It all started with the hunt. I've had the two texts and three or four calls."

"Okay, so zero help there," she says. "We need to check with Connor to see if it's the same phone that sent all of them the photo, but right now we need to move back to the clue you found at the art museum. It's taking us too long. Do you have any ideas?"

"The other clues have led me to places important to Declan and me in some way. I just can't think of anything that matches this one."

"Let's read it again," she says.

You want the future, not the past.
But your dreams and lies are blind.
Look for an old capital neighbor.
A doctor's gift, a citizen's find.

"Is it possible it's Mount Carmel West?" she asks. "It used to be a full-scale hospital, and it's the oldest in Columbus."

I wrinkle my nose. "We've never been there."

"Is there another hospital? Maybe a doctor's office near Capital University in Bexley?"

"I don't know. The only time a hospital was involved in our relationship was the time he sent me to one. And he wasn't there."

"Okay, let's take a step back and start again."

"Are there any other major locations with doctor in the title?" I ask. "Is there even a way to search for something like that?"

"We can search for anything we want. Phones are magic."

She reads off the name of a florist, a candy shop, a couple of things that sound dubiously like escort services, and a tiki DJ of all things.

"None of that makes any sense at all," I say. "I don't even know how to start cracking this one."

"Let's look at neighbors. Things near the capitol, maybe?" She clicks on her phone again. "The Planter's Peanut store? Columbus Commons? LeVeque Tower?"

"None of this," I say. "The only thing near there that we even visited was the park where we've already been. Maybe you're on to something with Capital University?"

"It's in Bexley."

"But what about the law school? Isn't there part of it that's downtown sort of near the art museum?" I ask.

"Yeah, but I can't think of anything..." Hope trails off, scanning something on her phone.

"Did you find something?"

"Yes," she says. "Apparently Capital University wasn't originally located in Bexley. Did you guys ever spend any time in Goodale Park?"

Images flash through my mind. Declan making me dance in the path. Declan walking on the edge of a fountain. Declan, giddy and happy and buzzing with energy, but also—drunk. Definitely drunk. And then our first fight—the first time he called me names and pulled his hand back. I don't remember what we said, but I remember snow on the ground and a look in his eyes that warned me to be afraid. He wasn't violent then, but it wouldn't be long.

"It's the park," I say. "Goodale Park."

"Are you sure?"

"We spent time there," I say, and we did. Walks and talks and cupcakes on benches. It was the first place we slow danced, while street musicians played by the fountain. But it was also the first place he made me flinch. "It's the park. I'm sure of it."

Hope's fingers fly across her phone screen. Seconds later, she grins and pops up on the balls of her feet. "I think you're right. Goodale Park was donated in 1851 by *Doctor* Lincoln Goodale."

"A doctor's gift. Let's go," I say, grabbing my shoes. Then I look down and realize I'm still wearing Connor's T-shirt and a pair of threadbare running shorts. "Maybe give me five minutes to change?"

"Take your time. I'm going to pull up a map of the park."

I head for my bedroom and change in record time, pulling my hair into a sloppy, wavy mess of a ponytail. I brush my teeth and swipe on some deodorant. On my way out, I glance at Connor's door, closed tight, his room empty.

For the first time in a while, I wish he was still at home. I wish I could poke my head inside to see him reading some thick, boring-looking book on business or leadership, and then I could tell him what's been happening. Maybe I should tell him anyway.

I glance over at the photo of us on the wall, one from when we were little. He's only two years older than me, but in this photo the age difference is huge. We're beside one of those splash pads, and I think we're maybe two and four. Connor's brown arms are wrapped around my fish-belly white tummy, and even though I'm still a baby, our smiles are just the same.

Growing up, it was always a thing. Explaining that yes, he's my brother, and no, I don't call him my half brother and why the hell do people feel like it's okay to ask shit like this? Do they think I don't love him the same as they love their brothers? Why?

Because we have different, mostly absent fathers and the same self-absorbed, distant mother?

Aside from our Nana, Connor is the only person in the world I knew I could count on growing up. All of my earliest memories are of Connor. Connor pouring me cereal. Connor helping me up when I wrecked on my tricycle. Connor making us both mac and cheese when Mom and my Dad went missing on random afternoons. And when I was five and got a stomach bug, it wasn't Mom who sat in the bathroom with me rubbing my back—it was my seven-year-old brother.

I touch Connor's face in the picture feeling a pang in my chest at the distance between us. Maybe things aren't like they were then. Maybe I ruined that forever in West Virginia.

But so help me God, I will not let it ruin him.

TWELVE

32 HOURS LEFT

IT'S A NINE-MINUTE DRIVE, AND WE ARRIVE WHEN THE promise of sunrise is a bruise-colored smear in the eastern sky. The Short North—home to Goodale Park and loads of upscale restaurants and pricey real estate—is a cool district, but I'm not down here often anymore. It's a little pretentious and a lot expensive. It's also touristy, or as close to touristy as Columbus gets. Also, it's easier to park on the dark side of the moon than it is to find a spot along the park. Unless, apparently, you arrive before six in the morning when normal people are at home in bed ignoring their phone alarm for the third time.

We find a spot right along the park's east edge and step out into an eerily quiet not-yet morning. The tapping of our feet sounds extra loud on the sidewalk as we head for the entrance. Two stone towers—remnants of a time when the park was fenced—rise up over either side of the walkway. Trees stretch toward the sky behind it, dark and ominous in the meager light.

We step inside, and whatever illumination we gained from the street vanishes under the shade of the trees dotting the park. Birds sing to welcome the coming dawn from shadowy perches and squirrels scrabble up and down the trees.

We walk aimlessly for a moment. Or I walk aimlessly anyway. Hope doesn't do aimless. She has her phone up, which probably means she's cross-referencing four different maps and a satellite image, and maybe—hopefully—ordering us coffee to pick up when we leave.

"We have a lot of ground to cover," she says. "Do you have a specific place in mind? There's a statue of Lincoln Goodale, the gazebo, the elephant fountain, the shelter house, and dozens of park benches and picnic tables."

"The other places haven't all been that specific. The art museum wasn't, at least. I don't even think he and I saw that dress thing when we went."

"Maybe whoever's planning this doesn't know as much as they want you to think they do."

"Maybe," I say. A breeze kicks up, and I shiver. It's supposed to get to sixty degrees today, but it's still early and dark and frankly a little bit creepy in this empty park.

"Well, pick something," I say.

"Let's head for the statue," she says. "It's straight ahead."

I follow her, trying not to let the emptiness unnerve me. As a city kid, I don't like empty. I'm twice as likely to be freaked in a forest than I am in the presence of a few sketchy people. Sketchy people aren't likely to drop out of the trees to slit my throat.

Not that the squirrels here are murderous, per se, but in this light it feels possible.

I notice a woman jogging along the sidewalk around the park, and then a man getting into his car a few yards down across the street. My shoulders relax, relieved to find people nearby.

But then the hair on the back of my neck stands up. I hear someone running behind us, but my eyes are riveted to another jogger—one across the park wearing gray workout pants and a black hoodie.

I stare at the figure and take a tentative step forward and then they stop, pushing back their hood. It's a guy—a total stranger stretching his quads and minding his own business.

"I've seen that person before."

I startle at the sound of Hope's voice. For a second I'd been so wrapped up in the mystery hoodie person, I'd forgotten all about Hope. She's not looking at the jogger I was watching—she's looking left. I turn, catching sight of another dark hoodie. Dark pants. Already a good distance away.

"I think I saw that guy at the art museum," Hope says.

"You sure?"

"I think so. It could be a different person, but I could have sworn it was the same hoodie. Kind of frayed at the bottom. I think the shoes were the same too."

"Well, I saw someone at Audubon in a hoodie and then thought I saw them in the art museum. It could be the person who's behind all of this. We wouldn't both see a similar person in a similar outfit out of sheer coincidence, right?"

"No, you're right. This could be the guy," she says, eyes narrowed and angry. "Let's go find him."

"But they're gone."

She shakes her head. "If we both cut to the sidewalk and sprint around the perimeter of the park, we might see him heading to his car." Hope nods her head to the left. "I'll take that sidewalk and head north. You go to the other side and meet me in the middle."

"Let's go."

We break into a run in opposite directions, outward from the center of the park. As soon as I reach the sidewalk, I turn left and pick up my pace as I move around the perimeter. I see a pair of pugs being walked on the opposite side of the street, a runner in high-end gear, and a minivan working to parallel park along the side of the fence. I meet up with Hope at one of the corner gates.

"Nothing," she says.

"I wish I could have seen something distinguishable about him."

"We know it's a guy."

She bites her lip. "I think. I wouldn't bet money on it."

I sigh. "Well, at least *you* don't want a future career in forensics. I'm so crap at paying attention to people that I may become the victim of a violent crime before I get the chance to investigate one."

"Don't even joke about that right now," she says. "I don't trust this."

"I'm sorry," I say. "I know. It's freaking me out. But you're the one who told me no one would go through this just to shiv me in an alley, right?"

I wait for her confirmation, because I need her to still believe this. I've been stupid enough to wind up in a violent lunatic's grips before. If I'm really in danger…

"I don't think anyone wants to kill you," she says, "but every clue feels personal and threatening. We need to be careful."

"Well, who would fit the description of our hooded stranger?" I ask. "Maybe we can narrow down our list of suspects."

"That could be any guy we know," she says. "Or a tall girl. And frankly, we don't know if it's one person. It could be multiple people. Or one person with helpers."

I swallow hard, looking around. "I hadn't thought of that." And honestly, it's making my skin crawl. What if this isn't a person, but people? Plural. How many of them are there? Is someone watching me *right now*? "This whole thing is a nightmare."

"We're going to get there," she says. "If there's one thing I know about us it's that we don't lose."

We check the statue. A plaque informs us that Lincoln Goodale, who gifted the land for the park, was the area's first physician. It does not, however, offer the location of the next clue.

Hope starts searching the shrubs to the left, and I take the ones to the right. Plenty of cigarette butts and a discarded latex glove that skeeves me right out, but no gift. The gazebo, too, is a bust.

"What about the shelter house?" I ask.

She shrugs. "I think it's locked unless there's a rental, but we can try. Are there any other likely options?"

My eyes drag to the lake. "Do you think it could be in the water?"

There are no words for how much I hope that isn't the case. Forget the hell that went down at the river. Water and I do not mix. Not shallow water or pond water—I don't even like hot tubs.

"I don't think it would be in there," she says, gently, knowing my phobia well. "The boxes are cardboard, and they'd fall apart."

God, I hope she's right.

Because everything about this hunt is dragging me to the past. And given what happened at the river in West Virginia, I want to stay as far away from water as I possibly can.

"Let's check the shelter house first," I say.

The sky is brighter now, and more joggers are starting to trickle through the paths. A girl with pink headphones. A couple with matching gray athletic shirts. It's sparse, but it won't be for long. Weekends and city parks do not equal solitude.

We need to find this clue before someone else does.

We cut across the grass toward the shelter house. It's getting warmer, but the grass is cool and wet on my ankles. The birds are no longer in shadow now. Instead, sparrows hop along the picnic tables and benches, looking for remnants from yesterday's picnics.

We head for the parking lot entrance to the shelter house. From a hundred yards away, the building has the feel of a cottage with a brown roof and large arched windows overlooking the park. But the closer I get, the more the luster of the brick building fades. It looks like a rec center, albeit one with some throwback accents.

We start peering into the windows and the fourth window on the left—for no reason I can see—reveals a metal folding chair with a white box in the center. The green satin bow looks black in the darkness inside.

"It's in there," I say, pulling back from the window.

Hope presses her hand to the glass to look in, then steps back with a frown. "That's random. Were Declan and you ever inside there?"

"No, but maybe you were right. Maybe whoever is behind this doesn't know all the details." And then another thought occurs to me. What if this location itself is a setup? The shelter house isn't open to the public. Are they trying to get evidence of me committing another crime?

Hope clucks her tongue. "I don't really know if you can go in there."

"Maybe it will be unlocked," I say. "The park is all public property, right?"

"Yes, but they rent the shelter house for events," she says. "It's generally closed."

She's right, and she's really not going to like where I'm going next with this. When I jog up the stairs that lead to the entrance, I know it's going to be locked before I even jiggle the door handles to confirm it. I lean down to check out the lock, but Hope taps me on the arm urgently and clears her throat. Someone is coming.

I instinctively step back from the door and try to look casual. Hope is already halfway back down the stairs to the parking lot. There's a college-aged guy running hard across the asphalt. He doesn't look up, but I wait until he passes. I'm guessing it would not be the best thing to have folks in the park notice the two teenagers creeping around the shelter house at 6:40 in the morning.

"Let's go around the side," I say.

We follow the sidewalk and I feel tense and twitchy. People are wandering all over the park now. A mom with a stroller at the eastern edge. Pink-headphones girl making another pass through the center. It's fine. No one is looking at us, and even if they are, it's a public park. I'm allowed to look at the shelter house. Heck, I'm allowed to be in the shelter house, for that matter.

I'm just not allowed to break into it when it's locked.

Which is exactly what I'm planning to do.

To my dismay, the side door is just as exposed to the park as the front door. It's locked too, but this isn't the same situation. The front door was closed with a hearty steel deadbolt. This side door is old, and there's a whole lot of wiggle in the handle. I learned about locks watching a police video training series. Turns out training police on processing burglary scenes offered a lot of information about how thieves break in.

I pull my wallet out, and Hope visibly stiffens. "What are you doing?"

"This is barely locked," I say.

"It's *definitively* locked."

I pull out my student ID, which is probably the sturdiest card in my wallet, and since I'm graduating in a few weeks, easily the least useful. "I'm just going to give it a tiny jiggle."

"And then tiptoe on into a felony?"

I roll my eyes. "I'm entering a public building."

"A *locked* public building. What are you going to say if someone asks us what we're doing?"

"That I thought it was the bathroom?" I push the card in between the door frame and the door. It's not quite as easy as I remember, and I'm trying to be cool about it, looking at Hope. Checking my phone. Wiggling it left and right and feeling for that metal latch.

After a minute or so of fruitless fiddling, I'm not sure it's going to work. Then I feel it click into place and—bingo—the door opens.

Hope looks at me with horror as I move to walk inside. "I can't believe you're going in there."

"What choice do we have? We *have* to get the clue, Hope. Whoever this is, they're not just putting my future on the line.

They're threatening Connor for something he had nothing to do with. I can't let that happen."

Her cheeks go softly pink, but she nods. "Okay."

Still, Hope's a consummate law follower with a fear of committing a crime that rivals my fear of water. I don't need her freezing up and balking every inch of the way. It'll only make it worse.

"You stay here and keep a lookout okay?"

"Just hurry," she says.

"I'll be right back."

I slip inside and pull the door behind me, not quite shut, but close enough that my ears hum in the sudden quiet. I'm in the main hallway, dark and mostly empty. A few stacks of chairs tower in a corner. A corridor leads off to the right with signs directing me to the hall or the dressing room. Maybe that's where the brides get ready?

Goodale is home to lots of weddings. When I was little, I saw a wedding here and told my mom I'd get married here too. She laughed and told me to choose a location where I can have an open bar.

I walk quickly toward the front entrance, trying to steer clear of the windows. And there it is. This box isn't perched anywhere special, and I don't see anything tucked in the ribbon or left on the seat when I pick it up. It almost feels like a mistake.

I'm tempted to open it, but I need to get out of here before some park ranger or yoga instructor or whatever shows up to open the building. I retrace my steps and stop when I find the side door closed. I twist the knob, but it resists, and then I hear Hope's voice through the wood, muffled, but clear.

"I take it this isn't the restroom," she says with a nervous laugh.

More distantly, a lower voice replies, a murmur I can't make out. I freeze, releasing the doorknob slowly as I hear Hope's steps as she walks away from the door. Her laugh sounds genuine, but I know it's forced. And before I even see anything, I know what's going on outside.

Someone official looking must have shown up. They probably asked Hope what she's doing lurking around the definitely-not-a-bathroom shelter house, and she's probably having a cardiac event trying to cover my tracks.

My heart thumps a little harder too. Okay, new plan. My palms go slick with sweat and I turn around, trying to figure out where to go.

There are windows all around me. If I step in any direction I could be seen. I inch away from the side door, trying to use angles and shadows to keep myself invisible while still catching a glimpse of the situation outside. Because maybe it's nothing. A curious jogger. A friend from school.

But then I see it. Grass. The edge of a tree. The shiny rope of Hope's ponytail.

And the tall, white-shirted police officer in front of her.

THIRTEEN

31 HOURS LEFT

I PRESS MYSELF AGAINST THE WALL AS HOPE MOVES down the walk. She's talking loud and clear, and, God love her, she is a nervous wreck. Once in sixth grade, I got in a yelling match with our gym teacher, and Hope was so scared she started crying and apologizing before I was even done shooting off my smart mouth. Lying to a police officer has got to be killing her.

I hear her going on and on and see the glint of morning sunlight off the officer's badge. He's stalling. Probably because she's being weird as hell.

Okay, so what do I do? Walk out and plead ignorance? From what I can see of the officer's expression, he's already a little irritated. I'm not sure I want to risk a trip to the station or a call to my parents. Wait. Would a write-up at the police station hit my background check? My breath catches at the possibility. This was not my brightest decision. I've got to find a way out of here.

Preferably before Hope breaks down and confesses, providing my full name, description, and a list of everything I've ever done wrong.

I edge along the wall toward the front entrance, tucking the gift in my shirt. A patrol car is parked in full view of the front doors. Hope appears with the officer, looking guilty of high treason.

I swallow hard and try to think. Both doors face the parking lot. A police officer is currently in that lot, giving my best friend the third degree, and I'm standing inside guilty of breaking and entering because I wanted a gift-wrapped clue. I try the door to the banquet room and—thank you, sweet Pappy Johnson—it's open.

It's also…not the fairytale wonderland I'd dreamed up as a kid with future wedding plans dancing in my eyes. There are round, ugly folding tables stowed in a corner and stacks of tattered brown chairs along the wall. Still, the view from the windows is lush and green, overlooking the paths full of strollers and dog walkers.

Lots of strollers and dog walkers.

How am I going to get out of here without being spotted? My phone buzzes, and I jump so hard, my bones nearly exit my skin.

Not now.

Please not now.

I pull it out with shaking hands, dreading the Unknown

Caller that will be dancing across the top of the screen. But it's not the mystery number.

Connor: Hey.

Bzzzz.

Connor: Did you and Mom move the coffee?

Bzzzz.

Connor: The good stuff.

Bzzzz.

Connor: Can only find shit decaf.

Bzzzz.

Connor: And some hazelnut garbage.

I have no idea why Connor is back at the house, or why he's incapable of texting like a normal human being, a fact I will kill him for later. But if I don't reply, he will follow this rapid-fire text vomit with eighteen versions of *Hello, Are you there?*, *Coffee?*, *Just answer me!*

Me: Cabinet above the toaster! Stop texting me!

To my intense relief, he does. Though I'm still not sure why the hell he's back at the house. He couldn't possibly need another shirt. Maybe he's coming back to stay for a while?

I really have to talk to him about what's happening. What if the guy who's been breaking in comes back while Connor is there?

I startle at the sound of an engine in the parking lot. A car door opening. I swallow and my throat squeezes. I can worry about Connor when I'm *not* arrested. I turn my focus back to the problem at hand—getting out of this building. I scan the windows overlooking the park. They open, but they're really visible. And there are at least four dogs on leashes out there. Even if some of them don't see or hear me, at least one of them is going to be all too happy to bark out an announcement of my arrival on the lawn, killing my plans for a stealthy escape via window.

Maybe the police are gone and I can get out the front? I slip across the room to peek out front. The first officer has been joined by a second, and worse still, there's a city vehicle now parked next to them. A sturdy-looking guy dressed in a navy blue polo starts heading toward the door, travel coffee mug in one hand and keys in the other. My heart thunks.

Got to go. Right freaking now.

I've officially been in here way too long to play at not knowing that the completely dark, locked building wasn't open to the public. I rush for the windows in the banquet room, trying to find the latches. They're old and stubborn, and am I going to wind up in jail because I can't open a window lock? The lock on the last window is busted, and I can see it's open a few inches at the bottom.

This is how the hoodie guy got in. This is how he left the clue. My fingertips hover over the latch, shaking. If I had a kit, I could look for prints or clues. I could finally turn the tables if I could just figure out who's screwing with me. And with Connor, for that matter.

Footsteps. A key tumbling in a lock and the creak of a door

being opened. I push the window further open. It's a floor-to-ceiling window, but only the bottom portion opens, and I can see there's a bit of a drop to the ground. Too late to worry about it now and beggars can't be choosers.

Faint whistling adds to the footsteps. I hear the doorknob to the banquet hall twisting. It's now or never. I shove both feet though and flip to my stomach so I can get out feetfirst. The frame pushes my shirt up, and then some part of the fabric catches on metal. I'm stuck.

Oh my God, I can't get out.

I wriggle wildly, flailing with my legs. Squirming with every muscle I have and several I'm not sure I've ever used in my life. Metal scrapes into my ribs in my struggle, hooking onto the underside of my bra.

I see those sturdy, shorts-clad legs walking toward the open door. Ranger legs. I rip hard at the fabric until my shirt tears enough to let me through. I push myself the rest of the way out and drop to my feet and then my knees. I scrabble away from the building on all fours. The window is still open, and a lifetime of living in an iffy neighborhood tells me to close it. But I have no idea where that city worker is now. Or the cops for that matter. So, I keep crawling.

The grass is wet and slick from the dew, and it's so cold I'm shocked I'm not crawling over frost. I make it to the corner of the building and spring to my feet behind a juniper bush. A mom with a stroller looks at me and frowns. I wave at her dark-eyed toddler, who's chewing her jacket sleeve. The see-I'm-harmless-and-friendly gesture works. The mom nods and keeps moving down the path.

I brush the grass off my knees and palms and start a brisk jog toward the convergence of the paths. My phone bounces in the waistband of my shorts, and I'm half desperate to call Hope, but first things first. I need to look like a legit runner, not a terrified fugitive who just ran from the scene of a crime.

The quote from Edward Locard shoots into my brain. "Every contact leaves a trace." That includes me.

Shit. I'm sure there is some proof that I was in there. A hair that fell out of my ponytail. Threads from the fabric where my shirt ripped. There could be skin cells on the window frame from where it scraped me. I feel fizzy with panic, but I force myself to breathe. I need to calm down. The police aren't likely to bring a forensics team out to assess a harmless case of trespassing.

I push my pace faster than normal, and once I've put some distance between myself and the shelter house, I pull out my phone. Hope's message is all business.

Hope: I'm at the statue.

Me: On my way.

I double back to meet her. The box is a little mangled now, the satin ribbon crushed and damp with sweat. Kind of gross, but when I catch sight of Hope, her shoulders sag so dramatically, I burst out laughing.

"It's not funny," she protests.

"Uh, you didn't see your face. It was definitely funny."

"You could have been arrested!" she says.

"But I wasn't. I got lucky." I feel the smile slide off my face and I swallow. Because now that I'm outside, I realize how close I'd gotten. All this work to try to clear my name—to settle some debt with an unseen collector—and I almost tossed my future away to break into a party house.

How did my life turn into this mess?

"Well, I'm glad you're out," she says. "How *did* you get out, anyway?"

"Through a back window. I think that's how our mystery person got in. Did the cop ask you anything concerning?"

She shakes her head. "They got another call, so they left to deal with that. I got lucky too."

"Good. And for the record, if we're ever caught in a morally dubious situation, let's remember you are not the member of our team that should try to lie to the authorities."

"Definitely not," she says, then she nods at the gift. "So, what is it? And what happened to it?"

"Escape from Goodale Alcatraz happened to it," I say. Then I tug the wrinkled ribbon off the partially mashed box. "I haven't read it yet."

Nestled in the box is the white paper that's become standard issue, but I don't even look at the clue. I'm looking at the lid. Or what's stuck to the lid at any rate. This time I know I'm not imagining a connection to Declan. This isn't a mass-produced gift shop bracelet. This is a business card from Daredevil Rafting in West Virginia. The same rafting company that hosted the trip where Declan drowned.

"What is it?" Hope asks. I'm sure the horror is written all over my face. I turn the card so that she can see it. The light catches the slogan printed underneath the address, the second half underlined with a thick, hand-drawn Sharpie line: *Take on the River. Live to Tell the Tale.*

My eyes focus on the last five words of the slogan. Live to Tell the Tale.

The fleeting thought—the curling smoke—the thing that felt impossible. Now it rises on steady feet in my mind. Did Declan survive?

I saw the river take him. Heard him scream and watched the water—angry and frothing—drag him under the bridge. But I *didn't* see him drown. Remote as the chance feels, he could have made it through the rapids, to a slower section. There could have been a log, a lucky catch—something that got him out. Declan could be alive.

I could even see him staying away all these months. He'd know that it would be my word against his, but that video of Connor? That changes the game. Declan would see it as a chance to prove that he was the victim. And I know him well enough to know that if there's a reasonable chance of winning, Declan will always come for his two pounds of flesh. He would want revenge.

I pull out the clue and read.

Do you believe it's over?

Do you really think it's through?

Find the silent people waiting.

Find the lies he wrote for you.

My eyes return to the first lines. Because I know it isn't over now. No matter how much I want to put Declan behind me, this hunt is dragging me back.

"Why now?" Hope asks. "Why is this happening after all this time? Is it because it's been a year?"

"I think it's the video. That video found its way into the wrong hands, and it looks like some kind of proof."

"What does it prove?"

"Some could say it proves it wasn't an accident. Connor looks like he's covering my tracks."

Because he *is* covering my tracks. That fact burns me with more shame than anything else. It's bad enough knowing what I did, but now I dragged Connor into this mess.

They were friends once, Declan and Connor. That's how Declan came to live with us in the first place. They'd met working at Greenscapes. Declan was newer in town; some awful family thing—parents in rehab and every other imaginable sob story. When he started running out of places to stay, Connor stepped in. A few months later on holiday break, his big-brother instinct told him something wasn't right. He didn't like that we were dating. Liked it even less when he saw how much Declan drank.

But Connor learned how bad things really were in West Virginia. No details, but enough. I swear I thought he'd try to kill Declan. In the end, I guess I took care of that. Or at least it sure seemed like I did.

"Cleo." Hope's voice pulls me out of my mind. She's reading the clue and her eyes are soft and worried when she looks up. "If someone really does want to hurt Connor with all of this..."

"I know." I think of the photo on our hallway wall, my brother's arms right around my tummy. I start walking. "Come on. We've got to tell him."

FOURTEEN

30 HOURS LEFT

CONNOR'S BIKE IS STILL IN FRONT OF THE HOUSE WHEN we arrive. Something tells me this unusual double visit is because he knows Hope is with me. I still don't exactly understand this situation between them, but looking at Hope now—stalling on getting out of the car while she stares at Connor's motorcycle—I wonder how I've missed it for so long.

"Hope, I know you said there was just the one kiss…"

"It's complicated," she says.

"But it's not 'no big deal', is it?"

"No," she says with a sad, soft laugh. "No, it's definitely not that."

We head inside and I say a brief prayer that Connor is making pancakes. I'm starving, and Connor is the only person in our house who has innate ability in the kitchen.

Hope waits at the door until I move past her to open it. One breath, and my pancake dreams are crushed. I smell clean laundry and nothing that even resembles food.

We enter to find Connor standing between the living room and the dining table, shirt off and headphones on. Three dress shirts hang on the backs of chairs around the dining room table, collars crisp and buttons shiny.

I didn't know we had an ironing board. Hell, I didn't even know we had an iron.

"Hey," I say, loud enough for him to hear us.

He turns, pushing his headphones down around his neck. "What's up?"

"Nothing," Hope says automatically. "I mean, not nothing." Out of the corner of my eye I can see her fidget when Connor reaches for his shirt, tugging it on over his shoulders.

Look, I get that my brother isn't hard to look at, but this whole thing is going to take some getting used to.

"We need to talk about this scavenger hunt," I say.

He smirks. "Do I get to solve a rhyming riddle?"

His smile falters when his eyes drift to Hope. He covers it quickly, running a hand through his curls. They spring back into his eyes with a mind of their own.

"So, spill it," he says.

"This scavenger hunt has some elements of blackmail," Hope says. "Elements that relate to Declan."

"Declan is dead." My brother's eyes are hard and flat, his

inflection making it clear that he is good with this fact. "What is there to blackmail?"

"Evidence that might suggest Declan's death wasn't an accident, for starters," Hope says.

"And maybe there wasn't actually a death," I add. Hope wrinkles her nose at that.

"What are you talking about?" he asks.

"I have a business card from the rafting company," I say, showing him the underlined portion, "and a bracelet that Declan used to wear. And all of the clues are places that meant something to us."

He frowns, looking concerned. "What's the blackmail piece?"

"The clues indicate that someone was watching when Declan died," Hope says. "That there's more to the situation than people know."

"They are threatening to tell if I don't win this hunt," I add.

Connor shakes his head. "Nah. A threat isn't blackmail. Screw them."

"There's more," Hope says. "Whoever's doing this took pictures of us when we were on our way to one of the clues. And pictures of Cleo sleeping."

"How'd they take pictures of you?" Connor takes a small step toward me, an automatic shift into protective-brother mode. I check the window behind him—the one where the photo was taken. It's still shut tight, curtains drawn as I left them this morning. Because I'm not supposed to talk about this with anyone but Hope, so I don't want someone spying on the convo.

"Here." I pull up the text stream on my phone and offer it over.

He scans the images and texts, his jaw growing tighter with every second. "You do a reverse phone search on this shit?"

I shake my head "No—"

"Yes," Hope says. "It's a blocked number. It could be one of those pay-as-you-go phones."

I don't know when she did this but I'm not surprised. Nothing is more Hope-like than handling stress through intense research.

"And what's with the Monday at 2:00 thing?" he asks.

"It's the one-year anniversary of his death," I say.

"What time did it happen?" he asks. His voice is hard. Flinty. "What time did he fall in?"

I shrug. "Sometime in the afternoon. I guess 2:00 is possible."

"It was close to that," Hope says.

"Then you need to look at the people who were in West Virginia," he says. He's throwing his shoulders back a little, that natural-leader streak in him wanting control of the situation. "Anybody there would know the day and time. They could get the business cards and say things to spook you, but there's no evidence. If they had something real on you, you wouldn't be playing a stupid game. The cops would be here."

"I thought maybe that was true too," I say. "Until we got the video."

Hope shows him the video at the river, and I stare as he watches it. On the phone screen, Connor drags his feet across the dirt, covering my footsteps. Cleaning up my mess. He leans down to pick something up out of the grass and images roll through my mind like thunder. My hair tie.

I remember the press of it in my palm.

And it's like I'm back there in the woods, waiting on him all over again. Sometimes I feel like this movie will never stop playing in my mind: Connor emerging from the trees. Back like he promised. I was shaking all over and then he curled my fingers around that hair tie, and I cried so hard I thought I'd choke.

I can still hear him talking to me, his voice steady and even and true.

"Breathe," Connor said. "Just breathe. We're going to get you cleaned up."

My face was snotty and tear streaked and my throat throbbed and burned. I couldn't imagine ever being cleaned of any of it, so I didn't answer.

Connor waited, no hushing noises or sympathy pats. He kept his hands on my shoulders, and his face was steady and calm. He was a rock, and so, I leaned.

"It's my fault," I whispered.

"None of this is your fault, Cleo. None of it."

He said it like a command, but I shook my head, because I knew the truth. I knew what I did.

"No. Connor, I—"

"Whatever happened, it was an accident," he said.

I shook my head harder, my sobs chopping my sentences into chunks of nonsense. "I was there. I didn't mean it. We were fighting. He grabbed me. I didn't know what—I was scared."

Connor's fingers grazed my throat and I could feel him shaking. Could see the rage and regret shifting over his face as he assessed the damage. His expression broke my heart.

"I didn't want this to happen," I whispered. "I don't want to be this person."

"You're not," he said. "He was drunk. He fell in. That's the end of it."

"Connor, it wasn't—"

"It was an accident," he said. "You didn't know what to do. Whatever else is true, that's the truth too. And that's the end of it. We move forward. You hear me? We're going to move on."

The river raged in the distance, but Connor's eyes were still and warm and I wanted the quiet they promised. I licked my bleeding lips and nodded. "Okay. We'll move on."

The iron hisses softly, and I am jolted back to the present. Connor is slouched against the dining room table, but he's not looking at Hope's phone anymore. From the expression on his face, I'm guessing he's put together all the bad things that video could do to his future. And mine too.

The line of freshly pressed shirts trail out beside him like flags of the kingdom. Promises of a new life, clean and crisp and full of possibility. Connor didn't let what happened with Declan chain me to my past.

Which is why I will not let it steal his future.

"We need to call the cops," he says. Hope takes a breath to speak, but he holds up a hand to stop her. "I can't have somebody creeping around taking pictures of you. No way I can live with that."

"And I can't live with this video getting out, because we both know *you* had nothing to do with Declan drowning," I say.

"Cleo, I don't give a shit."

"Yes, you do," Hope says. "I know you want to take charge and control all of this, but you can't. You're smart enough to know that a video like that sent to the wrong people could pull you out of this internship. You're working for a state prosecutor, for God's sake."

He shrugs, trying and failing to hide his concern. "So what? I'll find another internship."

Hope scoffs. "Oh, sure. Let's pretend you didn't spend half the winter going through that application process. You worked hard for this! It matters."

I look between them again, the weight of their connection heavy in the air. And then I clear my throat. "Give me until tomorrow to try to solve it. I'm asking for one day."

He looks reluctant, but Hope jumps in to support me. "If we figure it out, maybe that will be enough for them. Maybe all they want is for Cleo to face the music, and then they'll let this go. Either way, we'll know what they really have and what they're after, and that's better than we have right now."

I don't know if I buy that. Something tells me I'm going to

pay for what I did one way or another and right now, I don't even care. Connor is not going down because of me. Full stop.

"One day," I say again. "That's all I want."

He shakes his head. "I don't like it. Who would be doing this? Who would have a tape like this?" Connor asks. "Valerie? Aiden? Jack?" He nods at Hope. "Hell, you?"

Hope shifts uncomfortably, her pale cheeks gone pink. "No. Obviously."

Connor narrows his eyes, and I know the same impossible thought is in his mind now. Is it possible that Declan lived? Is it possible that this is him?

"They ever find his body?" Connor asks quietly. He doesn't need to clarify what body he's asking about.

"He's gone," Hope says. "Declan is dead. Period. We were all there. We all know what happened, right?"

"We thought we did," Connor says.

"I need to play you something," I say, and I pull up the voicemail and play it twice in a row. I can see his brow furrow the first time he hears it. The second time, his eyes shoot up, locking on mine.

"That him?" he asks.

"I think so," I say.

"I know what you're both thinking, but we have no idea what that is," Hope says, sounding impatient. "It could be a voicemail or a recording. We need to stop chasing conspiracies and look at the probabilities here. The likelihood of Declan surviving that river, staying in hiding, and then pulling off something like this is *beyond* remote."

"I know it's remote," I say, because she's right. There are rules about letting the evidence lead you too quickly for a reason. Even a single hair can change the entire trajectory of an investigation. "We don't have all the pieces yet, so we can't jump to conclusions."

"I hear you," Connor says, "but I know Declan is the only son of a bitch mean enough to do something like this. Who else has ever messed with you like this? Hurt you like this?"

"This isn't how he hurt her," Hope asks. "If he survived that river, he would have shown up and attacked. Maybe he wouldn't call the police, but he had zero reason to stay away."

Connor's expression shifts then, his eyes dropping. "That might not be entirely true."

I move in front of him to make sure he answers me. "What do you mean?"

"I mean I might have given him a good reason to stay away."

FIFTEEN

30 HOURS LEFT

"WHAT GOOD REASON?" I ASK.

Connor tilts his head back and forth like he's loosening up his neck. Or deciding if he can frame this to keep everything under control.

"Connor." My voice is a low warning and he puts his hands up.

"Fine. I told him that when we got back I didn't want to see him. I told him to stay the hell away from you."

"Or what?"

He shrugs. "Or I promised to rip off his arms and beat him to death with the bloody stumps."

"What the hell?" I ask. "Why would you threaten him?"

"Threaten him?" He scoffs. "You're lucky I didn't make good on my promise right then and there. He put fourteen stitches in your head!"

I whirl on Hope, furious. "You *told* him?"

He'd known there was pushing. Violence. No specifics. Or so I thought.

"I was scared!" she defends. "We were *all* scared for you. I thought your mom would have mentioned the stitches to Connor. That he would have put it together."

"Well, she didn't," I say. "She still thinks I fell."

"Well, I didn't know that," Hope defends. "And I didn't prep for secret keeping because you and Declan were *supposed* to be broken up. But then, *boom*! Declan is coming rafting. I told Connor because he heard us arguing at the gas station."

I remember it. She'd been quiet on the ride, and when we stopped for gas, I asked what was up. We got into it a little. Because I hadn't even talked to her about Declan until the night before.

"We didn't talk about stitches at the gas station," I say.

"And I didn't tell Connor about them until he flipped out and started demanding details."

"I didn't flip out," he defends.

She rolls her eyes at him. "You literally threatened to throw us all back in the van and drive home if I didn't tell you what the hell was going on."

I shake my head, still betrayed. "You swore you wouldn't tell."

"Hey!" Connor steps between us. "You want to get pissed, get pissed with me. I had every intention of extracting the information out of Declan myself. She's the one who convinced me not to pound that little shit."

"Threatening him isn't much better, especially with this video floating around," she says, giving him a look that quiets him. "Did anyone hear you talking to him?"

He goes very still. Waiting. Thinking. "I don't know. Possibly. Shit," he says, because it is one more stick to add to the fire of Connor looking guilty.

There is a long, strange beat where shame burns me from the inside out. I caused this. All of it. And now, to make matters worse, I realize Connor knew all along how much I put up with from Declan. Is this why Connor's been so strange with me? Does he see me differently now?

"You should have told me," he says softly.

And I don't say anything, because he's right.

"That doesn't matter right now," Hope says. "We need to focus on finding out who took this video."

"It had to be someone that was there, right?" I ask. "So that means Aiden, Valerie, or Jack."

Hope shakes her head. "None of them makes sense. Aiden was wasted and looking for Declan. Valerie was... I don't know, doing Valerie things. And Jack was on a phone call."

Connor's all in now, stalking back and forth in the living room. "Well, it had to be one of them."

"Unless it's some random stranger. Someone who was on the bridge and took the video and then realized later it might be important?" I shake my head, because I know that can't make sense. "I can't imagine a stranger having any reason to do this though."

"Even if they had a reason, how would they connect it back to us?" he asks. "How would they know enough details to get this video to someone who would want it?"

"Plus, anyone who wants justice or whatever would take it straight to the police." I shake my head. "It doesn't make sense. That's why I just want to get to the end of it. I want to win it and see what the hell is going on."

"Fine. Then win it already," he says. "What's the next clue?"

Hope reads it out.

Do you believe it's over?
Do you really think it's through?
Find the silent people waiting.
Find the lies he wrote for you.

"What lies?" he asks.

"I have no idea," I say. "I don't remember Declan writing me lies. Or any other guy for that matter."

"Can you remember him writing *anything* for you?" Hope asks.

"Not really." I sigh. "God, none of these are easy."

"What about silent people?" Hope asks. "Maybe a cemetery?"

"Creepy," he says.

She arches a brow. "Well, there are silent people there, right?"

"I don't remember being anywhere near a cemetery with him."

My phone rings, and I pull it out, checking the screen absently. It's the Unknown Caller, and the details tell me it's the same ten digits from earlier. The number that's been calling me since this scavenger hunt started.

"Guys," I say. They look at me and I show them my phone as it vibrates again. I think of the voicemail and the music. Declan's voice.

You ready?

"Answer it," Connor says.

My pulse kicks up. On the third ring, I slide my finger across the screen to accept the call and hit the speaker button immediately. Tinny music pours from my speaker. A different song, but still one Declan would play. The lyrics familiar and hollow.

"Hello?" I say.

I hear laughter behind the music. Indistinct. A rustle like the connection has gone bad or someone's muffled the speaker. It still sounds like a pocket dial. But I can hear that laughter. Voices in the background.

"Hello?" I repeat.

"Turn it up," Hope says, but it's already at full volume.

And then: "*This is going to be so great!*"

Connor's eyes lock with mine as the laughter and music continue. One split second, but I know he hears it now. That is one hundred percent Declan's voice.

Suddenly, the sound mutes. The silence is unsettling. I check the screen and find Call Ended displayed.

"Call him back," Connor says.

Not them. Not her. *Him.* He believes it's Declan now. And all the arguments I had against this insane possibility are dying.

I swallow, my throat dry and clicking, and press the screen to redial. I leave the phone on speaker, still turned up loud. Each ring is a jarring electric buzz, an audible jack-in-the-box, sending my nerves jumping.

On the fifth ring, an automatic voice informs us that she's sorry but the subscriber has not set up their voicemail. I disconnect and close my eyes.

"Was that Declan's voice?" Hope asks.

"Yeah," I say. No one argues with me.

"I don't get it. Why call and not talk to you?" Hope says.

"Because this is who he is," I say. "This is what he does."

"It could be someone with a recording of him," Hope says. And she's right. It could be.

"Who else would want to screw with her like this?" Connor asks, speaking my mind for me. "Who else would be motivated to do this?"

We all go quiet then. Declan is the only one with motive to make me pay. Because other than Connor and Hope, he's the only one that knows the truth.

I settle onto the couch and let my gaze drift around my filthy house. The freshly pressed shirts. The cat clock with its swinging tail. The shelf crammed with cookbooks and tools and cans of spray paint.

I freeze, my eyes glued to one of the cans. Red cap, drips of dried paint like blood streaking one side. I remember the hiss of the paint can and my chattering teeth. I'd been so cold that night. So afraid. And the flashlight shook in my hands.

I stand back up abruptly. "I know where it is," I say. "I know what the clue is."

"Where?"

"The old department store building on High Street, just south of Long. I think it was called Madison's."

"That shit's been boarded up for years," Connor says.

"I know. We broke in." I swallow. "Declan and me. He worked there before Greenscapes, so he had the code."

Connor shakes his head. "Son of a bitch did everything he could to get you in trouble."

"Wait, how are you sure it was there? What about the silent people?"

"The mannequins." I shudder. "There were display stands and old mannequins piled up in the corners. They really scared me."

"This is a date for the two of you?" Connor asks. "Cleo, that's a damn hellscape."

"Yeah. Well. Not really a nightmare I was hoping to revisit, but I guess I don't have a choice."

"I'm coming with you," Connor says.

I immediately shake my head. "No way."

"We're both coming," Hope says.

"No. It's dangerous. And it's illegal. And Connor, you're not even supposed to know it's happening. If whoever this is finds out that you do, they might release that video. We've got to try to keep it hidden."

"They won't know."

"They're following us," Hope points out.

"Well, then maybe it's time we turned those tables," Connor says. "Maybe it's time someone tries to follow him."

I can tell by Connor's smile that he's already got a plan.

SIXTEEN

28 HOURS LEFT

AFTER A BREAK FOR COFFEE, GRANOLA BARS, AND dishes—nothing like having to wash out mugs before you can have coffee to remind you of just how messy your house is—we head out. Connor takes off on his bike ten minutes before we leave, but since a growly motorcycle doesn't stand much chance of going incognito, he agrees to park it downtown and hang near the Madison's building on foot. Hope and I head straight to the abandoned store. We park in the alley off Gay Street, just like Declan and I did. The front entrance is on High Street, but it's boarded over and way too busy for a break-in. Plus the construction access keypad is on the back door in the alley.

Of course, the last time I was here, it was eleven o'clock at night, not ten in the morning on a Sunday, so if I felt conspicuous then, today is a whole new ball game.

Hope tries to play it cool, but it takes her five tries to park the car—the easiest parallel-parking slot I've ever seen—and then she just sits there, a white-knuckled grip on the steering wheel and her lip bitten hard enough that I'm sure she'll draw blood.

"You don't have to do this. I'm not sure I want you to do this."

"No, I'm doing it. It's cool. I just..."

"It's not technically breaking in," I say, feeling my cheeks go a little hot. "There's an electronic lock. Declan worked on-site for a while so I have the code."

"Wait, that was over a year ago. Won't it be finished?"

"The whole project has been stalled for way over a year. It's some kind of legal mess. It's been in the news."

"You sure it's still abandoned?"

"Not totally, but I think so. You can still see the lockbox on the back door."

"And you remember the code?"

"Yeah, Declan told me, because it was so easy—seven-forty-seven like the plane."

"Okay," she says.

"We're going to be quick, and we're not going to be suspicious, okay?"

"Okay."

She's so nervous her chin is shaking.

I touch her arm and resist the laugh bubbling up. "Okay, tough guy, I really—"

"I'm doing this." She lifts her chin. "You're right, I'm scared. But I'm doing it."

Five minutes later we're standing by the door. Construction fencing blocks us on the left, but on the right we're wide open, and there's enough traffic on Gay Street to keep my nerves jumping. My fingers shake on the code box, and on the first try, it doesn't work.

Dread rolls through me like a wave. Could they have changed it? Declan swore they never changed stuff like this. That it was too difficult to tell everyone and besides, no one wants to hang out in a shitty, dirty work site if they aren't getting paid.

A car drives by on Gay Street, and I feel Hope tense. "Try to be chill," I say. "I've almost got it."

Seven. Four. Seven. The lock tumbles, and I crack the door open. "We're in."

"Cleo!"

I freeze at the sound of her voice and then feel her hand in my sleeve. Yanking. She wrenches me away from the partly open door and starts marching down the alley without explanation. I follow, stumbling at first, not sure why or what's happening.

And then I look back over my shoulder and see the back end of the police car rolling past the alley.

"Did they keep going?" she asks, slowing.

I stop and wait the span of a breath. Another one. A Buick rolls past. A guy on a sleek racing bicycle. No police. "I think we're good."

We return to the door, which is still unlocked, both of us slipping quickly inside. I push it closed behind me, and we are plunged into a darkness so complete it's shocking. Fortunately, after years of escape rooms and other various mystery experiences, darkness is neither new nor worthy of panic. Hope gets her flashlight on first, illuminating the long, narrow, windowless back room. There is nothing here but walls, floor, and a pile of nondescript shelving at the far end. I see a rectangular cutout in the wall ahead.

"What is this place?" she asks.

"A storage room, I think. We need to be careful to keep the light on the ground once we walk through there. That's the front of the building, so someone might see the light."

"But it's boarded over."

"There's still some glass," I say. "And it's High Street, so it's busy."

Hope shivers. It's cold in here, and eerie. We're in a skeleton of a building, staring at empty space and cracked linoleum tiles. The emptiness is interrupted by occasional beams and hunks of bare concrete in the floor where large display cases have been removed. A sign reading PETITES still hangs on the south wall, but the west wall is covered ceiling to floor in abundant, colorful graffiti, overlapping names and designs, giant swooping letters and at least a dozen versions of a penis and testicles done in yellow paint.

A few smaller display cases have been shoved into a far corner, and heaps of broken drywall and other building detritus are piled everywhere. A pair of slim escalators, hunks of metal tread missing off several steps, climb to a large second-floor balcony. The handrails slope upward like the segmented backs of millipedes, gray and dusty in the dim light. Other than this and a few scattered beer cans and liquor bottles, the room is a bare, hollow shell. But I know where I'm going.

"I guess you weren't the only ones who knew that code," she says.

"Yeah, he said a lot of the guys told their friends. Nobody cared about the graffiti because everything was getting torn down."

"Where's Declan's graffiti?"

"Upstairs on the balcony," I say. It's a sagging, terrifying mess of a second floor, but it held both of us then. Surely it can hold just me now.

I see Hope's eyes grow wide as her gaze drags to the escalators and then up to the pitch-black balcony. I don't remember it being so dark up there before. Then again, I was with Declan. Laughable as it feels now, back then I felt safe.

"The escalators seemed sturdy enough," I say with a shrug.

"Your vast experience in structural engineering reassures me," she says.

In truth, I'm not feeling reassured. "Maybe you can just hang out at the bottom?"

"Sure, I'll just get cozy," she says, gesturing at the piles of rubble.

I laugh, but halfway up, I hesitate. I don't really have a thing with heights. Not like Hope. But I feel like I'm climbing a ladder that's two hundred feet high, and I'm suddenly very aware of how attached I am to the idea of all of my bones being intact. Plus, I'm pretty sure I feel a draft coming from some of the boarded-over windows, which adds to the I'm-up-too-high factor.

I check back to see Hope chewing her thumbnail at the bottom. "Cleo, I don't like this," she says. "It's too dark up there. There's no railing. This is dangerous."

She's right. The half wall that likely once ran the length of the balcony is torn entirely off on either side of the escalator. And is the floor attached to the escalators sloping downward? I can't tell, but with no half wall to keep me from slipping off the edge, even the question is making me feel every inch of the thirty-foot drop to the ground. My mouth goes dry looking into the darkness beyond the balcony edge.

Anyone could be back there. Declan could be waiting in that darkness.

I swallow, and my throat clicks painfully. A single beam of sunlight makes its way through a sizable crack in the front door, casting a bar of illumination directly across the next three steps of the escalator. I pause just below that light, staring at the darkness of the balcony beyond it. Then I remember what Bennett said about making sure my cell phone is charged.

My battery is more than half life, but my bars are low up here. I flip on my cell phone flashlight, but I'm not close enough yet for it to penetrate the shadows.

"Do you have cell phone signal in here?" I ask.

"Yes. Why?"

"Mine's low. I want to make sure we can get a call out, just in case..."

"Your contingency plans are not comforting. Is someone up there with an ax?"

I laugh softly. "No, nothing like that. Just want to be careful."

I look at the sunbeam where dust motes swirl slowly through my field of vision. Once I'm past the sunlight, I can see the dimmest outline of shapes in the balcony. My cell phone beam illuminates a pile of what might be the original half wall and some shelving. I step from the escalator onto the balcony floor and—

I see someone.

Shit!

I step backward, my stomach wadding up tight. I try to scream, but I can't make a sound. I can't even breathe. And then my light catches the figure more clearly. A bald head and slim arm. The hand motionless, two fingers severed at the second knuckle.

It's a mannequin. I put my hand to my chest and try to push my heart back to a normal rhythm. I use my other hand to let the light trail over the mannequin's form. I let out a shaky breath. Another. Adrenaline loops in a wild circuit through my limbs.

"Are you okay? What's going on?"

"Fine," I say. "It's just mannequins. They scared me."

I continue to look them over. The closest one—the one that startled me—is bald and pale, one painted eye chipped and the sculpted nose cracked, revealing the white interior. Another headless mannequin leans beside the first, neck bent at an unnatural angle. Several others in various states of disrepair lean against these two or are piled on the floor. My gaze shifts from one horror to the next, backward-bent arms, broken limbs, and wigs pulled half-free revealing the scalps beneath. A pile of mismatched limbs rest on the floor in front of the mannequin, a macabre scrap yard of department stores past.

"Connor was right," I say. "This is a hellscape. I can't believe I let Declan bring me here."

"It sure looks like a fun date," Hope says sarcastically.

"Oh yeah," I deadpan. "The best." I turn slowly to search the back wall inch by inch, looking for the words he wrote.

Part of me expects them to be painted over, but they aren't. They are still there, dripping and red like he just finished. Like I'll turn and see him standing here again, that paint can in his hand and a cryptic smile on his face, part pleasure at his creation, part amusement at my fear.

But Declan isn't here. Just his words: *C & D forever. Find the lies he wrote for you.*

Mission accomplished. Forever certainly didn't turn out to be true.

At the bottom of the wall, I find the white box I'm looking for. The bow curls smooth and clean over the edges.

"I've got it," I say.

I cross the floor quickly, grabbing the box. I look around, wondering if there's any other evidence here I don't want to miss. Any footprints or telltale trash. Any neon lights that would tell me if this is Declan. If he's back from the dead and determined to make me pay. But there's nothing but smeared footprints and a few random cigarette butts.

"What are you waiting for?" Hope calls.

"Sorry. Coming."

I head toward the escalator on the right side—spotting the discreet Down arrow on the base. Two steps down, the stairs shudder. I freeze, trying to determine what I just felt. But the escalators are still now. Everything is quiet.

And then something snaps, and everything jerks again. Violently this time. Hope and I both scream, and I grab the handrails to keep from falling. The white box—thrown in my terror—sails over the edge of the escalator, landing with a soft thump. Another shudder rattles the treads beneath my feet and the bones inside my body.

"What's happening?" I scream.

"The escalator is coming loose! Get down here! Go!"

My knees have gone to water. I force myself forward, and my legs almost buckle at the first step. Something on the balcony crashes. I can hear things rolling. Sliding. A cloud of dust has risen, and I cough, but I look back. The balcony is still dim and mostly as it was, but a new jagged rip separates part of the floor from the escalator. The balcony—sloped before—is deeply bowed in the center, the floor sagging a full six inches below the top of the escalator.

I inhale sharply and hold it. I'm afraid to move. Afraid to even breathe.

"Cleo!"

"Get out," I say very softly, forcing myself to take another step. "Get out, Hope, it's going to fall."

She's crying now. "I'm not leaving you! Go to the other side."

"Just go." I speak very quietly. Afraid that my voice will be the final straw, the gust of wind that sends this house of cards toppling.

"Shut up and climb over the middle!" Hope shouts. "The other side looks stable."

My heart is hammering at my ribs, a fist of instinct beating to get me out, out, out, of this building. Out of danger. Out of the darkness. More clattering from the balcony, and I see something up there. Movement. Something brown and shiny rolls off the edge. A bottle? I tense as it falls and then shatters into a million glittery pieces.

"Go to the other escalator!" Hope yells. "Right now, Cleo!"

Her voice is a starting pistol, and I practically vault myself onto the divider between the escalators. I crawl over the handrails, thinking of coiling snakes and other scaled things. I have one foot on the good side of the escalator when everything shudders again. I close my eyes and swear. Hope screams. Shouts instructions, but I just hold on tight until it passes.

More things are moving on the balcony. Something heavy. I hear it groaning and scraping at the floor. Wood snapping. Everything is unstable now, the shift of the floor sending the whole balcony off balance. Something clatters, more movement at the edge. I spot the plastic fingers of a mannequin arm, beckoning me back to the darkness.

I don't look again.

As soon as both feet are on the more solid half of the escalator, my strength returns. I descend in the span of a breath. Grab Hope and sprint for the back room.

"Wait," I say. "The clue."

"I've got it," she says, and then she yanks me into a quick, hard hug. She pulls back and I can feel that every part of my body is shaking. But everything else is quiet again.

"Let's go," she says. "Let's get you out of here."

It's maybe thirty seconds until we are outside, the air cool and crisp, tinged with the smell of garbage and gasoline. I breathe deep all the same. Hope steers me quickly to the car and pushes me into the passenger seat.

"Put your seat belt on," she says.

I comply, feeling like a little kid, and then she's getting behind the wheel, fastening her own belt and pulling out her phone to text Connor.

"Don't tell him." My voice is a shock in the quiet.

She looks at me, and I understand now why she's so steady. She's not calm. She's angry.

"I'm not going to tell him," she says. "I just want to know if he saw anyone."

She taps out a message and shortly after, a response buzzes in.

Hope's mouth goes tight. "He didn't see anyone. Says there are too many people on the big streets. He's been circling the block."

"You're angry," I say.

"Yes," she says. She sounds dangerously calm. "When we find who did this, who put you through all of this? I'm going to make sure they have nothing that can't hurt you or Connor. And then I'm going to ruin them."

SEVENTEEN

26 HOURS LEFT

WE'RE BACK AT THE HOUSE DRINKING COFFEE WHEN Connor rolls back in, yanking off his helmet and looking seriously annoyed.

"You're sure you didn't see anyone?"

Connor shakes his head, his bouncy curls making it difficult to take his anger seriously. "Can I ask you something? Is there a single asshole in downtown Columbus who isn't brunching on a Sunday morning?"

"Some of us like to break into abandoned department stores," I say.

"Not funny," Hope says. She hasn't shaken that cold fury from her face. I've seen Hope mad—not often, but it happens. But this is something else entirely.

"What's the clue say?" Connor asks.

I read it.

One Two Six Two Zeroes Four.

You'll find your clue behind this door.

They say the truth will set you free.

You're getting close.

Are you ready to see?

Hope frowns. "What's the phone number that's calling you? Is one-two-six part of it?"

I check, but shake my head. "Might be part of some phone number, but not that one."

"Is the number familiar?" Connor asks.

"Not off the top of my head," I say. "Maybe map coordinates or an address."

I don't jump up to check. Honestly, I'm rattled and queasy, and I don't want to do this anymore. I feel like Declan is waiting in every shadow now, his laugh echoing around every corner.

"I'm going to go clean up and change, I think," I say. I don't really need to change, which they might notice if they weren't eyeballs deep in all the long looks and silent drama that's hanging between them. But they nod, and so I slip off to my room and sit on my bed.

It's hard to be still. I fiddle with my end table. Straighten pillows that are already straight as if enough tidying will solve my problems along with my clutter. I remember feeling this way at the end with Declan. Sick with dread, my nerves jumping at every sound. I was always waiting. Wondering when he'd snap. I press my fingers to the scar in the back of my head and squeeze my eyes shut against the past.

I call Bennett because I don't want to think about the end with Declan. I want to feel normal.

"I was starting to think you were a myth," he says, and I realize I've ignored a couple of his texts.

"I'm beginning to feel like a myth."

"How goes the hunting? Are there more creepy photos I should be worried about?" Bennett sounds hopeful that this scavenger hunt is back to being a charming, quirky birthday gift. Why wouldn't he hope for that? He still thinks I'm ordinary like him, a girl who doesn't have dangerous enemies or dark secrets. And I want him to continue believing that.

"No, no, it's all fine now," I say, knowing it's almost certainly not fine. "But I don't really know where it's leading."

"Well, that's the part you like about mysteries, right? The intrigue! The excitement!"

I laugh, but it's half-hearted. "I guess. I think I'm just a little tired. So, how was the yarn store?" The background is loud again. Like he's outside, maybe in a crowd. I frown. "Where are you, anyway?"

"I want to talk to you about yarn and other assorted craft supplies, but not yet," he says. "For now, I think you need to see something. It's very serious."

I sit up. "Okay."

"I need you to brace yourself."

My chest goes tight. Because I thought he was kidding, but now I'm not so sure. Did someone send him the video of Connor?

My heart double thumps. If there's a video of Connor, is there another video? One of me?

"Are you braced, Cleo?"

"I guess so."

I feel my phone buzz and open it to see a photo of Bennett with the largest ice cream sundae I have ever seen. It's easily twelve scoops of ice cream, mounds of whipped cream. Cherries everywhere. And Bennett's nose and eyes over the top. He looks ridiculous.

I burst out laughing.

"It's not funny. I ate this in twenty minutes."

I continue to laugh.

"You're quite insensitive. Frankly, I might die."

"You won't die."

"Eight scoops of ice cream beg to differ with you." He sighs. "So give me *your* scoop. What's happened since we last talked? Other than scavenger-hunt shenanigans."

"Totally boring," I say, wincing at how easily the lies pour out of me. But then I think of something I can be honest about. "Hey, can I ask you something?"

"Shoot."

"I know you haven't been around us all that much, but have you ever noticed anything between Connor and Hope?"

"Are you referring to all the weird sexual tension?"

"Ew! Oh my God, am I the only person alive who didn't know about this?"

"Eh, I figured it was one of those sibling things. It's impossible to see a brother as anything but the little twerp that wrestled you for the last Pop-Tart."

I laugh again. "Who says twerp?"

"Only the coolest people."

We chat for a few more minutes about mundane things and possible birthday plans after he's back in town. It's nice to think about something else. To remember my life before this hunt upended everything.

When we hang up, I look at the ice cream photo one more time before I decide to check on Connor and Hope. Maybe they've had enough time to talk. My bedroom door is still open a crack, so I stop to listen. It's awfully quiet out there and I really don't want to see my best friend and brother making out on the couch, so I pause.

Connor's voice drifts out of the living room, breaking the silence. "It's not why I didn't call you," he says, settling that fear.

Hope sounds tired. "I said we don't have to talk about it."

"Right." Connor laughs but it's clear he isn't amused. "Why talk about it?"

"I tried. I texted you every day for a month," Hope whispers.

"I'm shit at texts. And I told you how weird everything's been since..."

"I get that. And I was okay with it until I realized weird just means you don't want to admit what this is."

"What this is? You won't let *this* be anything!"

"We can't do this right now," she says. "We have to figure out these clues so we can end this nightmare."

"I hate the idea of someone having something on her," he says.

His words squeeze at my heart. And even though this is straight-up eavesdropping, I can't force myself to walk away.

"Has she told you any more about what really happened?" Hope asks softly.

"No. I don't give a shit about the details."

"You might if there's more to that video."

My arms and neck feel tingly and cold in the silence that follows. Connor doesn't ask her what she means because he obviously knows. Because if they have video of Connor cleaning up the scene, they might have video of the thing that needed cleaning up. Video of me.

I turn and press my back to the wall beside my door, my eyes drifting to the Michigan State brochure on my desk. I know I need to tell them, but how do I explain? How can I make them understand that five minutes can change your whole world—that five minutes can drive you to kill someone?

I close my eyes and let myself remember:

Another mosquito needled my arm. I smacked it and leaned to my left, catching sight of the campfire. The campfire would keep the worst of them away, but Valerie was the only one there. I kept myself hidden behind the tent. I'd just spent forty-five minutes hiking along the river with Valerie having the weirdest conversation of all time, and I was not interested in more alone time. Where was everyone?

Birds chirped shrill warnings as I wandered the narrow footpaths that crisscrossed the woods along the river. I heard a murmur of voices in the distance, but they quickly faded to quiet. And then nothing. Nothing but the water, brown and angry and churning.

And then, he was there. Declan.

Tears streaked his face, and his pupils were blown wide. He was on something. Drunk. High. Take your pick. He jabbed a finger at me and I could see it shake.

"Cleo." My name stretched loose and strange in his mouth. The scar on the back of my head—still pink and tender—prickled with pain. My new warning that danger was near.

"What's up?"

"What's up?" He laughed, rubbing a hand down his face. I scanned for an exit. Thorn bushes to my left. Trees on my right. The river—hungry and growling—waited five feet behind me. My heart pounded behind my ears. In the tips of my fingers. I was in trouble.

"I'm headed back to camp. Hope's waiting for me." I moved to pass him, and that was it.

No warning. I saw the flash of his teeth and then he slammed into me.

I hit the ground back first, landed so hard that light burst across my vision. The pain was a shock—it was all a shock—but I rolled over, seeing the bridge ten yards away, the edge of the earth, and the water rushing below me.

No. Not that. I had to get away from the water.

I pushed up to my knees, trying to stand. Declan leaped on my back. My teeth clacked, catching the side of my tongue. Blood, warm and coppery, filled my mouth. I tried to scream, but his hands were on my throat.

"Did you think you could do this to me? Did you think I'd let you get away with it?"

The river roared on, reminding me that no one would hear this. No one would hear me. I felt his weight shift off me. My neck was free. My hair had come loose from my ponytail. I inhaled hard, dragging air into my greedy lungs.

I had to go. Move! I tried to scream, but only gurgled and coughed. I tried to scrabble away, but he'd gotten my ankle. My leg. He yanked me over like a rag doll, and now he was on my chest, heavy and choking me.

Choking me.

"You planned this!"

I blinked my eyes open. He was apoplectic, red-faced with drops of spittle on his chin. And he swayed over me, or maybe my vision was going. My lungs burned like I was underwater. My throat throbbed.

I clawed at his arms, squirmed. The river ran eight feet below us, water gushing around the bend.

"I'll kill you, Cleo." He gritted the words through his teeth. "I'll kill you."

I knew now, this is where it would end. Him. Us. Me. I didn't hear the water or see his face. Everything went dark and quiet. But my heart still thumped hard and frantic. A drumbeat commanding me to fight.

I jerked my leg up, rammed my knee into his groin. Elbowed his mouth. He wobbled and groaned above me. I covered my face instinctively as he spit. Blood and saliva spattered the backs of my hands, warm and wet.

I gulped a few painful breaths, and my vision swam back, light leaking into the gray. The river was close. Churning. I flopped to my side, and felt him reach for me, but then I was up. Up!

He snagged a handful of my hair and slammed me into a tree. I was too close to the edge. I was going to fall. Oh, God, I couldn't get away from him.

"You scared of that water, Cleo?" he snarled. "Let's put you in there and see how you do. You think anyone would hear you scream?"

His voice was mockery, and his fingers squeezed hard around my arm. He started to drag me. I screamed, wrapping an arm and then a leg around the tree. That cruel laugh was in my ears, and I could feel the spray of the water and then some desperate instinct—hunger to live—fired new adrenaline into me. I released the tree and jabbed at his eyes. Then his throat.

He howled. Rage, terror, and pain contorted his features. He stumbled, and I remembered the kitchen. My hands slipping on my own blood.

But Declan was slipping this time, backward down the bank. He reached out to me, and I looked him in the eyes and pushed—one hard pop, just like the one he gave me. But he didn't fly like I did. He slid back and down and then the current had him, pulled him from the shore into its greedy, frothing mouth.

I saw it happen. Watched his eyes go wide with terror, his hands outstretched, long fingers splayed wide. The river sucked him down, rolled him under, this boy I once loved.

I didn't do anything. I didn't make a noise. I watched him disappear in the rapids. And then I ran.

I ran until my head swam and the world went gray. I ran until my knees hit dirt and the gray darkened to black.

I woke up with Connor standing over me, my own blood in my mouth and Declan's blood on my hands.

EIGHTEEN

25 HOURS LEFT

THE MEMORIES LEAVE ME SHAKING AND ASHAMED. I make my bed, though it's already made, pulling the comforter tight and arranging the pillows just so. I straighten my shoes in the bottom of my closet and startle when Hope pushes open my door without knocking. Her face is flushed, and her ponytail is swinging, and I need to tell her the absolute truth. That I didn't watch—I wasn't just there. I pushed Declan in.

But something intense in her expression stops me.

"What's wrong?" I ask.

"I figured it out. The clue is leading us to Valerie." Seeing my confused look, she waggles the clue and reads it again.

> **One Two Six Two Zeroes Four.**
> **You'll find your clue behind this door.**
> **They say the truth will set you free.**

You're getting close.

Are you ready to see?

"Okay." I don't really know where she's going here, but I'm listening.

"Do you remember the triple date?" Hope prompts. "You and Declan, me and Jack, Valerie and Jana."

"I remember it was awful," I say. Mostly because of Declan. We got into it. Story of our relationship.

"Do you remember what day that was?" she asks.

"Right after New Year's Day."

She grins and nods. "Right. January second. One. Two. And I'll bet you can guess Valerie's address."

"6004 Town Street," I say. "Let's go."

I push my feet into my shoes and grab my jacket in case it cools down later. Connor is right behind us when a call comes in on his cell phone.

"Mr. Kunzig," he says. And then he pauses, presumably to listen. "Yes, I believe Maya took that deposition last week. Would you be willing to hold on for one moment?" He covers the speaker and looks at us. "Give me like ten minutes."

Hope waves him off. "We've got this. It's only Valerie."

"Go be a hot-shot lawyer person," I say.

"I'm just an intern," he says, but then he gets back on the phone and pulls a laptop out of his bag. "Actually, sir, I've been keeping an online database of interviews, depositions, anything recorded for that case. If you'd like I can take a look and send you a link."

Another pause.

"In the office now? Sure, I can come in." He covers the microphone. "He wants me in. Just for a bit."

"It's fine," I say. "Go!"

"Just keep killing it," Hope whispers. "We'll catch up soon."

He grins and his eyes follow Hope all the way out the door.

Once we get in the car, I turn to her. "Okay, I'm going to talk to you about the thing with my brother, and I'm going to channel every mature, not-dramatic bone in my body to do it."

She smiles. "Well, there's a first time for everything."

I stay the course. Because I don't want her thinking I wouldn't be okay with this. "Look. I know I reacted weirdly. I mean it is Connor. I remember when he told my entire kindergarten class that when I was little, I sometimes pooped my pants."

"Isn't that still how Connor introduces you?"

"Ha ha," I deadpan. "Don't change the subject. I need to say that I'm sorry. I love you. You know that. And I love Connor. So if it's real and it matters, then I wish you the best."

Her cheeks are a touch pink now, and the joking twinkle is gone from her eyes. "Okay."

"I wish you'd told me though," I say.

"It was just weird, you know? We started talking a couple of months before West Virginia. He came into Starbucks a lot. I worked pretty close to one of the libraries where he used to study."

"Does he really study at libraries?"

"Not usually, no." She's really blushing now. "But we laughed a lot that day and talked about my business idea, and he was really into it, you know? He said he had no idea I thought about things like that."

I nod, because I can see this now. I love them both—surely I noticed some of the similarities between them. Both of them are so focused and driven, so good at everything they try. I guess I just never imagined it would be those same similarities that pulled them together.

"So, what happened?" I ask.

"Not much. We took walks sometimes, but it didn't feel like a thing we could do."

"Because of Jack?"

Her brow crinkles. "Well, yeah. Jack. But also, I knew about stuff that was happening with you and Declan. After a while, he sensed I was hiding things. And in West Virginia…"

"He found out what those things were." I sigh. "I'm guessing that put a damper on it."

"There are lots of things that stand between Connor and me," she says. "We're still friends. I still helped him over the phone with his application. It's something, I guess."

And then she turns on the car and puts it in reverse, and I know we're done talking about this. Soon enough, we're parking in front of Valerie's for the second time.

Valerie answers the door looking a little sweaty and beat, rosin staining her wrists and her T-shirt still clinging. Since her

Sundays usually include a good six hours at the gym, her appearance isn't surprising. I don't know how she's even upright. But then she smiles like the cat that ate the canary, and all the exhaustion seems to melt away.

"I knew you guys would get it," she says. She pulls a white box with a green bow from behind her back and hands it over.

"Are you the one behind all of this? Is this all you?" I ask.

"Ugh, I wish I could take credit for this. I have no idea who this is or how they knew to leave this thing at my house." She waves her hands. "Just open it. I'll tell you everything in a minute." Then she turns and hollers up the stairs. "Aiden, Hope and Cleo are here! Come down!"

Mrs. Drummond breezes through with a basket of laundry. "Hi, girls! Aiden's still at work."

"Oh," she frowns. "I thought he'd be back."

We take our normal places on the couch, but this time Hope is closer to me. I slide the ribbon off, but pause. I'm still not convinced this isn't them. It has to be Valerie or Aiden, doesn't it? But if it is, they're determined to keep it quiet.

So, I have to play along and wait for someone to slip.

"Do you know it's been a year since our trip?" I ask quietly.

Valerie heaves a sigh of relief. "I know. I'm glad you said something. I didn't want to bring it up, but I've been thinking about it. With Aiden and all…"

"I think this hunt might have something to do with what happened in West Virginia," I say.

Her face tightens. "Look, I don't mean to be insensitive, and I'm sorry for how hard that was, but I really don't want to bring that up around Aiden if he gets here. He's just…"

She trails off, but I nod because I know what she means. Aiden and Declan were close. Well. Aiden was close to Declan. They met as soon as Declan moved in, and though Aiden's usually the poster child of melancholy and strange, he lit up around Declan. Declan pulled him out of his shell. Got him laughing.

Got him high, if we want to get to the truth of it.

And when Declan was gone, he sank deeper into that sad, quiet boy he was before.

I turn the gift around in my hands and decide to cut to the chase. "So, you're sure this isn't your handiwork?"

Valerie's laugh is genuine. "I barely have time to shave my legs, and you think I'm putting together a scavenger hunt? Sorry to disappoint, but no."

"Then how did you get this thing anyway?" Hope asks.

"Aiden and I found it on the porch when we got back from the gym today. Maybe the better question is why *I'm* part of your scavenger hunt?"

Is she lying? I think of her dragging me into the woods in West Virginia, that long, winding conversation about nothing and everything. The whole thing felt like a setup—like she was killing time with me. Is this a setup too?

"It's a mystery," I say.

"Sure is," Valerie says, holding my eyes. No smile now.

The hair on the back of my neck stands upright. Something changed with Valerie after that trip. Was it the video? The hunt? I'd bet money there isn't a question around that will get me a straight answer.

"How did you know we'd come for it?" Hope asks.

"There was a note attached telling me not to open it and not to say a word unless you showed up here looking for it." She pulls it off the end table to show us.

I sigh. It's the same paper and font as the clues. Absolutely zero help.

"Are you going to read it?" Valerie asks. She looks amused. Or I'm reading all kinds of crap into things. Either is possible.

I read it.

Past the bricks, before the fountain.
Up the stairs, through a haunt.
Time to see what really happened.
Because your guilt isn't what I want.

"Oooh," Valerie says, grinning wide. "Sounds mysterious."

It does sound mysterious. It also sounds vague as hell.

"Do you guys have a doorbell camera or anything?" Hope asks. "So we could see who left this?"

"Mom would never go for it." Valerie rolls her eyes. "She's all about believing in the goodness of people or whatever. Do you think this might be Bennett? He's a smart cookie, and he's sweet enough to set all this up."

I laugh at that. Valerie has no idea how very not sweet this hunt is. "No, it's definitely not Bennett. He's with his grandma this weekend."

Valerie starts to shake her head, but then stops. "His grandma?"

"Yeah. Antique stores and stuff."

She laughs awkwardly. "Sorry, I thought I… Never mind. I'm sure I read it wrong."

"Read what wrong?"

"Nothing, I thought I saw a thing… Forget it. It's no big deal." Valerie stands up. "Did you guys want a Coke or anything?"

Hope and I exchange a look, and Valerie isn't with us as much now, but she knows us. We were all a group once. We went to our first homecoming together and drifted around the same Halloween parties and shared rides after school.

Valerie sighs. "I don't think he's driving his grandma around."

She pulls up her phone and taps something into the screen. Then she turns a social media page toward me. A picture of a couple of our classmates and Bennett's friends, Ty and Owen. They're all wearing New York paraphernalia, hats and T-shirts of every team and logo I can think of.

The caption reads: "Good luck in the Big Apple this weekend!"

Bennett is tagged.

I double-check the date. Bennett's name. Then I shake my head. "I don't know what that's about, but he's not in New York. He was at a yarn shop earlier today."

But then I remember the noise I heard on the call. Was he really in New York? Is he lying to me?

"Who knows," Valerie says. Now she's all bright eyed and grinning again. "Maybe he's throwing everyone off the trail so he could plan this scavenger hunt for you. He's probably going to be waiting at a cabin with flowers and dinner when you get to the end."

Given the things we've found so far, he'd be waiting at that cabin with the police and my alcoholic ex-boyfriend returned from the dead.

"My sister thinks the whole world is a romantic comedy," Aiden says.

I turn to spot him in the doorway. He's still sporting dark circles beneath his eyes, and his hair needs a meeting with the business end of a pair of scissors. I'm also pretty sure he was wearing that same shirt yesterday.

I never totally understood his connection with Declan, but it was real. Even before the drugs, they sort of clicked. For a while I thought maybe Aiden was in love, but Valerie told me it was less like that and more like hero worship. Worship worked just fine for Declan, but Declan trusted Aiden too.

Maybe enough to tell him things about us?

I look at Aiden and try to imagine a world where he'd do this.

Type up clues and tie bows on boxes. I don't know if I could see it, but I don't think it's impossible.

"Hey, would you show Valerie the other clues?" I ask Hope.

"Sure," she says, reading my mind. "Come out to the car with me?"

Valerie hesitates, giving a reluctant look at Aiden before following Hope out. She looks nervous, and I get it. If it were my brother with hollow eyes and a perpetual frown, I wouldn't want someone dragging up traumatizing memories.

When the door closes behind them, I take a steadying breath. Aiden is watching me, so how do I approach this? How do I find out what he knows or if he's involved without triggering some sort of spiral?

"You want to talk to me, right?" he asks.

"What?"

He's fidgeting with his pockets and nods toward the front door. "Hope and Valerie. That seemed weird, so I'm assuming you wanted to talk to me alone."

"I did." I squirm on the couch, suddenly feeling uncomfortable thinking of what Valerie said. "But I'm second-guessing it, honestly."

"Because you want to talk to me about Declan?"

I flinch and he looks at me, but only for a second. Then his eyes are back on the ground, his thin fingers still plucking at the edges of his pockets, pulling threads loose.

"I never talked to you much after that," I say.

"You never talked to me much before that."

"Point taken," I admit. "It felt weird, especially at the end of things with Declan."

"Because he was hitting you," he says.

"It wasn't—" I cut myself off, because I have to stop this. The details of whether it was hitting, shoving, whatever the hell, aren't the point. The point is, he knows what was going on. This big secret I thought I was hiding? Everyone knew.

My face burns and it's my turn to look down. "I didn't know you knew."

"Secrets have a way of getting out," he says.

I half expect him to say he's sorry this happened. To apologize for not stepping in. For not rescuing me. But he doesn't, and that's better. It isn't just the shame that keeps me from telling people. It's the pity.

"So, what do you want to ask me?" he asks.

"Do you know anything else about what happened to Declan?" I ask. "Anything you maybe remembered or heard about later?"

Or didn't tell the police when we were there? I don't add that part but he knows that's what I'm asking. Aiden was on probation when we were in West Virginia. It was a stupid case, shoplifting or something, but the judge threw the book at him. When the cops arrived on the scene, Aiden was higher than a kite, sick with grief, and breaking probation by being out of state. I know he didn't say a word, but I don't know what he saw.

"What are you talking about?" he asks tightly. "Is there something you know, Cleo?"

My chest feels too tight, but I force myself to stay calm. I choose my words very carefully, aware of Valerie outside. The slope of Aiden's shoulders and the suspicion in his eyes. Does he know something? Is he starting to suspect me? "I think this scavenger hunt has something to do with what happened to Declan. I think there's more to this that some of us don't know and whoever's doing this hunt is dragging me back through it."

"What's the point in that?"

"What do you mean?"

"He's still dead, isn't he?" He watches me very carefully. "You know very well he isn't coming back from that river."

His expression feels like an accusation, or maybe that's just guilt. Aiden had to cover his ass in West Virginia, so he didn't say so much as two words to the officers milling around camp. I always assumed he hadn't said anything because he hadn't seen anything. But now I'm not so sure.

Now I wonder if Aiden knows exactly what I did to Declan. Because he'd definitely be a person who'd want me to pay.

NINETEEN

24 HOURS LEFT

HOPE AND I GRAB A LATE LUNCH AT SUNNY'S DINER. I don't know how to talk to Bennett about the New York post thing. I also have no idea what to do about my suspicions about Aiden, especially without explaining to Hope in crystal-clear detail that I *pushed* Declan into the river—a fact that would certainly give Aiden a reason to be upset if he'd witnessed it. Here under the bright lights and the smell of bacon grease, none of these conversations hold much appeal. I'm just tired. Tired of suspecting every person who had anything to do with West Virginia of wanting to serve me a cold dish of vengeance and tired of vague-ass clues that leave me stumped and frustrated.

I have breakfast, because I'm firmly convinced there is no food on earth that rivals the glory of pancakes, eggs, and bacon. Hope has a tuna sandwich, because even her lunches follow the wholesome rule. While I drag bites of pancake through a river of syrup, I fill her in on the Aiden conversation. She looks thoughtful but unconvinced.

"Think about it," I say. "He could have taken the video. He was there."

"But he was obliterated," she says. "Like so high the paramedics were looking at him and whispering. Do you remember?"

"I do," I say.

"Plus, he loved Declan. If he thought Connor was covering something up and had proof, he would have said something."

"He couldn't have said anything because he would have been in huge trouble over that trip. They both could have been. He wasn't just breaking probation. He forged a guardian signature on Valerie, remember?"

"Oh, that's right," Hope says. Valerie's parents hadn't signed all the right forms, so when we were getting everything in order, Aiden signed for her dad, and she agreed to play along.

"Neither of them would have wanted to have the police asking questions."

"Fine, but why not tell someone in the group?" she asks. "I get not talking to the police, but wouldn't they have wanted to talk to one of us?"

"I don't know," I admit, but I remember his words. *What's the point in that?* "Maybe he didn't see the point of it because Declan was gone either way."

I cringe at the thought that Aiden might be wrong about

that. Declan could be alive and currently executing the most terrifying scavenger hunt of my life.

"I don't know," she says, "but if it's Aiden behind everything, it makes it less scary, right? He has his issues, but I couldn't see him hurting anyone. Maybe he's just lashing out."

"Maybe."

"What about the clue?" she asks.

I read it again:

> **Past the bricks, before the fountain.**
> **Up the stairs, through a haunt.**
> **Time to see what really happened.**
> **Because your guilt isn't what I want.**

"The brick makes me think of German Village, so maybe it's past that, but before the big fountains on the waterfront?"

"I don't think there is anything between German Village and that park," I say. "I mean, other than the freeway."

"The Brewery District? Does anything there seem significant?"

"Not really. Declan worked in German Village. At Katzinger's. I don't think there's a fountain near there."

"I'm going to search German Village." She pulls out her phone and starts tapping. "Whoa. Check this out. Have you been to Schwartz Castle? Because it's in German Village, it's brick, it has plenty of stairs, and it's apparently haunted by a naked apothecary owner."

"I'm sorry, what?"

She turns the screen to show me and sure enough, there it is. A towering, unfamiliar castle on Third Street with a history of a naked man sitting in the glass turret at the top of the mansion, mourning the lover who jilted him.

"Does it look familiar?" She asks.

"Not really. But everything down there looks like that, right? We did take some walks."

"Maybe we should drive by," she says. "Let me run to the bathroom really quick first."

"I'll get them to split it," I say.

"No, I'll get it," she says. "Just sign for me."

"Hope, you have to let me get the next one."

She nods, but I don't know that she's paying attention. She always pays, which is nice, but it also makes me feel a little like the Walmart tank top I'm wearing.

I sign her name on the slip and leave a tip, and then someone with dark, floppy hair and wide shoulders walks in. For a second, I think it's Bennett. It's not, of course. Bennett is at antique malls and yarn stores.

Or so he said.

All of my couldn't-care-less chill factor about Bennett's whereabouts suddenly fly out the window. I call him. Three times when he doesn't answer, because apparently, I'm hoping to major in Paranoia and Controlling Behaviors in college.

Bennett doesn't call me back, but he does text.

Bennett: Are you trapped in a well?

Me: I need to talk to you.

Bennett: That doesn't sound fun.

Me: I'm not sure it will be.

Bennett: I can't talk now. In a store.

Me: In New York?

The replying dots appear and then disappear. Do the same thing three more times. My face is so hot, I'm sure if I open my mouth, steam will roll out. He knows I'm on to him.

And that's—God, it's ridiculous. This is Bennett. *Bennett.* He's not some douchey guy with girls on the side. He's ridiculous and a little dorky and generally the kind of boyfriend moms like Mrs. Deb try to set you up with.

Except that he's lying to me now.

"You okay over there?" Hope asks. She's back from the bathroom and zipping her jacket.

My phone buzzes.

Bennett: I'll call you in an hour.

"Just dealing with my lying boyfriend." I bite my lip and drop my phone in my purse as we get into the car. "My whole world is turning into mysteries and deception this weekend."

"Okay, melodrama llama. He's really not with his grandma?"

I sigh. "No idea. I think Valerie might be right."

Hope buckles up and starts the engine. "Just talk to him. If he is, there's got to be an explanation. Maybe they changed plans."

"You're right, he'll tell me what's up," I say.

"Do you want to talk about it?"

"Not yet. Distract me."

"Okay, let's put aside Bennett and go back to German Village. Katzinger's is on Third, right?"

"Yeah."

"Did you guys walk around down there much?"

"Well, sometimes when he'd get off we'd get a coffee at Stauff's. Or I'd drag him down to the Book Loft."

The Book Loft, our city's crown jewel of cool, is a towering, meandering maze of books—thirty-two rooms of heaven to be precise.

With bricks. And stairs. And a fountain.

Past the bricks, before the fountain.
Up the stairs, through a haunt.
Time to see what really happened.
Because your guilt isn't what I want.

The Book Loft has brick steps leading to the entrance, and there's a fountain just past the front entrance. I've heard it gurgling when I looked over the outside tables. And I did that with Declan. More than once, coffees in hand and weird flute and harp-heavy music pouring from the speakers.

"It's the Book Loft," I say.

Her eyes light up and she turns left at a traffic light. Heading south toward German Village. "You might be on to something."

I nod. "I am. The bricks and the stairs. And not to mention the fact that Declan took me here on Valentine's Day."

She hangs a left on Third Street. "I thought you told me once that he didn't like books."

"He didn't, but he thought the Book Loft was cool."

"Everyone does."

He wasn't a reader by any stretch, but he did like the way the building felt like a maze. He was always wanting to sneak into the restricted areas and would check the windows to see if we could get out onto the narrow balconies that trim the front and side of the building. On Valentine's Day he tried to steal me a book of poetry, but I wasn't having it.

It wasn't our first fight, but it was the first time he really shoved me. Not hit. No slap or punch—he was careful about that. Just a push to my shoulder to *move me* out of his way. It had been happening here and there, brushing past me a little too hard, snatching things out of my hands. Not violent, but rough. Back then, I was stupid enough to believe it was no big deal.

"Did you spend a lot of time in one room?" she asks. "We're going to need to find something specific. There are thirty-two rooms in there."

Hope's phone buzzes and her mom's face appears on the screen. She answers on her headphones. "Hey, Mom!"

She gives me half an eyeroll, but it's not in earnest. Mrs. Deb is great. She's funny and smart, and she's always sweet to me. "No, I'm just out with Cleo. We had lunch."

She looks over at me. "Mom says hi."

"Hi, Mrs. Deb!"

"No, we're just... Oh, crap. I'm so sorry, I completely forgot."

Her mom says something, but I can see Hope shaking her head before she's even finished. "No, no, I'll come. I completely mixed it up. Let me drop her, and I'll be there in a minute."

Hope pulls to a stop behind one of the pedal buses, full of midday drinkers pedaling their way from one bar to the next. She finishes the call with her mom, and we move slowly along behind them.

"So, I've got to make a detour."

"Everything okay?"

"Mom's getting her car worked on, and I was supposed to pick her up. I'm going to drop you and come back if that's okay."

"Sure, of course."

She pulls to the curb across the street and frowns. "I'm really sorry about this. Maybe I should call Connor so you aren't alone."

"It's fine. This is a bookstore next to a coffee shop in the most touristy part of town. I'm not going to get shanked by the cookbooks."

"I don't know," she says. "Connor would kill me if I let you go off on your own right now."

"Connor won't know anything about it," I say. "Just text him an update about the Aiden situation and tell him we'll check in as soon as we're done. It's fine. I swear."

"All right. It'll be an hour max. Text me if you find it."

"I will." I hop out and look across the street, and Hope laughs.

"Hurry your butt up—there's traffic!"

Someone honks behind her and I laugh too. "See you soon."

Hope pulls away and I look across the street at my destination. A red cloth banner hangs over a tall black iron gate. It reads: *Willkommen—The Book Loft.*

The first time I visited the Book Loft was when Hope turned ten. We had a Big City Birthday, and Mrs. Deb took us to a fancy downtown Italian restaurant. I don't remember it well, except that there were candles on the tables and long, white tablecloths that I was terrified to stain. But I remember my first walk through this bookstore perfectly. It felt like magic then, and it still does.

I step off the sidewalk to cross the street and hear the screech of tires on pavement—a car trying to brake. I whirl like I'm underwater, like my limbs are weighted and moving in half-time. Sunlight flashes on a windshield. A gleaming red bumper shudders toward me. I lift one stone-heavy leg and hurl myself left. The car veers right, but I know it's too close.

I'm not going to make it.

I'm going to—

The car squeals to a stop, and I crumple, going down on one knee. My palms kiss asphalt, and I open my eyes. The bumper is inches from my nose. The engine idles, and I push myself up, smelling fear and gasoline.

I hear the engine rev as I stand. I raise my hand to assure the driver I'm okay, but the car jerks forward. I leap back, stunned, and then the car guns it, squealing tires as they pull around me. I sprint to the sidewalk and try to make out what I can about the driver. They're too far past. I can only see a small, pale hand raised outside of the window, the middle finger raised in my direction.

My heart is pounding so hard I feel it in my throat as I look both ways again and carefully cross the street.

"Are you all right?" a woman asks. A barista from Stauff's coffee shop is standing in the open door. Her apron is stained with dark blotches, and her tired eyes are full of concern.

I nod, not capable of speech.

"I've never seen anything like that shit," she says. "That idiot almost killed you and then got pissed like it was your fault."

I still feel a little breathless. "Did you happen to get a license plate?"

"Sorry, no. It was an older Mustang. Not sure if that helps."

"Thanks," I say. "I appreciate it."

"Come in when you're done calling the police. I'll make you whatever you want on the house."

"Thank you. I will."

Though in truth, I won't be calling. The downside to learning about forensics and crime investigation is…well, learning about crime scene investigation. Calling the police to report a red Mustang that almost hit me is the vehicular version of reporting a needle in a stack of needles.

I turn toward the Book Loft, and my phone buzzes. I fumble to pull it out of my pocket, sure somehow Hope has seen what happened. That she'll ask if I'm okay and rush back over. But it's not Hope. It's a picture of me taken getting out of her car. Hope is behind the wheel, her ponytail a bright yellow ribbon behind the windshield.

Unknown: You should be more careful.

Me: Are you threatening me? Was that you?

Unknown: We both know what can happen when someone goes walking alone.

I pause for a moment, staring at the screen, knees still wobbly from the car that almost ran me over. And now this. I look around in every possible direction. I don't know anyone who drives a Mustang, but someone saw this. Someone took a photo.

Me: Is this Aiden?

Unknown: Finish the hunt, Cleo. Or I'll make sure Connor's school knows about his out-of-state activities. And maybe Michigan State needs an update on what you've been up to.

I swear, pacing a short loop in front of the coffee shop. My phone buzzes one more time.

Unknown: Stop pacing and get moving.

I look up, chills rolling down my spine. I check every car on the street. Every window. I see nothing, but I feel invisible eyes on me everywhere.

I try to remember that this is supposed to be a game. A scavenger hunt.

But it's hard not to feel like I'm the one being hunted.

TWENTY

22 HOURS LEFT

I STEADY MYSELF WITH A HOT MOCHA FROM STAUFF'S and do a little snooping in case my spy is grabbing coffee too. After searching every table at the coffee shop, and even the courtyard on the side—still not opened for spring—I find nothing. Outside I realize there are at least a dozen businesses or buildings nearby. Finding the person who was watching me is more than a long shot. It's a lost cause.

I pull myself together and march toward the bookstore. It's after four o'clock. In less than twenty-four hours, this game will be over, win or lose. And since losing could cost my brother and I both everything, I intend to win.

I look at the clue one more time, making sure I have every word fresh in my head.

Past the bricks, before the fountain.

Up the stairs, through a haunt.

Time to see what really happened.

Because your guilt isn't what I want.

I walk under the familiar red banner and up the brick steps that will take me to the bookstore entrance. It's beautiful, but I don't take time to enjoy it. I keep moving. As I approach the covered entrance, the tables come into view, stacks of books with familiar orange price stickers. I run my fingers over a pile of Bill Bryson books next to old copies of *The Hitchhiker's Guide to the Galaxy* and another stack of *The Awakening.* But no white box and no ex-boyfriend back from the dead.

True to my memory, there's a water fountain, small but gurgling pleasantly. It's a simple two-tiered design, definitely a fountain, but just as definitely not hiding a clue, so I go in. The Book Loft is a labyrinth, with all the cramped atmosphere that word implies. Books and products and gifts line every inch of wall space in the entrance, and the stairs that lead up to the right are only three or four feet from the cash register counter.

I consider going to the left, a wing that leads through rooms of random discount titles, cookbooks, and eventually magazines and calendars, but the clue says up the stairs, so I head to the right. Each step squeaks under my weight, familiar and homey. At the top, I check one of the maps helpfully hanging from the ceiling and double left to head up more stairs, then down a long narrow hallway with a variety of fiction. No box. I slip into a closet-sized alcove with shelves stuffed with Agatha Christie, Mary Higgins Clark, Sue Grafton, Louise Penny—all the big mystery names, but again, no box.

I move on to the poetry room. It's larger than the others, but after a thorough search of every shelf, nook, and cranny, I come up completely empty. Ugh, what the hell did we even do here? Did he buy something? Did I? I remember nothing, and I do *not* have all day to wander around this place.

I retrace my steps, flipping through any section that looks familiar. Literary socks and tote bags hang along the stairwell railing. I search that area for a bit, dodging customers every two seconds, looking for a place a box might be hiding. After that, I walk into another wing, heading ultimately for the stairs that lead to children's literature.

I worm around a couple with their heads bent together and their voices hushed as they pore over travel guides. My phone rings, and I check the screen. Bennett. On time as usual. I slip past the couple into the art room—which is always quiet—before I answer.

"Hey," I say softly.

"Hey," he says.

There's a weird pause where the normal version of us would insert witty commentary or teasing questions. But that version of us didn't include him lying to me.

"So, you've figured out I'm in New York."

"The social media post from your buddies made it an easy guess."

More dead air on the line.

"I think we can rule out a future in spy work for me," he says.

I don't laugh, but the statement lets me breathe. This is still Bennett. Then again, he still lied.

"Where are you?" I ask. "I mean, are you on Wall Street, or maybe taking a ferry to the Statue of Liberty, or..."

He sighs, and I can hear him stop walking. Then I hear him fumble with his phone. A couple of seconds later, my phone buzzes. I check it and find a photo from him.

A selfie. Bennett looking sheepish and a little cold in a Columbia University baseball hat. An imposing gray-white building rises behind him.

"Are you at Columbia? Like *the* Columbia?"

Another picture comes through. This one is a selfie in an enormous long room, with lamplit tables on either side of the main walkway. Giant circular chandeliers hang from the ceiling, and I half expect a wizard to pop into the frame with him.

"To be fair, that one's from yesterday," he says. "But that's Butler Library. It's incredible."

"It's beautiful," I say. "But can we go back to the 'why are you there' part of our conversation? And maybe add on why you told me you were going antiquing?"

"I'm sorry," he says, "I didn't want to say anything before I knew this was a real thing I was looking at and not just a fluke."

"The real thing is you visiting Columbia? Was it a last-minute change of plans?" I struggle to keep my voice even. To resist the urge to remind him of all the details he gave me, like the gift shop at the Amish restaurant. Who would *do* something like that? And why?

"No, it wasn't," he says, sounding contrite. "I'm sorry."

And then I soften a touch, because he's not the only person in this relationship hiding something. And something tells me he isn't lying about an ex-girlfriend who died at his hand.

"Can you just tell me why?" I ask.

"Yes," he says. "I should have told you before. The trip was planned, but I was afraid to talk about it. Remember that chemistry camp I told you about?"

"You talked about going to one before you moved here."

"Right. Well, they reached out to some of us. Invited us to take a tour, and I went. But it felt stupid. It felt like, I don't know...like I was bragging and I might jinx it."

"If you have a shot at getting into Columbia, I think you have a right to brag."

He gives a soft, breathy exhalation, and I can hear him walking again. There are people nearby. Students probably. I could see Bennett somewhere like Columbia. And it makes me remember why I want it too. Not Columbia, just...college. Real college with the green lawns and brick buildings and old libraries with leatherbound books.

Bennett is only four months younger than me, but a year behind me in school. He started kindergarten late, so he's one of the oldest in his class, and I'm one of the youngest in mine.

College is still a year away for him, and I remember how busy that year felt. How exciting.

But I can't imagine how it would feel to have places like Columbia on the table. Hope got into Vassar, but she was rejected by Yale and Brown. And this is Hope. Head of the class, fastest on the team—she's pretty much perfect. It was the first time I'd ever seen her fail at anything, and the first time I realized how competitive some schools are.

"Why didn't you talk to me about this?" I say. "Hope's going to Vassar. I'm not angry with her. I'm proud of her. I'm proud of you too."

"I know," he says. "It's not that. I knew you'd be excited for me. But when all those scholarship applications got rejected, you seemed so upset. All you wanted was to go away to school and then you couldn't. Talking about Columbia felt like rubbing it all in somehow."

"But I told you about the criminal justice scholarship. Why didn't you tell me then?"

"Because you were so excited. The last thing I wanted to do was start talking about myself," he says. "It was dumb. I can see that now. I know they're going to finish up the background stuff and send your letter and then we can celebrate together. If you forgive me."

Celebrate together? I'm going to be lucky if the background check doesn't end with a warrant for my arrest at this rate. Scholarships do not get awarded to people who kill people, accidentally or not.

"I was stupid. I know you," he says when the silence goes on too long. "I just didn't want to be a smug jerk."

"So, lying jerk is preferable to smug?"

"I'm rethinking my theory on all this jerk business," he says. And then, more sincerely. "I'm sorry, Cleo. I really am. But the long story short is that I was invited for a tour. We got to sit in on a chemistry class. And they invited me to apply for early decision."

"I get it."

"You do?"

"Of course. It's great. Columbia is great. Really great." I cringe. Great is apparently the only word I know now. College is great. Columbia is great. Lying is great. It's *all* great.

"I wanted to tell you," he says, not buying my enthusiasm. "I just didn't want you to think about my bright happy future until yours was one hundred percent secure."

"I get it," I say.

"But it will be, Cleo," he says. "They're going to finish all the checks any day now, and then you'll be in. I know you will."

Except he can't know that, especially since he doesn't know what kind of secrets I'm hiding.

"Do you hate me?" he asks.

"No," I say. "I wish you'd told me."

My phone buzzes, and I flip it over to check the screen. It's Bennett. Another selfie, an extreme close-up this time, his frowning face filling the frame. I laugh.

"I forgive you already," I say, glad for our normalcy and the relative innocence of his lie. We exchange our goodbyes, and I slip out of the art room and take the stairs that lead to children's items. I need to get back to this impossible clue. Every minute this goes on feels more dangerous to my future.

Halfway down the steps, I realize something. Declan did buy something when we were here. A book. I remember seeing it when we were walking back up the stairs. A children's book? I can't quite remember, but it was a book, and we got it down here. I speed up, wishing I could conjure that day more clearly. But after a loop past jigsaw puzzles and a shelf stuffed full of ancient-looking Nancy Drew books, I feel a rush of déjà vu.

This feels familiar. This whole section of the store. We were down here. He actually browsed around this area. This is where he got the book.

I close my eyes and try to remember the path we took, but it's all a blur. I was caught up in my own shopping. My memory down here includes the sunlight coming in through the front windows, and then seeing him later with the book. I'd been surprised, but he'd shrugged off my questions.

God, what was that damn book?

I lean in to get a closer look at some puzzle books, and someone grabs my shoulder from behind. I jerk back from the shelf, whirling with my hands raised. Ready to fight or run.

A redhead with braces, maybe fourteen, holds his hands up in horror. "Sorry, sorry! I thought you were someone else."

I try to tell him it's fine, try to at least manage a smile, but my heart is pounding in my ears, and I can barely see what's in front of me. I'm turning into her again, that girl who flinches at every touch. Who sees monsters in every shadow.

The redhead skitters away, and my stomach squirms in misery. I don't want to go back to this. I square my shoulders and take a deep breath. Correction, I'm *not* going to go back to this.

I'm going to win this stupid hunt, face whoever the hell is doing this, and I'm going to leave Declan where he belongs. Behind me.

TWENTY-ONE

21 HOURS LEFT

I'M HALFWAY AROUND THE CHILDREN'S SECTION, wondering if I've dreamed up Declan buying a book and also wondering where the hell Hope is. It's after 5:00. How long can it take to run to Jiffy Lube or whatever?

None of this would be so annoying if I could just remember the book I'm looking for. God, why don't I pay better attention? I want to be a forensic investigator, for crap's sake! I move quickly past a couple of bookcases with graphic novels and pink, glittery journals. None of that feels right, but when I hit the middle-grade section, I remember.

He stopped here. He looked more carefully. My fingers drift over different covers. A somber owl, a castle and a scroll, and then an older cover with a boy in a bed, surrounded by ghostly figures. I pause on the last one, examining the cover.

Have I seen this book before? I study it, and my skin begins to tingle as I look at it closer. I haven't read this book, had never seen it before. But I remember now. This is the book he bought.

He held it under his arm and when I pulled it out, he would barely offer a comment.

"*We had it when we were kids.*"

He bought the book—funny how he didn't try to steal that one, but maybe he had figured out by then that I was going to be a pain about any attempted theft. I asked about the book, hoping he'd tell me more about how he grew up, but he changed the subject.

I pick up the book, but it's not big enough to hold a clue box inside. I pull out more copies from the shelf and find nothing behind it or behind any neighboring books either. I touch the hollow under the shelf above, my fingers tapping wood, wood—then cardboard. *Bingo.* I feel out the edges with the pads of my fingers, finding the rim of the lid. And then the satin bow.

I pull the box free, hearing the satisfying rip of Velcro being undone. A small black square on the bottom fixed to another square stuck to the shelf above.

"Hey, you can't move all the books like that."

I startle, looking over my shoulder to see a girl in a red Book Loft polo watching me. My cheeks go hot, and I tuck the box discreetly behind the pile of books. "Sorry, I'm buying one for a friend. Wanted to get a good one."

The clerk nods and moves on, and I chew the inside of my lip looking at the $12 price tag on the book. I have a twenty-dollar bill in my pocket and nothing else to my name unless Mom mailed me extra birthday cash, which is about as likely as me learning French by tomorrow morning. I put the book back and make my way outside.

I head past the fountain to the back half of the patio—the quieter entrance. It's cool and quiet here. Birds chatter overhead, and I sit on an old wooden bench and take a few moments before I pull the box open. The card seems to be the only thing inside. I pick it up and another piece of paper is folded underneath. Narrow and white.

A receipt from the Book Loft. February 14th of last year. The only item listed is the book Declan bought. My lungs feel squeezed and tight, my breath trapped in a vise. I read the clue quickly.

Seven went in. Six came out.
And now it's been a year.
Think new clubs and old trains.
You'll find the rain drawn here.

I jolt, looking up to see Hope standing over me. She has two iced mochas and frowns when she sees the nearly empty cup I'm holding.

"Don't worry," I say. "I'm going to need another."

"You found the clue," she says.

"It's Declan," I say. "Now I know there's no other explanation."

"Wait. What happened? What changed?"

"This." I hand her the receipt.

"What is this?"

"It's the receipt from the book Declan bought when we were here on Valentine's Day. No one would have this, Hope. Just him."

"But I mean, somebody could have found it," she offers.

I laugh. "A receipt? Someone happened to find a random Book Loft receipt from a year ago and they just knew to keep it?"

Her face goes pale. "You're sure, aren't you?"

"I can't think of a single other person it would be," I say.

"What about Aiden?" she asks. "Declan could have left this book at Aiden's house and left the receipt in it. Half the books in my house have receipts for bookmarks."

"Doesn't that feel random?" I ask.

She nods. "It does, but it also feels possible. What doesn't feel possible is Declan getting out of that water, Cleo. It was..."

"I know," I say. "I was there. I know."

I let out a shaky breath and get up, leaving the box on the bench to throw my cup away. I take the new iced mocha from her and watch her brow furrow. I know Hope well enough to catalog the emotions that flicker over her face as she reads. First, skepticism. Then, certainty. Then, worry.

"I don't like this," she says. "It feels like a trap."

"I know it does, but what am I going to do? Screw up Connor's amazing internship? Give up on Michigan State and let Declan leave one more shitty mark on my life?"

"I hear you," she admits. "I just don't see how this ends well for you."

"I don't either," I admit, "but I have to try. I have to try for Connor if nothing else." But my heart is racing. What if there isn't a way to protect Connor from this? What if this is all just an elaborate set up and the video is getting released either way?

I set down my mocha and push my hands through my hair, pacing back and forth.

"Are you okay?"

"Yes," I say, but I don't feel okay. I feel like I'm losing my grip. I look at Hope, so good and earnest. So determined to help me, but she still might not realize exactly what I did.

I feel something squirming in my chest. The secret wanting to get out. "Hope, when I talked to you earlier about what happened, I don't think I was clear. I told you we were fighting and that I didn't do anything…"

"But that's not all of it," she guesses. She doesn't sound surprised.

I close my eyes and tears roll down my cheeks. "I pushed him. I *really* pushed him. God, I was terrified. The only way I could be sure I'd get away was to shove him into the river, so that's what I did. It wasn't an accident. I saw my chance, and I took it."

Hope has that same eerie calm about her. "You mean, after he threw you into a kitchen cabinet. And after he left bruises on your wrists. And after he tried to choke you to death, and let's be clear. He would have done it, Cleo. He wouldn't have stopped until you quit breathing."

I don't even ask her how she knows about me being choked. Connor told her, of course, and right now I can't make myself care. I nod, numb and sick.

"You were defending yourself," she says. "No one would have blamed you. Honestly, I don't understand why you didn't say anything then."

"I was afraid," I say. "Connor found me, and I was so terrified and ashamed of who I was. Of what the whole thing had turned me into. Connor didn't know and he kept telling me it was over, and it didn't matter, that there was no need to go into it because it would all end the same."

"It was obviously self-defense."

"Funny how much that feels like murder some days," I say.

"Cleo, I know this is hard to hear, but what happened to Declan happened because he was reckless and high and *because he attacked you*. You did what you had to do. And if someone wants you to pay for what they think is murder, then we can't handle this ourselves. We need help."

"I know," I say, and then I get to the point of the thing that's been loosely formed in my head since I first suspected that it was him. "But Declan wouldn't plan to kill me. At the river, he had totally lost control. I know he was violent, but he didn't plan out his attacks. They were always impulsive. He would plan out ways to make me miserable, though. Putting me through this hunt feels possible. And if revisiting all of this crap gives him some sick sort of satisfaction, then it's worth it to me to keep Connor safe. And to protect my future too."

"This can't be Declan," she says. Still so certain. "But even if it is, how can we be sure your misery is enough? What if whoever is behind this wants more—"

My phone rings, cutting her off. I gesture to her to hang on a second, because it's Connor, and since he's probably back at the house and probably worried that Hope and I are dead in a ditch at this point, I'd better answer.

"Hey, what's up?" I answer.

"Did you get into Declan's old room?"

"Yeah, the police officer walked in there yesterday, remember?"

"No, I remember that. Have you been in there again?"

"No," I say. It feels like something is crawling up my arms. "Why?"

"You need to come home and see for yourself."

TWENTY-TWO

19 HOURS LEFT

AFTER I HANG UP WITH CONNOR, WE RUSH BACK TO MY house, and he leads the way to Declan's room. I don't know what I expect. Maybe something like one of those movie-worthy thrashings—overturned lamps and drawers dumped all over the floor. It's nothing like that, but it still makes all the hairs on the back of my neck stand up.

Everything is exactly as it was before. Closet door open a few inches. Bed made. The whole of the room untouched. Except for the corkboard behind the desk.

Mom had carefully removed the few photos and things Declan had left in our house and mailed them back to his family. Other than an old Ange's Pizza menu and a random fortune-cookie fortune, it had been an empty expanse, a few brightly colored pushpins dotting the pocked surface.

But now it is covered with three plain sheets of typing paper, each one bearing a single word.

Left. For. Dead.

A single photo is pinned beneath the papers. It's Declan, and it's unfamiliar. Only his head and shoulders are visible, the background an indistinct blur of sky. But I can see tilt of his head, his pale hair, and those sharp, sharp cheekbones.

"Did you see anyone? Did you hear anyone break in?" I ask.

"I'd only been here five minutes when I called," Connor says.

Hope exhales slowly. "They could have done this hours ago."

"Or twenty minutes ago."

I turn away from Declan's eyes in the photo, feeling the scar on the back of my head prickle. "What is this about? What's the point?"

"Not a damn clue," Connor says. "But I think it's time to call this asshole's bluff."

"You think I should quit?" I ask.

"Hell, yeah. If this is a game, it's sick. You're the one who's getting hunted here, and I doubt the point is to get to the end where we all hold hands and sing 'Kumbaya.' Somebody wants something out of you, and I'll be damned if they're using me as a threat to get it."

"I pushed him," I say plainly. "Declan. I pushed him into the river."

Hope tenses for an instant, but Connor just shrugs.

"I figured as much. Still don't care."

I tilt my head. "If he has video of you, he could have video of me too."

Connor goes quiet. I know what he's thinking. Because Declan isn't patient, but Connor knows he's cruel. If he's waited a year to do this, he'll hold his high card until playing it would do the most damage.

"You think it's him?" He's looking at me. "Is that what your gut tells you?"

I see no point in beating around the bush with this. "Yes. All of the clues are locations significant to us, to our relationship. There's stuff no one could know. That bracelet he wore. A receipt from a book Declan bought when we were together."

"People can figure shit out, Cleo."

I conclude with a sigh. "Look, I'm not saying we know for sure it's him. I'm saying he would want me to pay. He would torture me like this. And he's the one person—the *only* person—who really has a good reason to not take it to the police."

"Why the hell not?"

"Because he tried to kill me," I say. "You saw my neck. For all Declan knows, I talked to the cops in West Virginia about what he did to me."

"He didn't get out," Hope says softly. "Declan could not have survived. There's no way."

"We could go round and round about this all day," I say. "It's not going to matter. We just need to finish this damn thing and find out what we're up against."

Hope nods. "You can't fight what you don't know."

"Screw that. This is fucked, Cleo. Look at this!" He stabs a finger toward the ominous message on the corkboard.

"I'm not throwing away your future!" I drop my voice and try to breathe. "I have to try to figure this out, Connor. You saved me that day. Please let me try to help you now."

Connor shakes his head, furious but relenting. Hope looks at the photo of Declan pinned beneath the message, her expression cool and calculating.

"What we need to figure out is who took that video," she says.

"Truth," Connor says. "Unless one of the three of us needs to make a confession, the video we were sent wasn't taken by anyone here and it wasn't taken by Declan. That leaves three people."

"Valerie, Aiden, and Jack," I say.

Connor nods. "We find out who's behind the video, I'll bet we find the same person is behind this whole damn hunt."

"So, what should we do next?" I ask. "How do we find out?"

"Easy," Connor says. "Bring all three of them over. See if somebody fesses up."

Hope cocks her head. "Hey, do you hear that?"

"What?" Connor asks.

I listen hard for voices, noises. I hear the clicking clock. My own breathing. But there's something unfamiliar behind the regular rhythm of my house. Something new. A slow, quiet trickle.

Connor shakes his head, "I don't hear sh—"

"Water," I say. Hope's eyes lock onto mine. "I hear water."

"The bathroom," Connor says.

He flings the bedroom door wide and freezes, one hand up to keep us from moving. I hear it more clearly now. I don't know how I didn't notice it when we got here, because it is a steady sound.

"Have you been in the bathroom?" I ask.

He shakes his head. "I told you. I got here ten minutes before you. I checked the outside of the house to see if anyone had broken in."

"The carpet's wet," Hope whispers behind me.

She's right. I can see a half circle of darker carpet around the bathroom door. Connor swears and starts moving, his feet squelching when he reaches the bathroom. I'm right behind him.

"Maybe we should—"

Whatever Hope was going to say is cut short when Connor yanks open the door. The trickling sound is almost a gush in here, an insistent spilling.

"What the hell," Connor says softly. He stands frozen in place. The floor is shiny with pooled water. It's coming from the bathtub.

My throat goes dry.

"What the hell," Connor repeats. His low voice sends goose bumps up on my arms.

He moves in and pushes the curtain back far enough to turn off the taps, then makes a choking sound and stumbles away, the curtain slipping back into place. Soft plinks of water splash into the tub.

"Get some towels," he says, sounding rattled.

I drag the ones off the towel rack and toss them both on the floor, faded palm trees and parrots turning darker as the water soaks through. But my eyes drag back to the bathtub, to the hollows in my brother's face. Something is in that water.

Connor pulls more towels out from underneath the sink and chucks them on the floor, his hands trembling. I take another step, and he looks up at me.

"What is this, Cleo?"

I grab the edge of the curtain and quickly, like removing a Band-Aid, rip it open. A scream claws its way up my throat. It's a body. Nude and beige and slender and—not real. I swallow my scream. Press my hand against my heart and let my mind repeat it.

It's not real. Not real. Not real.

"Oh my God," Hope gasps from the hallway. I can see her turn away, but Connor shakes his head.

"It's not real," he says. "It's a doll."

"A mannequin," I say. My voice cannot belong to me. The shaking fingers that reach and touch that ice-cold water—they can't be mine.

I blink and try to clear my mind. Try to make sense of the scene before me. The bathtub is full, water draining through the silver circle near the spigot, the one that can't possibly keep up with this volume of water. The body inside is crammed and contorted, torso wrenched away, legs bent at terrible angles, neck twisted backward.

One green eye stares up at me from under the surface, the pupil chipped white in the center.

"Where did this come from?" Connor asks, his voice gravelly.

"From the store," I say. I swallow hard. "They were all over."

"From the old Madison's building," Hope clarifies. Her voice trembles. "The place downtown."

Connor reaches in the water, and I cringe. But he just shifts the mannequin aside to twist the plug open. Water begins to pour down the drain, and I turn away.

"What's that on its chest?" he asks.

I force myself to look, to examine the curving lines of Sharpie splayed across the mannequin's half-visible breast. I can't see what it is and I can't—*cannot*—touch that thing. It's Connor again who swears, pushes his big dark hand into the acrylic chest and flips the mannequin flat on its back in the half-drained tub.

It's an outline. A Sharpie-drawn handprint splayed right in the center of the chest.

TWENTY-THREE

18 HOURS LEFT

AFTER A HELLISH ARGUMENT, CONNOR RELUCTANTLY agrees to let us see it through, as long as we get everyone over here for a chat. We clean up the worst of the water while Hope makes the calls. He shuts the curtain tight but refuses to remove the mannequin.

"If someone starts looking squirrelly, I'm going to drag that son of a bitch out and see who squirms," he says.

"Who wouldn't squirm? That thing is a horror," I say.

Hope hangs up the phone when we emerge; she looks composed once more. "They'll be here in thirty minutes. Pizza should be ready in twenty."

"They're all coming?" I ask.

"I told them it was a last-minute birthday thing," she says.

"It's free pizza," Connor says, and I buy that more, except…

"Jack does not care that much about free pizza." I say.

"Yes, but he owes me," she says. "Big-time."

Connor agrees to grab the pizza, so I spend a few frantic minutes tidying until I feel like the worst of the clutter and mess is hidden. Then I sink onto a kitchen chair with my phone. Bennett texted me a couple of more pictures—on the subway and eating a giant bagel. I stare at them over and over, wondering if I'm still the girl I was when he left on Friday. God, I hope so.

"I need to tell you something," Hope says out of nowhere.

Or maybe not nowhere because when I look up, I realize Hope hasn't said a word since Connor left. I've been gawking at my phone, but she's just been sitting here, not looking at her phone or watching TV—just staring.

"What's wrong?" I ask.

"It's about Jack." And then she sighs like she's made a difficult decision. "I want to talk to you about this, but it's not my secret and I don't want to break his confidence."

"If it involves what happened with Declan..."

"Only part of it."

"Just tell me," I say.

"First, Jack is gay."

I try to hide my shock, but don't entirely manage. The guy has been dating my best friend for years. "Gay? Since when?"

"Since always?"

"But you guys have been together forever."

She tilts her head back and forth like she's weighing the truth of my statement. "We haven't ever really been together. Haven't you noticed that we aren't very physical?"

"I guess. But you've never said anything."

She waves it off. "He was really paranoid, and it's not like you were great buds. We pretended to date so people wouldn't ask questions, because he wasn't ready to come out."

"Because of his parents," I say.

Hope's grin is wry. "Baptist churches aren't exactly the most embracing of such things."

Worry and guilt wash over me. "Did Jack think that I wouldn't…that I would have had some kind of problem with that? Because, Hope—"

"No, no." She shakes her head. "It's just his parents, but he has to get over this. That's why we've been getting into it so much this last year. He wants to keep up this ruse, and I'm tired of him waiting. He's had a boyfriend for over a year."

"And you want to be with Connor."

Her cheeks go pink. And then crimson. "It's complicated."

"It's not *that* complicated," I say, because it's clear she's in love with my brother. Beneath the weirdness, it makes my heart hurt to know she's held that possibility at arm's length for so long. I sigh. "Hope, listen. I know I say crap about Connor all the time, and I maintain the man *is* a complete slob, but he's a good guy."

"I know," she says. "For the record, I wanted to tell you, but it just… If I told you about Connor, I'd have to explain about Jack. And that wasn't fair. I was the only one who knew until Matt."

"Matt is his boyfriend?"

"Yes. He's great." She smirks. "He's been way more patient about all this than me."

"I'm glad you told me so I can be careful," I say, "but I don't understand why I need to know now."

"Because Declan found out about Jack in West Virginia. Jack went off after dinner that first night to call Matt. It was a video call. And Declan walked by. I don't know the details. I just know Jack was in a dead panic and Declan was making it awful. Mocking him. Asking what the good old pastor would think."

I feel sick. This is on me. Declan wasn't even supposed to go on the trip, but I invited him. Forgiveness and another chance and all the rest of the bullshit I bought. I dragged all that to Jack's doorstep—to everyone's doorstep. And now we're all living with it.

"It was the final straw for me," she says. "That's the reason why I asked everyone—"

The door bangs open, and Connor steps in, heavily laden with pizza and a bag of breadsticks.

"A little help here?" he asks. I can see nothing but his curls over the top of the pizza boxes.

"Coming!" I say. And as I get up, I squeeze Hope's arm and whisper. "Just talk to him."

Hope's face falters, but then she offers a tight smile and gets up to help.

Fifteen minutes later, we're all enduring the weirdest pizza party in the history of pizza parties. We eat in near silence, and the awkwardness is so thick I should serve it up on dessert plates. I put my half-eaten slice down, my appetite gone, and look around the room.

We've pulled three chairs from the dining room into the living area. They're right in front of the TV, directly across from the couch. I sit in the chair closest to the hallway. Hope is in the center, Jack is in the corner chair, tucked between Hope on his left and Connor against the side wall in Dad's vile, stained recliner.

Valerie and Aiden sit on the couch, and the empty cushion between them makes me think of the picture of the seven of us. It doesn't take a genius to figure out how strange it is to be together pretending like there isn't a Declan-shaped elephant in the room.

It's worse because Valerie is trying to make up for our silence with an endless stream of chatter that singsongs up and down and all around, covering fascinating subjects like her friend Alicia's ankle injury, Jana's ever-shifting major plans, and some concert update about a band none of us listen to. Hope, God love her, nods and makes reassuring noises. Aiden looks confused and a little uncomfortable beside her, though he dutifully nods when she slaps his arm and includes him.

"And then this guy—" Smack to Aiden's arm. "He's working all the time and will have zero student loans at this point. And he totally fixed the class-tracking database for his history professor."

"It's just a spreadsheet," he corrects softly. "I've only taken a few classes."

"So what!" Valerie grin at him. "You'll be the next Steve Jobs one day."

Aiden flushes brightly and looks miserable. I don't know why she's laying it on so thick, but Connor looks nauseated and Jack has checked his phone eighty-four times since he sat down—after frowning at every single item in my home, thank you very much—so I feel like I have to get to the point of all this.

"So, some of you guys already know that Hope and I have been doing a scavenger hunt."

"Did you win a birthday pizza party?" Jack asks.

"No, we haven't won anything yet," Hope says. "We're not quite sure there is a prize."

I nod. "That picture everybody got? It's about the scavenger hunt. To be honest, whole thing seems to have something to do with what happened to Declan in West Virginia."

"Cleo thought maybe we should all talk about it," Hope says.

The mood in the room stalls. Everyone goes quiet. Or quieter. But I can feel people's eyes seeking others across the room. Not just Aiden and Valerie or Jack and Hope. This is a silent game of visual tug-of-war happening with everyone here.

Except me.

"Let me get to the point," Connor says. "Someone filmed a video right around the time Declan fell into the water."

Aiden looks up at that.

"Filmed where? And by who?" Valerie asks.

I pick up where Connor left off. "It was filmed on the bridge near our campsite. And we don't know who, except that it wasn't me or either of them—" I pause to motion at Connor and Hope.

"So, which one of you three did it?" Connor asks.

"You're accusing us?" Valerie asks. She puts her slice of pizza down on her paper plate.

Connor shrugs. "I'm calling it like I see it. The six of us were the only ones there."

"Unbelievable," Jack says under his breath.

"The thing is, if someone knows something about the video and didn't tell the authorities when we were down there..." Hope trails off.

"It might look a little like accessory to a crime," Connor says. "Or maybe accomplice? I'm not a lawyer yet, so I don't know all the details of the legal system like some of us."

Aiden flinches, his face registering shock and then pain. Valerie stiffens and reaches for Aiden's arm. She opens her mouth to speak, but it's Jack, of all people, who makes the first sound. He laughs, and it is a cold and humorless noise.

"Accessory to a crime." Jack repeats the words with so much derision, I feel like I've been called a dirty name. "Do we really want to talk about *our* role in what went down at that river?"

"Jack." Hope's voice is a warning.

"No, Hope. You asked me here, so I'm here," he says. "We all went down there not knowing shit about the lunatic that was in the boat with us. Declan wasn't supposed to be there."

He looks at me and holds up a hand. "I'm sorry, Cleo. I know what it's like to be in a screwed-up situation, but none of us were part of that mess until you made us part of it."

He looks back to Connor and Hope, shaking his head. "Instead, we were dragged down to the middle of God knows where so we could play our parts in some desperate save-Declan Hail Mary when one look at that guy would have told anyone he was way past saving."

"Your compassion is touching," Aiden mutters, looking venomous.

Jack shrugs. "Look, I didn't throw the guy in the water. I'm just not surprised he fell. He was wasted every minute of that trip. You both were."

Hope starts in with *Let's just all take a breath*, but I'm barely listening. I feel like I'm curling in on myself. I look away, unable to face the shame of Jack's words. He's right about a lot of it. Except Declan didn't just fall.

"I'm not saying you're wrong," Connor says, the bite in his tone bringing me back to the present. "But someone took a video from the bridge, and none of us ever saw it until now. It had to be one of us."

"But..." Valerie pauses, and I can tell she's trying to control her voice. To be calm. "You're talking about the walking bridge, right? That's where the video was shot?"

"Yes," I say. "The green one not too far from our campsite. We went under it right before we pulled up to shore."

She nods, still speaking very carefully. "That bridge is the main connection between the campsites we were staying in and the state hiking trail. *Lots* of people use it."

"So, you're saying someone used that bridge, took video that might have pertained to Declan dying and didn't bother to turn it in, but somehow it wound up in someone's hands who is now using it in a scavenger hunt for Cleo." Connor says. "See how much sense that doesn't make?"

Valerie cocks her head, looking annoyed. "Well, if it was one of us, what possible reason would we have to hide it? Or, for that matter, why would *any* of us have even been on the bridge? Maybe you missed it, but after everything that went down, most of us just wanted to go the hell home."

"Who planned this hunt?" Aiden's voice is a strange shock. He'd been quiet for so long it was easy to forget he was in the room. He runs a shaking hand through his lank, greasy hair. "Is someone here behind it? Is one of you doing this? Because Declan is dead, and that isn't funny. It isn't a game."

The room is utterly silent, everyone looking at everyone else. No one confesses. Because there isn't anyone to confess. The person behind this scavenger hunt is supposed to be dead in a river in West Virginia. But I don't think he died in that river now.

"I don't have anything to do with this. And I don't have answers," Jack says. "But I don't see a big mystery here. Nobody wanted Declan to drown, but he was *wrecked*. What else did we expect?"

"They never found him, did they?" Aiden says. I shake my

head, and hope blooms in his eyes. "They shut down the dam, did all the things they do when this kind of thing happens, but they never found him, right?"

"No," I say softly.

Jack gets up and takes his jacket from the back of the chair. He looks at me, and his expression is unusually gentle. "I'm sorry, Cleo, but I can't be part of this."

On some strange instinct, I follow him to the door, but he moves fast and is on the porch by the time I get there. I stick my head into the evening air as he's trotting down the steps.

"Jack, wait."

He turns and looks at me, and I swallow.

"I know you don't want to talk about that trip, and I promise I'll never bring it up with you again, but did Declan say anything I should know? I mean, when he...when he talked to you?"

I see the realization dawn on his features, the moment when he understands I'm asking because I know when Declan and Jack were alone and why they talked. Which means I know his secret. I feel a surge of guilt and brace myself for him to explode, but he doesn't. His expression looks more like resignation. And then maybe something a little like relief.

I shake my head. "Please don't be angry with her. She was afraid I'd ask dumb questions in front of everyone and didn't want me to—"

"I'm not upset," he says. He looks a little surprised about it. "I don't know. I'm just not."

I nod. "I'm sorry. I know how he could be."

He shakes his head. "You knew better than me. He was drunk. A little dickish. Gave me shit and called me a fag. In the end, what's it even matter?"

"I'm sorry," I repeat. "I brought him and it was wrong. I shouldn't have done that."

"We've all done stupid things for what we think is love," Jack says.

"What we think is love?"

He shrugs. "Love doesn't make us do stupid shit, Cleo. Fear does that."

Jack leaves with his words still settling into my bones. Making me think. Back inside, it's clear Aiden and Valerie are getting ready to leave. Valerie doesn't look so bouncy now, and Aiden is standing close to Connor, looking near tears.

"Let's go," Valerie says, tugging his arm.

He just stands there, breathing hard. Valerie tugs his arm again, and he yanks himself free. He looks desperate for something, and I'm not sure what it is.

"Do you..." Aiden's voice is a strangled rasp. His fists are balled at his sides. Shaking. He's looking right at Connor. "Do you really think he could be alive? Do you think this could be him?"

"I know he's mean," Connor says, "and you should never count the mean ones out."

"Can you think of anyone else who'd want to do this, Aiden?" Hope asks softly. "You knew Declan better than most of us."

Aiden looks at her like she's speaking another language. His brow furrows, and he looks so pale. Almost sallow under the yellow lights of our living room lamps.

"Aiden, come on," Valerie says, her voice soft even as her eyes stab at Hope like a weapon.

Aiden seems to come out of a trance then, nodding vaguely and shuffling toward the door. When he's on the stoop, Valerie stops behind him.

"Go ahead and start the car. I'm going to run to the bathroom really quick."

Aiden nods and disappears down the stairs, a wraith with sloping shoulders.

Valerie comes back in and I know by the set of her shoulders she is not going to the bathroom. She stops in the living room, her eyes smoldering.

"I have no idea how any of you can stand to look yourselves in the eyes."

TWENTY-FOUR

16 HOURS LEFT

MY MOUTH DROPS OPEN, BUT MY VOICE IS GONE. Probably buried under the metric ton of shock that's currently surging through my system. Valerie is standing in my living room in full-on rage mode. I've hardly ever even seen her annoyed, but she's way past that. She's *livid.*

"What are you talking about?" Hope asks.

"You! Her! Even you, Connor. Maybe especially you!"

"What the hell did I do?" Connor asks.

I have no idea what to say, so I stay quiet. This is uncharted territory for Valerie. She is bubbly to the point of annoying. Nice to the point of nauseating. And now she's standing here, practically vibrating with fury.

"You brought us here to ask us about that night? To ask about videos and to imply that somehow we had something to do with Declan dying?" Her eyes are flashing. "I told you we can't talk about this around Aiden. He thought it was just pizza! *Pizza!* And now he's walking out of here wondering if Declan is alive somewhere. You put that in his head."

"Valerie..." I don't know what to say.

"Do you have any idea what this year's been like? He lost fifteen pounds the first two months after Declan disappeared. Fifteen pounds!" She shakes her head. "No one reached out to him. Not one of you called or texted. Aiden might as well have disappeared right along with Declan, because ever since he's been gone, my brother has been invisible."

My chest squeezes, and I glance toward the window, but I can't see the car. I can't see Aiden at all. I can't even remember what he was wearing tonight. The reality of Valerie's words hits me like a hard punch to the sternum. She's right. Aiden is still invisible to me. What kind of person has this turned me into? Is this who I really am?

"I'm sorry," I say quietly.

"It's way too late for sorry," Valerie says. "Look, I didn't like Declan. And that's even before I knew what he was doing to you, Cleo."

I flinch, feeling my face ice over. But Valerie isn't looking at me. She's looking at the window where her brother is waiting in the car.

"But for Aiden, Declan was *it*—his one, true friend. And hell, that's more than I can say for us, isn't it? Because we aren't really friends at all."

"I—I didn't know," Hope says. She looks beyond distraught.

"That's because you didn't pay attention." Valerie's words land like bullets. "When I stopped calling and reaching out, we saw each other half as often. Then less than that."

Shame is burning me from the inside out. I swallow, feeling a fist squeezed hard around my throat.

"You're right," I say. "It was awful. It *is* awful."

She makes a dismissive sound, but she doesn't speak, so I go on.

"So, why have you been nice to us? Every time we call or text, you're always quick to invite us over or join us for lunch. You're always so…"

"Friendly," Hope finishes.

"Because I love my brother," she says firmly. "And I want him to see that even if things can't be normal anymore, they can be nice. We can laugh and smile and keep living, even if it all feels different now. Because we have to let go and move on."

Connor still doesn't speak. He keeps his eyes on the floor and his expression carefully blank.

"Everything about what happened tonight was wrong," Valerie says. Her eyes are watery and her chin is trembling. "But whatever this scavenger hunt is, it seems like a very messed-up game, and I think you should really consider why you're playing along."

"You're right," I say, closing my eyes.

"But what if he really is alive? What if he survived?" Aiden's voice is a surprise. I didn't even hear the door open again, but he's standing there, frowning.

He swallows so hard I can hear it fifteen feet away. Or maybe it's just that quiet in here. Either way, I'm careful to look him in the eyes. I don't want him to feel invisible anymore.

"Look I know Cleo and Connor believe—" Hope stops herself and changes tactics. "The thing is, the river was really dangerous there. It just... I can't imagine anyone without a life jacket surviving."

"Of course *you'd* think that," Aiden says, and his voice sounds like an accusation, "but what if you're wrong?"

It's our turn to not answer. Valerie gives us a final sharp look and then manages to usher her brother out. We watch in silence as her little silver car backs out of the driveway.

Connor crosses his arms. "She recorded the video."

"What?" Hope asks. "After all of that you think it's Valerie's video?"

"That was a distraction," he says. "I'd bet money on it. Valerie shot that video. She wouldn't have turned it in because of Aiden being on probation. But now he's a mess all this time later, maybe she thinks you owning up to what you did will give him closure or something."

"She doesn't want us to talk to him about it," Hope says. "Besides, she was at camp when it happened."

He shakes his head. "That's all deflection. I'm telling you, it's her. Did you see the way she grabbed for Aiden to keep him quiet? Besides, she left camp around the time I went after you. Everyone left after Declan took off."

"What do you mean Declan took off?" I ask.

"Hold on," Hope says to me, and then to Connor "Valerie and Cleo were out walking, but Valerie came back to camp. I saw her."

"She left again because Aiden was gone," he says. "It was after you and Jack both left, I went after you. She definitely had time to get there."

"To get where?" I ask.

"To the bridge."

"But why?" I ask. "What possible motive would she have to keep it quiet for so long?"

"She was worried about Aiden," Hope says softly. "He was probably her only priority."

"Siblings will do anything for each other." Connor looks at me. "We're proving that right now, aren't we?"

My chest clenches. "I guess we are, but I don't get it. Why wouldn't Valerie have said something later?"

"Because any criminal investigation into this would reveal that Aiden broke probation," Connor says.

"I'm surprised that didn't come out a year ago," Hope says.

"The police who showed up that night didn't even get all of our names," Connor says.

"Because they thought it was an accident," I say.

"It *was* an accident," Connor says.

My laugh is bitter, and I'm crying again. Maybe all of this is what I earned. I was the pathetic little abused girl who took him back. Who bought his bullshit promises and then had to do the unthinkable to survive the mistake of inviting him. Maybe I don't deserve a scholarship and a beautiful school—but my brother *does*.

Connor walks closer to me even as the tears spill over my cheeks, and I don't know if he's angry. It's hard to see him through my blurry vision.

"You did what you had to do. He would have killed you," he says, and then I feel his hand very gently on the back of my head. My scar tingles. "He almost did."

I sniff, and Hope hands me a tissue and gets us all water and forces us to drink.

"So, now what?" I ask. "If we think it's Valerie's video, do we confront her? See if she gave Declan the video or posted it somewhere or what?"

"Tried that," Connor says. "She's clearly not telling. I think all these clues might be freaking her out. She gave this video to someone, but I don't think she wants anything to do with this scavenger hunt."

"We could go to the police without the video," Hope says. "Just take what we know."

I shake my head. "No way. He is watching us. If we go anywhere near that station or make a single phone call, that video will go everywhere. And I'll bet he adds some commentary to go along with the video."

Connor scoffs. "I told you I don't—"

"Care?" I interrupt him. "You don't care about having your name smeared through the mud, but I do. If we call the police, I'll confess immediately to pushing him."

"It was self-defense," Hope says.

"A year later? After telling the police nothing?" Connor's laugh is hard and short. "Hell no. They will open some big fat investigation, and it will be all over the news and social media. It will be a *Dateline* story, and she'll be stuck in this damn house for eternity."

"I don't want that for her either," Hope says, a little defensive.

"But it's my life, so I choose," I say decisively. "And there are only two choices. We finish this hunt or I go in right now."

"It ends at 2:00 tomorrow anyway," Hope says.

"Fine. What's the clue again?" Connor asks.

"*Seven went in. Six came out. And now it's been a year. Think new clubs and old trains. You'll find the rain drawn here.*"

Hope checks her phone with a frown. "'New clubs' has to be Arena District or Short North, right?"

"Maybe the river," I say. "But we don't have any train stations."

Hope checks her phone again. And then again.

"You okay over there?" I ask.

"It's Jack. He wants to talk," she says. "And Mom is asking where I am."

"We can totally work on this and hook back up in the morning," I say.

"I don't want to leave you two. We're running out of time," she argues, but then her phone buzzes again. She checks it and frowns. "Mom again. I can call you as soon as I'm done with Jack."

"We'll start working on it," I say. "We'll call if we're stuck or if we find something."

"Besides," Connor adds, "we both know you're no night owl."

"True," she says, and they share a smile that doesn't feel so strange anymore.

Connor watches her go and then catches me noticing his staring. "What?" he asks.

I laugh. "Look at you. Trying to play it cool with all this Hope stuff."

"You know about that?" He doesn't look terribly alarmed or surprised.

"I know *everything*," I say, enjoying the way he squirms a little.

"Huh," he says. And then he slaps his hands on the front of his thighs and jerks his head vaguely toward the hallway. "Yeah, good talk. Let's drop it and do this Scooby-Doo thing. How does it work? Do we like, go to a library and create a spreadsheet of trains and rain and shit?"

I laugh again. "We usually mostly go with Google."

"Well, the first Columbus train station was downtown," he says. "I think it was where the convention center is, but not originally."

I tap in a quick search, having to reword it three times before I pull the right results. There's a reason Hope is the researcher around here. I pull up an article about Columbus's train station history and find the location of the first station, which eventually ended up at the convention center like Connor thought. It was originally built near a small park, though.

It's not exactly meaningful, but it is a place Declan and I would cut through if we were walking around downtown, so it's possible.

"I think we need to check out Sensenbrenner Park," I say. "That's the original site."

"I'm coming with."

"Fine, but we're calling an Uber."

He points toward the front of the house. "I have my—"

"I'm not riding on that crotch rocket of death. We're calling an Uber."

Fifteen minutes later, the Uber drops us at Sensenbrenner Park, which is ghostly and strange in the dark. It's also…not empty. A couple of homeless people are smoking cigarettes near one of the fountains, and another is carrying an oversized backpack slowly through the paths.

We walk past the bike racks and the fountains, and I remember making a wish and throwing in pennies I'd found with Declan. We wander for a while, but I eventually stop, suddenly sure this isn't right. Nothing serious happened here. We didn't talk or kiss or fight. This was just a layover on the journey of our screwed-up relationship.

"This feels wrong," I say.

"What, you're worried about the old lady with the backpack?"

"No, not that. It's just that this doesn't feel like a place he'd leave a clue."

"Let me ask you something, Cleo," he says. "Did you know that he'd hit you? When you first started dating him, did any part of you think that was possible?"

My throat is thick and tight but I force myself to answer. "No."

"People choose, say, and do things you wouldn't dream. That's all I'm saying. You never know what a person is going to do."

"Maybe we should check the convention center," I say, though I can't remember a single significant thing there either. "We don't have any actual stations left."

"Well, we've got the arch." When I look confused, he gestures vaguely. "The one by the ballpark and the arena. That's from the original station."

"I thought that was from the old prison," I say.

Connor rubs his chin. "Well, I'm not positive, but that's what I thought."

One quick Google search, and the results snap me out of my fog. "No, you're right. That arch is from the Central Train Station. It was torn down in the seventies, and that's the only significant piece of the train station we have left."

"So we maybe check it out?" he asks.

"That's the place," I say. "That's where we'll find it."

He laughs. "You sound pretty sure for a girl who didn't know it was there until now."

"We've been there," I say. "Declan and me."

Connor doesn't press, and I'm grateful. After he gashed open my head, I met Declan near this arch. It's where he sobbed out his litany of apologies, his desperate stories of his parents and how much he missed his brother and he was so messed up, and he never *ever* meant to hurt me.

This is where I forced myself not to pull him into my arms. That night I kept my face stony and my voice calm when I told him that I didn't know how we could go forward. That I didn't trust him and we would have to go slow.

I told him a lot of things in that park, but there was one word I didn't use. I didn't say *No*.

My phone buzzes, jarring me out of my thoughts. I check the text messages and shiver when I see the now familiar Unknown Caller again.

Two texts. The first is an image: Valerie and Aiden climbing the steps to my house. Goose bumps rise on my arms.

The second sends my heart into overdrive.

Unknown: Looks like you have too much time. Let's up the ante. You have three hours.

TWENTY-FIVE

~~**14 HOURS LEFT**~~

3 HOURS LEFT

WE BOLT TOWARD NATIONWIDE ARENA, TURNING LEFT AT the corner where billboards transform the bricked area into a glowing spectacle. My breath comes hard and fast, and Connor grabs my arm, forcing me into a walk.

"Calm down. Three hours is plenty of time," he says.

"We don't even know how many clues are left!"

He doesn't have a response for that, so we keep going in silence. This is another big-money section of downtown, an area with brick sidewalks, sleek iron benches, and a veritable buffet of upscale food and beverage choices. Most of the restaurants are closed, but the bars are still hopping. Once we get to the entrance of Wendell's, a bougie nightclub known to host jazz artists on Fridays and Saturdays, the arch comes into view.

"Do you see it?" he asks.

I don't know how I could miss it. The arch glows, four ornate pillars topped with scallops or ruffles—I don't know the architectural term for them, but they catch the light and cast beautiful shadows against the stone. It's gorgeous.

"God, what the hell kind of train station did we tear down?" I ask.

"All in the name of progress," Connor says, the disgust evident on his face.

"Aren't you a business attorney in the making?"

"There are ways to make a product and a dime without shitting all over art, culture, and history."

I laugh, but that look in his eyes makes me more determined than ever to make sure this doesn't affect him.

Hidden speakers mounted around the club's large patio are filling the night air with a duet of saxophone and soft piano. I pass a small group of people milling about on the patio and circle the arch, then the bench where we sat. Declan held my hand and told me he was terrified when I hit my head, that he'd only meant to get me off him so he could breathe. And I thought I was stoic and strong, the girl who'd never fall for his shit again. But I wasn't, and I did.

Nothing of interest pops out on, under, or behind the bench, so I circle the arch a second time and look up, seeing no crevice or ledge or anything that could be hiding a box. I don't get it. I read the clue again to make sure I'm not missing anything:

Seven went in. Six came out.

And now it's been a year.

Think new clubs and old trains.

You'll find the rain drawn here.

The jazz song changes to another and I sigh. The park is a long wedge, narrow at the arch and widening as it goes on. But there's nothing here but sidewalks, benches, trees, and grass. We check each of the benches, just in case, but come up empty.

Back at the arch, I heave another sigh. "Connor, I have no idea where to look."

"Maybe this isn't the right place?"

"I'm really sure on this one," I say. I still don't want to explain, but I add, "I think we've got to figure out the rain thing."

"Maybe the gutters, the downspouts on the buildings?"

"They're not really part of the park though."

I look around, spotting a few drainage pipes on nearby buildings. The jazz song cuts out, and a new song starts high-pitched guitar joined by shrieking punk vocals.

What the hell?

Connor looks up at the speakers and laughs, but I'm not laughing. Goose bumps rise on my arms in an instant. This is Declan's favorite.

"This song was playing on the voicemail from Declan," I say.

Connor's smile fades. "Are you sure?"

"I'm sure. I can pull it up now."

But Connor just nods. "I believe you."

People continue milling. The song continues playing. I'm waiting for Declan's voice—for those two terrible words—but his voice never breaks in. And then it's over.

There is a brief silence and then the low, warbling notes of a lonely trumpet spill into the night. Soft piano and bass soon accompany the sax. We're back to jazz.

"Maybe it was a glitch," Connor offers.

I don't even dignify the comment with a response. I march toward Wendell's, with its long narrow patio that flanks the park. The patio is empty now, but the lights are still on inside.

"Where are you going?" Connor asks.

"I want to know why they played that song."

"And you think the bartender at Wendell's is going to help?"

"The music is piping from their patio speakers, right? Maybe they're in charge of the station. Or maybe someone working there is in charge of the music."

"You can't really go in there. You're only eighteen."

"I'm just asking a question. I'm not ordering shots." I scale the steps to Wendell's and pull open the doors. The music I followed to these doors is the same that's playing inside, but at a significantly lower volume.

A pretty twentysomething hostess gives me a once-over. Her strapless black dress reeks of trying too hard, and after appraising me and then Connor, her smile wobbles.

"Welcome to Wendell's. Do you have a reservation with us this evening?"

Connor laughs. I shake my head. "No, sorry. I have a question about your music."

She tilts her head, and her wobbly smile disappears altogether. "I'm sorry?"

"Your music. Do you guys decide the music that plays through the park?"

"I believe our patio speakers do project music onto the gree space, yes, but I should tell you that we have a strict twenty-one and up policy."

"The *green space*?" Connor asks. His tone is comparable to an eyeroll. Connor hates places like this the way I hate the smell of cooking onions.

I smile at the hostess, who's looking at the door behind me hopefully. Another hostess arrives, adjusting menus in a basket behind the greeting station.

"I know this is odd, and I'm not planning to stay," I say, "but we noticed a punk rock song mixed in with all of this..."

"Jazz?" she supplies. Her smile has sharp teeth, and I have to remind myself that flicking this glossy little rich chick's upturned nose would be—however satisfying—a terrible idea.

"Yeah. It seemed like an unusual addition. Are you using a playlist or a station or..."

The second hostess turns toward us and I trail off, but she looks a little less tightly wound than the first hostess. "You're talking about that Green Day song?" Hostess Number Two says.

"Yes!" I say. "Are there a lot of songs like that in the rotation?"

The first hostess flitters off to heaven knows where to do heaven knows what, but the new, infinitely preferable hostess leans over her stand with a grin. "Hell no. Man, it's all Count Basie and Miles Davis and then—bam!—twenty-year-old punk."

"So, this song has played before?" I ask.

She laughs. "That song has been on the playlist *all weekend*. Every twenty-four songs—I've counted."

"Really?" I ask.

She nods and lowers her voice conspiratorially. "It's a playlist online, and apparently it was left public. Somebody looked it up and added that song in. And the best part? When our manager tried to fix it, he ended up locking the account, which no one can fix until we hear back from the club's owner because it's his account. So here we are."

"Classic jazz with an occasional side of old-school punk," I say.

She smiles and winks. "Exactly. The manager is about to lose his mind. It's delicious."

"Zara?"

Prissy hostess is back, and she's looking pointedly at Zara, who rolls her eyes and then grabs a couple of menus. "So, do you want to grab a drink? Or..."

She looks at me, and I can tell she's trying to figure out if I'm old enough to be here. Which I'm obviously not. Not that I could afford a drink in here if I was.

"Thanks, we were just curious about the music thing."

"It's the great Wendell's mystery," Zara says with another wink. Her eyes linger on Connor briefly, but he's already turning away. He clearly has it as bad for Hope as she's got it for him.

"Have a great night," Prissy says. Her comment is a dismissal if ever I've heard one.

I don't look at her, but when Zara gives us the peace sign with her fingers, I return it.

Outside, Connor is quietly staring at the lawn. "What did that clue say again about rain?"

I read the part he's asking about.

"*Think new clubs and old trains. You'll find the rain drawn here.*"

Then I frown at the lawn. "What happens in a park like this when it rains? Does it just flood everything? Make giant puddles?"

"No, they usually have drainage systems."

"How can I find them?"

"They're little grates. Built into the grass."

"Would the grates be big enough to hold a jewelry box?"

Connor's face sharpens with realization. "Inside the grates, maybe."

"Let's give it a shot," I say.

The paths are illuminated, but it's dark in the grass. We're reduced to scanning the park with our cell phone flashlights.

"Look close," Connor says, "They're usually brown or even dark green so they blend in. They might even be installed under the sod."

"What do we do to find them then?"

"Uh, we don't. But no one else would find them either," he says.

"Good point."

Ten minutes later, I've scanned what feels like a mile of grass, and my lower back aches from being bent over to look. Maybe they are under the sod. Maybe they have a different kind of drainage system. Maybe—

"I found one," he says across the park. "Nothing in it. The grate will be round. Dark brown, maybe black."

"Goody," I mutter, and then I lean back over and keep swinging my cell phone in a slow arc. Back and forth, take a step, back and forth, take a step. I lather, rinse, repeat this for what feels like hours. Maybe days. And then Connor, again.

"Got another one!" He's on his hands and knees in the grass. I hear him give a little grunt, prying the grate loose, I guess. Then he shakes his head. "Nothing. That pipe is definitely big enough though."

I sigh and roll my neck and take another step and feel something hard and flat under my toes.

I freeze and step back, scanning the grass with my flashlight. I can just make out the rounded edge of something dark. I use the sole of my shoe to push the grass back and there it is, a perfectly round grate.

"I found one!" I say, and I crouch down on my knees, trying to pry the grate loose. To my surprise it pops out easily, and when I shine my flashlight in the hole inside, I see a familiar flash of white. My heart jumps, and I adjust the angle of my light. I can make out the short end of another white box. Bingo. I reach for it and pain—sharp and shocking—stabs into the tip of my middle finger. I pull it back with a yelp, my phone dropping into the grass.

I cradle my hand to my chest in shock. Blood is dripping from my finger. "I cut myself on something."

"Are you bleeding?"

"Some," I admit.

Connor starts jogging over. "On what? There's nothing in those but water and mud."

I grit my teeth together as pain throbs through my finger. "Well there's something else in this one."

I root around in my pockets with my good hand, finding nothing. "Do you have a tissue?"

He pats his pockets, and I roll my eyes. This man doesn't have a tissue. I'm still feeling lucky that he wore a shirt on this excursion.

"Hang on," he says, and he takes off for the restaurant.

Hopefully, he'll get Zara, because I'm pretty sure Miss Strapless Dress is going to call some sort of authority figure if my brother asks her for a napkin.

I find my phone and shine my light back into the hole where

the white box gleams. It's turned upright and it's hard to see around the sides. I grasp the top with my left hand, careful to only touch what I can see. It's wedged pretty good, but I tug it until it's free.

Tucked in the back side is the culprit of my agony. A nail file.

I set my phone down so I can examine the file and the box. Even using my uninjured hand, I manage to smear blood on the lid. I turn the file over and notice the faded Santa Claus etched into the red handle. My stomach swings low. This isn't just any nail file—it's *my* nail file.

My mind rips the terrible images of it from my memory. Screaming. Running. Declan. The file.

Every contact leaves a trace, and this is mine. This is the evidence I left behind.

Something buzzes and I jump. My phone. I turn until I see the telltale glow of my screen from a patch of dark grass. It buzzes again as I reach for it, and the file slips out of my fingers. A single drop of blood lands on the screen, a dark stain on the blue-white glow.

It's the mystery number, a flashing incoming call that makes my chest squeeze and my stomach squirm. I try to answer, but the screen shifts to Missed Call and all is quiet.

My heart thumps rabbit-fast in my chest. My finger throbs, the blood seeping into my T-shirt now. I use my good hand to search the grass, patting the cool blades until I feel the slim metal edge of the file.

I clutch it, the faded plastic Santa face leering up at me.

Declan and I always fought, but it didn't turn physical until February. There was Valentine's Day—that barely-a-shove in the Book Loft. I shrugged it off, but by the end of February, every argument was ending with a shove, a pinch, a yank of my wrist. No hitting—he was careful about that—but plenty of marks and bruises. I guess by mid-March, I'd had enough.

Connor was gone and Mom and Dad were in Connecticut on a job site. Things had been bad for a couple of weeks, and I had a massive chemistry project due. I was sitting in my bed filing my nails, talking to my lab partner, Daniel, about the final presentation.

When Declan walked in, we were laughing about something ridiculous our teacher, Mr. Weida, had done, and I knew there was going to be trouble. For Declan, Daniel wasn't a classmate or a study partner. He was a guy, and therefore he was a threat. Before I knew it, Declan had yanked the phone out of my hand and disconnected the call. In a matter of seconds, we exploded.

Raised voices turned quickly into full-fledged screaming. We were in each other's faces. Throwing threats. Calling names. It's upsetting to remember losing myself like that.

When I tried to get out of the room, he grabbed me by the back of the shirt and a fistful of my hair. My collar dug into my neck, gagging me, and I'd just had it. I was done. I got loose and ran for the front door. He stopped me, and in the struggle, I forgot I was holding that file. I forgot that I stabbed him—not on purpose, but I held it up when he slapped toward me, and it happened.

Or maybe it didn't just happen. I can't remember any of it clearly. Everything from those weeks is a blur of anger and violence. What I do remember is hearing him scream. Seeing it stuck in the palm of his hand. Feeling my lungs clamp down like they were trapped in a vise. Declan shouldered past me, slammed me into the door frame once, and again for good measure. And then he ran.

He didn't come back until the next morning. I don't know where he went. I never had the chance to ask, because the next time I saw him, I wound up in the emergency room.

"Hey," Connor says, startling me. I look up to find him offering a stack of napkins and a bandage.

He reaches for my finger and while he examines it, I tuck the nail file discreetly into my purse. I should tell him—I know that, but the idea of admitting one more violent act feels too terrible to contemplate. I don't know what this all adds up to. Am I still me, or am I just the sum of my worst sins? I clean up my finger and put on the bandage. I'm throwing the wrapper away when the drumbeat starts through the speakers. Then the guitar. I feel cold and sick and tired. So damn tired of this.

My phone buzzes, and I check it. My notifications list a bunch of unread messages—one from Bennett, one from Mom, and two from Valerie. More pop up while I'm holding it open. I scan quickly past Mom—Just checking in, sweetie!—and

Bennett, who sent me some sort of joke I don't have time for. Valerie's message is different.

Valerie: What is this? Is this the video you were talking about? Why are we getting this?

Valerie: You need to leave Aiden out of it. He can't keep getting stuff like this.

Unknown: Looks like you have a new helper. But you weren't supposed to tell, Cleo.

Unknown: Next time it will be the prosecutor and the police.

Hope: I just got a text from Jack. Someone sent him the video of Connor.

"He knows you're with me," I say. "He sent the video of you to Valerie, Aiden, and Jack."

Connor tenses and tries damn hard to hide it. "Because I'm helping you?"

"I think so."

Another text from Hope pops up:

Hope: Did you find the clue?

Me: Yeah. I need to talk to you. He shortened our time.

Hope: How much?

Me: Just call me when you can.

Hope: I'm in the middle of something. Will call soon.

The wind picks up and a roll of clouds blots out the stars on the western edge of the sky.

"Come on," Connor says, tugging my sleeve. "It's going to rain."

"Wait, I haven't even read the—"

I freeze, spotting movement at the back of the park, along the trees on the left. It could be a jogger. A resident. Whoever. It's a public park. But something about the way this person is moving in and out of the trees feels important.

I watch, even as the first drops spatter the ground around me.

"What's going on?" Connor asks, noticing my focus.

"I..." I stare at the section of trees to the left; I don't see anything now. No. Wait. There it is. An arm lifting. A shift of shadows. "Someone's out there."

"Where? Are you sure?"

I feel cold all over watching the trees. The darkness. And then one shadow pulls away from the rest. And he steps into the open. Dark hoodie. Long legs. A familiar silhouette. I can feel his eyes on us and I know this isn't a stranger. I've seen this silhouette before. A thousand times.

Declan.

TWENTY-SIX

2 HOURS LEFT

"CONNOR," I SAY. "I THINK THAT'S HIM."

"Look, I know we're both freaked, but don't jump to—"Then he stops and looks at him. I can see the recognition fall over my brother's face. "Holy shit."

"It's him, right?"

Connor gives the figure one long look, and then he bolts, full-out sprinting after Declan, who turns and runs as soon as he sees Connor. I'm chasing after them both, my legs pumping, my feet finding that old familiar rhythm of the run. Connor was not a distance runner, but he played three seasons as a running back, and he's fast as hell.

He's gaining on Declan. And I'm slowly closing the gap. But there's a difference between sprinting and distance, and within a minute or two I can hear Connor breathing hard. He's slowing. I catch up with him, and Declan heads left, ducking down a side alley.

"This way," I say, and we veer after Declan.

I see a sliver of dark hoodie and black-clad legs. Definitely a guy. But is it Declan? How do I know this is real? That I'm not dreaming all of this up?

"Declan?" I cry out before I can stop myself.

He falters, his body going tense. My heart drops into free fall and my hands turn to ice. It's him.

God, it's really him.

He picks up speed again and ducks into a parking garage attached to a business building. Behind me Connor groans. I turn back and he's grabbing his side. "Too long since I last ran."

"You can wait."

"Hell no," he pants out. "You're not going in there alone."

We jog into the parking garage and I stop just inside. It's quiet and dark, the first floor mostly empty. I hear the soft rhythmic pounding of footsteps heading up a flight of stairs.

"There," Connor says, pointing at the back corner of the garage. "The stairs are there."

Yellow lights flicker overhead and we jog toward the entrance of the stairwell, rain falling in a steady spray. When Connor reaches for the door, I touch his arm and shake my head.

"He's in there," he says.

"And he has to come out," I say, looking around the mostly empty garage. A blue minivan sits in the corner. Two black sedans are nestled against the far wall. But mostly it is gray pavement with the occasional flicker of a yellowing light overhead.

"Do you hear him?" Connor asks.

"No, but there are only two stairwells and the ramp leading up to the next level." I point to the opposite corner, where the other stairwell waits. The ramp is easy to spot, marked by yellow directional lines and a helpful arrow promising more parking on the next level. As we can get closer, there are bare spaces between the supports to the second floor, giving us a view of part of the level above us.

"We're just going to wait?"

"He has to pass us, right? There's no other way out of this garage."

"I don't like it," he says. "He had to have picked this for a reason. He could be parked here."

"He'd still have to stop to get out of the garage," I say, pointing at the lift gate near the payment booth. "We've got him, Connor. This ends here."

And then I stop, considering the rage in my brother's eyes earlier. "Hey, when he gets here, don't do anything. See what he says."

"See what he says? Are you out of your mind? He tried to kill you!"

"And he has a video I do not want getting into the wrong hands. Just...we'll listen. If anything—anything goes wrong, we call the police, okay?"

But Connor doesn't look convinced. I stand near the open door to the stairwell and let my breathing return to normal, but he paces tight circles. Checks his watch. I breathe in the smell of old gasoline and urine coming from the stairwell and listen to the rain outside, but I know beyond a doubt that if Declan shows his face, Connor is not going to be chill. It's going to be a nightmare.

What the hell do I do? My only hope is that facing it head-on will calm things down. Maybe seeing me miserable and scared will be enough for him.

I don't hear anything. Traffic purrs along in the distance. I hear an occasional noise from outside, but the garage is silent. Empty.

"I don't like this," Connor says again, shaking his head. He walks toward the ramp that leads up to the next level.

"What are you doing?"

"Checking to see if there's a bridge or a building entrance. We could be standing here for nothing."

I shift uncomfortably as he walks up the ramp, disappearing from view. I check my phone and watch as a minute passes. Two. On the third minute, I'm getting ready to call, but he heads back down.

"Nothing," he says, shaking his head. "He got out. He must have gotten into the building or—"

Crash!

The noise is an explosion, shattering the quiet and sending us both into an instinctive crouch. Distantly, I hear glass plinking against pavement.

"What was that?" I ask.

Connor crosses the garage, closing the space between us and—

Crash!

Car windows. Someone is breaking car windows on the floor above us. My heart pounds and I look up, wishing I could see what was happening. Wishing I could hear what's going on.

"I'm going up—"

"No!" It's a whisper scream, but I grab his arm too. "Think for a minute! If he's breaking glass, he's doing it with something."

"He didn't have anything," Connor says.

"Well, he obviously found something!"

Connor's face shifts into worry. "A car. He could be parked here and he could have gotten something out of his car."

"He's trying to scare us because he knows he's caught," I say. "We've got him. He's trapped. He's the one who's scared of us. That's why he's—"

Crash!

I feel my phone buzz, and even that makes me jump. I check it quickly, and sure enough it's a message from our mystery caller. Except he's no longer a mystery, is he?

I pull it up—an image of Connor, fairly clear. He's on the parking lot ramp, looking over his shoulder. A message pops up underneath as I'm staring at the photo.

Unknown: I bet the cops would love to see where Connor is right now.

Crash!

My heart pounds, my mouth gone dry.

"What is it?" Connor asks. "Is that me? What the hell?"

He moves again toward the ramp, but I grab him hard. "No! Don't! This is exactly what he wants. He wants you to lose it and do something so you can really take a fall. He's already threatening to call the police and blame you for whatever the hell he's doing up there."

"We can't just take this, Cleo! We're playing right into his hands."

My phone buzzes again.

Unknown: Finish the last clue, or I'll let him take the blame for everything.

A flashlight beam flickers in the far stairwell, and I listen. Someone's coming down. Is that him? Is Declan going to walk through that door and tear my world apart again? My heart is squeezing itself into my throat, making it hard to breathe.

There's a faint clunking nearby. I look up to the ceiling and then back to the stairwell, and my stomach flips over. Wait. That's not the same person. Unless Declan is coming back down. Is that footsteps?

There's a crackle of a two-way radio in the stairwell. The jiggling light seems brighter. It has to be a security guard from the attached building. He must be checking the lot. And then I hear a radio.

"...in progress, requesting immediate assistance."

It's a security guard.

"Connor," I whisper. My phone buzzes, but I don't dare pull it back out. I hardly want to breathe.

Connor is resisting, but he's looking at the stairwell, too, and I know he's putting this together. There is glass on the floor and a photo of Connor looking suspicious. If the police find him here, there's no way this ends well. This will end with Connor being questioned by the police at best, or in jail at worst.

"We have to go," I say. "Right now."

His jaw clenches. He's furious. In the far stairwell, the flashlight is much closer; I can see the beam and hear the guard's heavy breathing. And finally, finally Connor moves for the wall. We climb over and drop the four or five feet to the ground.

And then we run, bursting out of the garage and back into the rain. It's lighter now, barely sprinkling, but the pavement is slick and shiny. My legs feel heavy, and all the adrenaline has burned out of me. I'm breathless. Achy. Beaten down. We hold the jog and weave through the grass until we're back onto a clean, white sidewalk.

Connor slows, and I take a deep breath. We're near the river. I can smell it in the air, loamy and damp. We find a dry bench under a picnic shelter and slump onto it wordlessly, panting in alternating rhythm until our bodies slow and we come back to the here and now.

It takes long minutes before Connor speaks, his voice low and flat.

"I should have killed him before we ever went to West Virginia."

I flinch. "Stop. Just stop. You aren't that guy."

"I would be," he says, and my heart thumps. "You're my sister. He almost—"

"But he didn't," I say, touching his hand. "I'm here. I'm okay."

"And what if he comes back?"

"We just need to get to the end of it," I say. "Let's just finish this. Time's almost up anyway. We have to try."

He finally relents with a sigh. "Do you still have the clue?"

I nod and open the box. Right away, I know this one is different. There are eight lines instead of four, and there's something written on the back. I read the riddle first:

I know seven secrets.
One caused the fall.
One did nothing.
One saw it all.
One didn't care.
One used their head.
One played the hero.
One was left for dead.

My arms prickle with goose bumps. It's the seven of us that were in West Virginia.

"I don't get it," Connor says. "Is there a hint to a place in all that?"

"No, the secrets are us. The seven of us." I turn the letter over. An address is written on the back of the clue. All print. Black ink. I show him the address. "This is where it all ends."

TWENTY-SEVEN

1 HOUR 9 MINUTES LEFT

CONNOR LOOKS UP THE ADDRESS AND I SEE HIS BROW furrow.

"What is it?" I ask.

"That's the YMCA," he says. "The one a couple of blocks from here."

A rush of cold sweat runs up my back so quickly, I feel like I might vomit. I stand up and press my freezing hands to my both sides of my neck, trying to cool myself down. Trying to breathe.

The pool is where it started. Where *we* started. Of course he will end it there.

"It's the last one," I say. "This is it."

"You're sure?" he asks.

I nod, pacing tightly back and forth in front of the bench. "That's the first thing Declan and I did together. I invited him to a party at that pool."

Then I stop and sit down, suddenly urgent. "I have to text Hope."

Me: We're on the last clue and I got a text that cut down how much time we have. Can you meet us at the YMCA? But wait outside!

Hope: The one downtown? Where we went to that party? How do you know it's the last one?

Me: That's the one. Call and I'll explain. Do not go inside alone!

I consider explaining everything about Declan over text, but it's too much. And I don't think she's going to believe it until she sees it with her own eyes.

Hope: I'm on the phone, but I can be there in fifteen minutes.

Me: We only have two hours. Maybe less.

Hope: I'll hurry.

And then:

Hope: I think it's Aiden's video. I think he's behind it. I'll explain when I get there.

I frown. "She thinks it's Aiden and that he's the one who planned the hunt. And that it's his video."

"It could be *his* video," Connor says. "He'd have the same motives as Valerie, and he'd definitely send it to Declan if Declan reached out."

I nod. "If Declan called anyone, it would be Aiden. I don't think Hope can get her head around the part where Declan is alive to get Aiden's video and put all this together."

"Because Declan being alive feels illogical to her," Connor says. "No one found his body. No one has heard from him. Hope probably can't imagine anything thing other than him being dead."

"True. But we also just chased Declan through the park. That helped eliminate any doubts I had left."

"I feel that," he says.

The rain has slowed to the lightest drizzle, but it feels colder now that we're sitting. Our breath steams around us, and I pull my hands into the sleeves of my shirt to keep them warm.

"I wish I could just figure out who each of us is supposed to be," I say.

"What do you mean?"

"In the clues. Declan is the one left for dead. I'm the one who caused the fall."

"That's bullshit," he says. "You're not the cause."

I don't argue, and I don't try to figure out any more of the clues. I wait for him to talk.

"What was this date at the YMCA?"

"I invited Declan. It was a party with some school friends. Things were a little wild, and at one point, people were throwing each other in. He threw me—"

"You can't swim."

"He didn't know that then," I say. "After Hope and Valerie fished me out, I was embarrassed, and he came and sat with me. He apologized and I guess... I don't know." I squeeze my eyes shut, trying to block out the memory. "That's sort of where it all started."

When I open them again, Connor is clenching his jaw so hard a muscle in his temple jumps.

I flinch. "Look, I know I was stupid—"

"*You* were stupid?" He whirls on me with a hard laugh. "I brought that son of a bitch into our house. Into your life. That was on *me*. All of it is on me."

I gape at him. Not once did I ever think of it like this. Declan lived with us for three months before he even looked at me. He was quiet. Kept to himself. I was the one who gave him long looks, who wore T-shirts with his favorite bands and brought him his favorite soda any time I stopped at a store.

"I hate myself for letting this happen," he says. "I should have known."

"You couldn't. You can't read minds."

"I should have read the signs. I should have damn well known not to bring him home."

"You can't do this, Connor," I say. "We can't play the blame game. There's no way to go back. We can only go forward, right?"

He scoffs, looking unconvinced, but I squeeze his hand.

"He tore us apart this year," I say softly. "Even though he wasn't here."

"Yeah."

"So, let's deal with that shit. And we'll take it step by step from there."

Connor turns to me, and his dark eyes are glistening. "And what happens when we get to that pool and he's there, back from the dead with all his bullshit and all your shared history?"

I shake my head, though in truth, not much scares me more. I've been running from Declan for a year. From what I did to him. From who I was with him. Can I stop myself from becoming that girl again? Is that spell ever going to break?

"I don't know," I admit. "But I have to face it. I don't want to look back forever. I want to move forward. I want to find my way through."

"Yeah," he says softly. And then he squeezes my hand back. "I hear you."

We walk the four blocks to the YMCA and find Hope's car parked out front. It used to serve as home to residents, but now it's just a workout facility, and rumor has it that will be closing soon too. The building is tall, old, and sort of ominous, with dark brick and arched windows. The lights that usually illuminate the blue awnings are out, leaving everything shrouded in darkness.

We search up and down the street, but do not spot her. I call her phone a couple of times, but it goes to voicemail.

"What the hell?"

"She better not be standing around here by herself," Connor says, looking worried. I can't blame him. We are in serious sketchtown here.

If it was me, I would not want to sit in my car. Or stand on this sidewalk. I'd probably see if I could get inside the building.

I step over a pile of broken glass near the curb and then turn for the doors.

"That door isn't going to be open, Cleo. It's two o'clock in the morning."

"Well, Hope isn't out here." I try the main doors, but they're locked as expected. I move to the visitor entrance on the left and to my surprise, that one pulls right open.

"Huh," he says.

I check the edge of the door, feeling the smooth, rubbery texture of duct tape sealed tightly over the latch that would hold the door closed. "Looks like someone made sure we could get in."

We step inside and the door shuts behind us with a soft noise, the absence of the telltale click reassuring me that the tape is still doing its job. We can get out when we want, which is good, because it's dark and creepy inside.

"We need to be careful," I say. "I have no idea if there are cameras or what."

"I'm trying Hope again," he says, but four rings later, I hear her voicemail pick up.

I listen to Connor breathe and let my eyes adjust to the darkness. We're a little left of the main entrance in the professional section of the building.

"Where the hell is she?" he asks.

"Her phone might not work down there. The pool's on the lower level," I say, but I'm getting nervous. Would she really stay in here alone with it being so dark? Wouldn't she at least text me?

"We need to find her," I say. "But we need to be careful. He's probably already here."

"If he hurts her—" Connor sucks in a tight breath. "If he even touches her—"

"He won't," I say, and this I am reasonably sure about. Declan has always been an asshole, but he saved his violence for me. Still, I can't be sure he won't scare her to death. Or use her as bait.

"Get us down there," Connor says. "I don't want to wait."

The rooms are dark, but I remember the ornate woodwork and iron banisters in the stairwells. Now, the leather chairs are black in the darkness, the elegant details lost in shadow.

"I thought this was a gym," Connor says as we walk.

"We're only passing through this part. The stairs to the pool are just ahead."

A large exit sign glows just above them with an arrow pointing to the main entrance. We ignore that arrow and begin our descent.

In the stairwell, the grandeur gives way to white drywall and the familiar smell of a rec center. I inhale floor cleaner, chlorine, and grade school gymnasium as we follow the rubber-coated stairs past posters advertising swimming lessons and promoting hand hygiene. At the bottom, we pause outside the main hallway. It's completely dark and utterly silent. I spot the dim outline of a water fountain on the right and little else.

"She wouldn't come down all this way and not have turned a light on," I say, my stomach tightening with dread.

Connor paces, his hands rolled into fists. "I don't like this. Call her again."

Something clunks in the distance, so loud and sudden that I lurch. A deep, mechanical hum whirs to life. Just the heater. I sag in relief.

"My service is shit down here," he says. And then, he moves to the mouth of the hallway. "Hope!"

My heart leaps at his volume. I grab his arm, because Declan will hear us. But what's the point? Declan knows where we are. He's wrote the address on the back of the clue, for God's sake. He set this trap for me, but Hope is the one who walked in first. My throat constricts.

Connor moves forward, and I stay behind him. Hallways to the left and right lead to classrooms. Straight ahead, we'll find another set of double doors, the pool inside.

"Hope!"

The answering silence is unnerving. I turn around and check both hallways. My eyes play tricks on me with the darkness. Shadows seem to move. The heater could be hiding the sound of footsteps. I feel…watched.

"Where the hell is she?" Connor sounds scared now, and my teeth are starting to chatter.

Please don't let him have her somewhere. Don't let him hurt her like he hurt me, because I will never forgive myself.

I think I hear something zipping in the background. The buzz of a bee. The hum of a small fan.

Connor inhales to shout again, and I grab his arm hard.

"Shh!"

Bzzzz bzzzz bzzzz bzzzz.

My stomach drops. I know that noise. I've heard it before.

I hear it again, the insistent *bzzzz bzzzz bzzzz bzzzz* that I've heard in cars and locker rooms and my own bedroom countless times.

"What's that buzzing?" Connor asks. "Is that a phone?"

I can't nod. Can't speak because my tongue is sticking to the roof of my mouth. Because I want more than anything to say no. To be wrong. But I'm not wrong. I inch forward down the hallway, following the sound I've heard a hundred times. A thousand maybe. I follow it until I see the blue light of the screen, until I see the phone itself—cockeyed and discarded.

Connor's steps sound heavily behind me, but I can barely hear him. There is nothing beyond the roar of blood behind my ears. Behind the fear burning brighter with every beat of my heart. I pick it up, see the familiar metallic blue of the case, run my thumb over the new crack in one corner of the screen. I silence the alarm and put in her passcode that she hasn't changed in years.

The phone lights up, a photo of Hope and me filling the background behind the icons. Both of us look sweaty and spent. I have my arm slung around her waist, and she's wearing the gold medal, so this must be last year. The Springfield Invitational. She took first in that race.

My stomach clenches, and I blink away the tears collecting in my eyes. She wouldn't leave her phone. She wouldn't drop it here and not hear it. This wasn't an accident.

Hope is in trouble.

TWENTY-EIGHT

32 MINUTES LEFT

I HEAR CONNOR'S BREATH WHEN HE SEES THE SCREEN—when he realizes. He goes utterly still, and then slowly, very slowly, he reaches for the phone. His finger hovers over the image of Hope's face for the briefest second. And then the screen goes dark, and Connor's stillness breaks.

He erupts in a flurry of terror and movement. He calls for her over and over, her name coming out like a command. And then a prayer. He rushes back and forth and rattles doors on either side of the hallway, but while Connor's fear burns through him like fire, dread fills me like wet cement.

Desperate words tumble from Connor's mouth. "Say something—Hope, please—where are you—"

But I am still as stone, unable to move. To speak. My thumb runs over the broken corner of the screen. I think of the glass shattering in the parking garage. My hands slipping on blood on my kitchen floor.

Hope is down here with Declan. He has her, and I know where he'd keep her. I know exactly where this is all going to end. The same place it started.

"The pool," I say, my voice a steady shock in the midst of Connor's panic.

He meets me at the end of the hallway, and I push the double doors open. Cool, damp air hits me. I take a breath that tastes like bleach. Nothing has changed. The pool sits, blue and glowing in the center of the room. Dim emergency lights add just enough illumination to the pool lamps to make it easy to scan the room. The diving platforms form a line to my right, ladders directing divers to the low, medium, and high boards in succession. I move out of the shadow of the diving area to see the rest of the room. She has to be here.

But where?

There are equipment cages on the far side of the water, mostly lost in shadow. The doors are open and I can see a few familiar shapes inside the cages. A tower of chemical tubs. A stack of kickboards. A crumpled pool cover. On the right side of the water, wide bleachers rise into darkness, light from the pool casting strange shadows on the seats. In the corners, open doorways lead to the locker rooms.

My eyes lock on a bench beside the right opening—the women's locker room. That's where they took me when they got me out at the pool party. Hope's arm was slender but strong around my back and Valerie's hand a reassuring pat between my shoulder blades. And then Declan was there, a sheepish smile and an apology at the ready.

He was good with apologies.

He was even better at doing things that required them.

Connor rushes for the bleachers first, calling Hope's name, climbing with loud, clanging steps. I start slowly toward the bench, seeing nothing.

What am I looking for and where is Hope? If this is the end, what the hell am I supposed to find?

"Cleo," Connor says, his voice echoing off the bare walls, his face blue and strange in the pool light. He's standing on one of the bleachers, halfway up, and he's looking up from there.

"Is that one of the boxes?" he asks.

He's looking at the diving platform and as soon as I turn, I see it. There's no mistaking the curl of ribbon. I turn, walking swiftly for the diving board. I don't even stop to think, I just climb. I'm halfway up when a loud crackle shakes my focus. I freeze, looking around. Music blasts through unseen speakers.

It's the Green Day song. I twist, seeing nothing but Connor still standing on the bleachers. He's looking at something, so I climb higher, high enough to scramble up on the platform, to see the white box with its green ribbon at the far edge.

"There's a speaker!"

Connor has to scream to be heard over the music, but I follow the direction he's pointing. I spot the speaker near the wall, surprised it's large enough to be so loud. The song is about to rip me in two.

And then I hear the laughter.

My stomach shrinks tight. That is the laugh I heard when my hands shook before he kissed me. The laugh I heard every time he called me names. That's the laugh from the voicemail on my phone, and I'd know it anywhere.

"*Knock it off, Declan.*"

The sound of my own voice over the speakers is a shock. I cross my arms over my chest, still frozen on the platform. Declan's laugh rings out again, even though there was nothing funny about what I'd said.

"*What do you think, my man? Does she need to loosen up?*" he asks.

"*Sounds like.*" Aiden. Aiden's voice, and it's closer than the rest. Muffled. He's the one behind the camera.

If he recorded this, maybe Hope was right. Maybe Aiden was the one on the bridge. I shiver wildly and my teeth begin to chatter. It is so loud, so loud I can barely hear myself think.

"*We need to get moving.*" Me again.

"*True facts.*" Valerie this time, bright, but maybe tense around the edges. It's familiar.

"*What are we going to do with these women? Always nagging,*" Declan says.

"*You tell me,*" Aiden says, a soft laugh amplified by his closeness to the speaker.

Déjà vu rolls over me in waves. The song is ramping up, and I hear shuffling in the background. Things being moved. It's all familiar. I've heard this before, but where?

"*We need to get going if we're going to get there on time.*" This is Connor, and it is his voice that unlocks the scene.

This is the day we left. This was taken when we were loading the van. I can see it now, the stacks of backpacks and the two giant coolers. I can see the van, doors open, and the sun—bright and unusually warm for April—high overhead.

"*You ready?*" Declan asks. There is a brief pause—only music and laughter. And then.

"*This is going to be so great.*"

The sound cuts out, and a soft hiss pours through the speaker.

I'm too far to see Connor's expression, but he has stopped moving, because he gets it too. We both know what this is now. The song. The voicemail. This wasn't a pocket dial—this wasn't Declan. It was all sound from a video. *Aiden's* video.

Hope was right. I was so caught up, so sure Declan was alive, I didn't even see it. But who else would hide something like that? Who would be furious enough about Declan dying to want someone to pay? His words echo through my memory. *Secrets have a way of getting out.*

Aiden didn't answer Connor when he asked about the video. God, he could have even had the nail file. Declan could have gone to him. Confided in him. All of this could be Aiden.

I search the shadows, looking for his lanky form melting

into a corner or a shadow, but there's nothing. Nothing but the clue.

My body moves of its own accord, carrying me closer to the far edge of the platform. There's the box, small and white at the end of the diving board. I know this is the end. No evidence this time, just bone deep instinct. The answers are right there. As easy as bending down and grabbing them. I take the last step, making sure I'm steady. I'm not afraid of heights, but everywhere I look, there is water. I do not want to fall.

At the edge of the board, I pick up the box and tear the lid free.

There are only five words typed on the white paper.

Hope could have saved him.

I read it a second time. A third. It doesn't make sense, because Hope has nothing to do with this. I want the words to change into something else, but they stubbornly refuse. Footsteps suddenly thunder across the room. From the bleachers. My head swims when I turn to see Connor racing down the steps as fast as he can. He's staring at the cages.

"Hope!" His voice is frantic. A prayer. "Hope!"

In the cages, one of the pool covers moves. A slim pale arm extends, and I think of the balcony in Madison's, the mannequin's fingers curling upward.

"Connor, stop!" My voice is hoarse and small. "Stop!" I

scream louder, but Connor is off the bleachers, shoes slapping the pavement.

In the cages, those waxy fingers curl. The elbow bends. It's moving. A blond head lolls and pulls itself upright, the ponytail hanging off center.

It's Hope.

She groans softly, and Connor drops to his knees, crawling into the equipment cage to get to her.

"Look at me," he says.

I see his hands on her face, her pale fingers gripping his wrist.

Hope could have saved him.

I look at the paper in my hand and the words blur. Everything is confusion and nonsense. Hope wasn't there. Hope wasn't… Where was she? Where was Hope when I pushed Declan into the river?

Connor looks up at me. "She's hurt! She's been knocked out."

"I'm…okay," she says weakly.

They are still in that cage. Hope, moving so slowly. Connor checking her face. Her head. My heart thunks in a strange rhythm. I feel glued to this platform. Paralyzed by a thousand questions. Is this the big answer I've been looking for? There's no sense in any of this.

My knees give way, and I slump down to a crouch, my head swimming with confusion.

"Did you see me push Declan?" I ask, my voice echoing off the water. The platform is scratchy beneath my hands. The pool glows blue beneath me.

I had expected Declan. I had expected violence. And now I am faced with a quiet, terrible question instead.

"Did you..." I trail off and Hope takes a breath. I can hear her, even all this way across the water.

"I didn't see you. But yes. I saw Declan in the water," she says. "I was downstream from you. Past the bridge."

"You could have saved him?" I ask.

"I didn't try," she confesses, her voice high and cracking.

"Don't talk. Just breathe," Connor says, trying to take charge. Trying to get her on her feet. I can hear her struggling.

"I should have told you," she says. "I should have tried—"

"It doesn't matter!" Connor says. "He almost killed her. Declan deserved what he got."

"No!" The shout comes from behind me. I turn and see a shadow peeling away from the wall. A voice roaring out wordless, bone-deep rage.

Someone is running toward them, out from behind some shadow in the bleachers. I see the black hoodie and long legs. Aiden! I howl out a warning, but it is too late.

Connor spins just as Aiden slams the cage door shut with a clang. They're trapped. I reach out to them, futile and desperate from the platform.

I try to turn for the ladder, but I wobble.

Aiden turns, and time slows. My foot slips off the platform and my balance shifts. My world slides sideways as he steps closer, his hood down around his shoulders.

There is a terrible jolt of shock when I realize I was wrong. But I cannot say a word. I can only stare at his face in horror as I fall.

TWENTY-NINE

11 MINUTES

I DO NOT HAVE TIME TO TAKE A BREATH OR BRACE MYSELF. I hit the water badly, the side of my body smacking the surface and plunging under. Stinging—sharp and electric—blooms everywhere my body hits. I sink like a stone, the force of my impact pushing me down.

I pinwheel my arms and legs. I'm panicking, adrenaline charging through my veins, speeding my heart. I see the surface of the water above, a rippling sheet of gray. I am rising, bringing that gray closer. My limbs work automatically, thrashing forward and down, searching for the surface.

I reach for the light and feel my hand break the surface. Air! The thrill of it pushes adrenaline into my limbs. I kick and reach. And rise. My head emerges and I gulp in one greedy breath.

Another, but it is too short. Not enough.

Connor is screaming like a man possessed. My name tears

through the air, and I hear him slamming and banging at the bars, but I can't reassure him. I can't do anything.

"Help!" The word gurgles as I slip beneath the water again. My limbs move, blindly searching for leverage, for something to push me up—to get me *out*. I surface again, one more breath and then the water takes me. It's cold and heavy, dragging me down.

Long-lost swimming lessons come back to me, an echo of a command to *Kick my feet. Scoop the water*. I follow the voice even though I failed them all. I scissor my legs, move my arms up and down. My limbs are clunky and heavy, water sucking at my pants, my shoes, pulling at every part of me.

My lungs begin to burn, a steady and growing warning. I need to breathe. I need air. I struggle and kick, my fingers stretched out, clawing for the surface. I break through to the light. Breathe.

Too short. Not enough. I am submerged again. A cold burn wraps around my middle and pulls me deep. The burning in my chest rises to a throb, and pain overtakes me. My body curls in on itself, and the ache blooms into agony. Blinding pain beats in my arms and legs, pounding with my pulse behind my eyes.

I look up, the surface a shimmering ripple. A sliver of dark curls through the water above. A green satin ribbon, floating like gossamer above me.

My lungs scream for air, my heart a hummingbird beating wild and small behind my ribs. Darkness pushes my vision into a tunnel. Into a pinprick. I close my eyes to the light and surrender.

And my body grazes something narrow and rough—a cord dangling into the abyss.

No. Not a cord. A rope.

My eyes open and I reach, my fingers clumsy and weak. I graze the rope with my fingers. Try to grip but miss. I try again, pushing my whole body at that rope. I give everything I have to pulling myself up, reaching with my other hand even as my lungs ignite. My limbs go stiff, and my body forces my mouth open. Biological instinct overrides my command and sucks water into my mouth, my throat.

I pull with all my might, and my head breaks free. I gag and cough, inhaling water and air and vomiting half of it back up in a convulsive rush. Over and over, until I am spent and shaking, my arms precariously wrapped around something at the top of the rope.

A float. It's part of a lane separator, but it is not enough. I am still going under, my head held at an awkward angle, face up in hopes of staying afloat.

"Cleo!" Connor and Hope scream my name together. Connor swears and screams and jerks and rattles at the cage.

My hands are shaking. Slipping. This will not buy me much time. I will drown.

I try to call out, but gag and cough, gulping air. I try again.

"Help!" I cry, my throat raw. "Help me!"

"Cleo!" Hope's voice. The rattle of metal. "Help her! God, please, help her! Please!"

I blink water out of my eyes. I'm seized by another fit of coughing, and my grip slips. I hear Hope screaming again as I go under, but I still have the float. It's not enough. I bicycle my legs as hard as I can, but I'm failing. I can barely keep my head above water. I have to get to the side. My brain is sluggish, my thoughts a jumbled fog behind my need to live.

"Help," I gurgle weakly, slipping under again and kicking back up, my hand shaking on the rope.

I see the cage. The edge of the bleachers. And then I see his feet and I want to be wrong. I want it to be Aiden. Even Declan. I want it to be anything and anyone but what I'm seeing. But as my eyes follow the black sneakers up to the familiar face, my heart shatters.

I force myself to look into his eyes, to try to make sense of him being here.

"Bennett," I say. His name is a shock. A prayer. A cry. "Please. Help me."

He just stares at me, his eyes hollow and hungry. A warning whispers, vague and muddled in my brain. I can't make myself think, can't make sense of why he would do this—what possible reason he could have to hurt me, to hurt any of us.

"You're killing her!" Connor screams.

"Nooo..." Bennett drags the word out, his voice low and sure. "I'm not killing her. I'm just not doing anything to help her. Nothing wrong with that, is there, Hope?"

Hope sobs, and Connor growls, rattling the cage and then

swearing. He is raging inside that metal box, but he cannot control this. He'll be forced to watch me like Hope watched Declan.

But these pieces still don't fit together. Bennett doesn't even know about the river. He doesn't even know about Declan.

Except that's not true, is it?

Water fills my ears, laps at my cheeks. I tip my head up and drink deep, greedy breaths. And then I look at him again. The same eyes from the ice cream picture. The same mouth that asked permission before he kissed me. The same hands that have never, ever hurt me.

"Why?" I ask him, the pain blooming through my middle.

He tilts his head and his smile, for the first time, is strange and cruel. Familiar in its coldness. *He* is familiar in a way I have never noticed until this moment. His broad shoulders. His high cheekbones. The way he tilts his head when he's smiling. He looks like—

"Can you imagine what you'd do if you heard that someone drowned Connor?" he asks. "If you knew it didn't have to be that way, that he could have lived—started again. Fixed his mistakes. You would do anything for your brother, Cleo."

Brother. The word rings in my head over and over. Brother.

He smirks. "I would do anything for my brother too."

"Bennett, please," I say softly, automatically. But my heart knows there is no use. He is not here to help me.

"My name isn't Bennett," he says, and then he steps back from the edge. Away from me.

His eyes stay locked on me, and my grip slips. "Think of him, Cleo. I hope you think of my brother when you drown."

Connor and Hope are screaming again—so much noise. So loud. But I am sinking, my legs weak and heavy. I can't do this anymore. I can't. Before my head goes under, I hear Bennett's laugh.

He sounds just like Declan.

THIRTY

TIME'S UP

THIS TIME I DON'T KICK OR FIGHT. I AM SO TIRED. MY BODY is heavy and exhausted. I am a terrible joke. A believer of lies. A fool who deserves this truth. But it feels too heavy to bear.

I release the rope and my body drifts, my eyes shutting to the light. Pain wraps iron bands around my chest and squeezes tight.

You ready?

My eyes fly open. Declan's voice is so clear I half expect to see him in front of me, floating in the water. Bennett will get his wish after all. I am thinking of Declan, and thinking I am the girl he always wanted me to be.

Powerless and weak.

But I wasn't always this way. I've put in ten-mile running days in cross-country. I've lived on my own for weeks at a time while my parents were away. I've dreamed a future for my life, picked my place and planned my way.

I was strong once. Is any of that left?

We have to find a way forward.

I remember Connor next to tonight, his eyes bright with tears. His hand squeezing mine. Declan tore us apart, but we found our way back.

Could I find my way back too?

Could I be something else?

A girl that survives?

The idea pushes the tiniest surge of strength into my limbs, and I use it. I find the rope with my hands and kick, pull, drag myself up. Every cell in my body is screaming when I break the surface, taking a deep, greedy breath. And another.

No waiting this time. I keep kicking and put my eyes on the nearest ladder. I don't see Bennett. I don't hear Hope or Connor. There is nothing outside of my own determination. I'm going to get to that ladder. I'm going to get out of this water.

I'm going to walk on green lawns and sit on campus benches. I'm going to live.

I force weak scissor kicks, holding the floating ball. I am slow. I go under. But I come back up, and I keep pushing, inching, dragging myself through the water toward that ladder.

When my fingers graze the metal, I lunge with the little strength I have left, heaving myself against the rungs. I gag and cough. My whole body aches. I am painfully, terribly, blissfully alive. There's a voice, a soft sobbing, and it's me. My own cracked, bleeding heart screaming its way back to life.

"You're supposed to be dead by now."

I recognize Bennett's voice at the same time that he looms into view above me, his face swimming in my smeared vision.

"You're supposed to be at Columbia."

He laughs. "I was. Six months ago. A few pictures is all it took to fool you. Ty and Owen were helpful with that post, though—giving me cover for a made-up girl on the side."

He winks, and I am repulsed.

"But your grandma. The yarn store."

"See, I thought you might start to suspect I wasn't being entirely truthful. Or hell, maybe you'd run into my grandma. So, I set up the backup story. Because what would make you believe in your boyfriend again more than a heartfelt confession like mine?"

I hear something in the distance. Soft, hiccupping sobs. Connor. Hope. I can't see the cages. I'm near the diving platforms, in a corner too far for them to see me either. I want to call out, to tell them I'm alive, but I'm not sure I can do that yet.

Because I haven't figured out how I'm going to stay alive. Bennett crouches by the ladder, close enough to reach me. There is no violent burst of energy; he is not like his brother. He plans and waits. Bennett takes his time. But when I see him tilt his head, I know he's ready to finish this.

"You fought harder than I thought you would." He clicks his tongue. "But I'll hold you under if that's what it takes."

And then his hands are on my shoulders and he is pushing

at my arms, dragging me off the ladder by my shirt. My hair. It's the river again, another boy trying to push me to the grave. And just like I did then, I wrap my limbs around the ladder holding on with strength I do not have. Connor shouts in a sudden burst of rage and grief.

I think I hear something in the distance. The faintest thumping above us. Bennett looks up, and I realize this is it—my one chance. I cannot swim away, so I do the only thing I can think of.

I pull him in.

Bennett's body tumbles over mine, almost dragging me off the ladder. I hold on, barely, and heave my body up one rung of the ladder.

"Cleo! Is that you?"

Connor. I groan, dragging myself up another rung. I hear something above us for sure. Is someone up there?

"I'm here," I croak out.

And then Bennett wraps his arms around my legs and yanks me so hard my chin hits the top rung. Blood and chlorine flood my mouth, and I am underwater again, tangled in the ladder. I manage to get my head up.

"Nice try," he snarls, slapping one large hand on the top of my head. "But unlike you, I can swim."

I hear the doors to the pool burst open as he pushes me under. I am still caught in the ladder, one foot pinned between the metal rungs and the wall of the pool. I am trapped and saved in the same moment, unable to be dragged under, but unable to climb out. Bennett suddenly releases my head, and his whole body shifts. He's going for the ladder. Climbing.

I pull my head out of the water and grab at his foot. He tries to kick me loose, but I hold.

"What are you doing?" Bennett screams. "Get the hell away from them."

I have no idea who he's talking to, but I hear footsteps. Commotion.

And then Connor's voice, clear and eager. "Get it open! The key! It's right there!"

Hope, pleading. "Please!"

I don't know who they're talking to. If someone is trying to help, Bennett will stop them. Unless I stop him first. He's on the top rung when I hook my arm hard around his leg. I put my whole body into it—finally wrenching my foot free, dragging with all of my weight.

"Get off me!"

Bennett pulls his foot free and kicks me square in the chest. There's a commotion at the other end of the pool. Voices. I'm slipping under when I hear footsteps. Running. Connor roars and there is an awful crashing. And then the clean splash of someone diving in.

I scrabble desperately underwater, disoriented. I can't see. I don't know where the ladder is. I don't know who's in the water, but if it's Bennett I can't fight him off again. This will be the end.

An arm hooks around my waist and I thrash, but there is no

use. I'm moving quickly, being dragged backward in sure, heavy strokes. I can see and hear nothing but the rush of water. And then my head is above the surface. My arm is hooked over the top of the ladder.

"Can you hold on?"

Hope. It's Hope's voice, and I don't understand. She was locked in the cage.

"Cleo, can you hold this? I'm going to get you out."

I try to answer, but I launch into a coughing fit that makes me gag and gasp. She climbs out and then grabs me under the armpits, dragging me up rung by rung. I flop onto the floor like a rag doll, and Hope stretches me out, rolling me to my side. My coughing slows, and my eyes open. The world is a dark smear.

I hear voices. Shouting.

My vision clears, and the scene unfolds with a shock.

Aiden is here. Aiden is near the bleachers, still holding the locker keys. And Connor is kneeling over something, his arms moving. Punching something. I blink and drag myself up. He's hitting Bennett.

"You're killing him," Aiden cries.

"Piece of shit." Connor is panting. He isn't hitting him now. His arms are rigid. "You piece of shit."

There is a dark smear of blood on his mouth. His shirt is torn at the collar. But his hands are wrapped around Bennett's throat and Bennett is choking. Arms flailing.

I remember blood and dirt in my mouth. My vision going black at the edges.

"No," I croak. And then, much louder, "Connor, no! Stop!"

My brother looks over at me, relief transforming his face in the span of a breath. His eyes soften, and he loosens his grip. Bennett bucks. Anger renewed, Connor turns back to his task with a grimace.

"Stop!" I roll onto my stomach and push myself up with quaking arms. I'm on my knees, Hope behind me. "Don't do this. Stop!"

"The cops are on their way," Aiden says. "I called them as soon as I heard shouting."

"Connor," I say again, because his jaw is clenched, and I can tell he's still squeezing Bennett's neck. Maybe not hard enough to kill him, but close. "Please don't do this. We have to move forward. Remember? We have to move on."

"Please," Hope says, and Connor's eyes flick to her.

Anguish fills his features, and he releases Bennett. Lurches back.

"Block those doors," Connor says to Aiden. He's nodding at the set of doors that leads into the pool. There's a second door on the left—a service door—but when Connor leaps off, that's exactly where he goes.

Bennett launches to his feet and looks around like a wounded animal. His left eye is horribly swollen. Half of his mouth too. It still makes no sense to me, this monster spinning in circles, desperate for a way out. How is this the silly boy who ate Lucky Charms with me and asked about toothpaste flavors? How is this the boy who introduced me to his grandma?

"What's your name?" I ask him, my voice like parched gravel. "Your real name."

Because I have kissed this boy. Held his hand. Stayed on the phone too late and shared pints of ice cream. Before tonight, he was good and kind. He was my way back to normal.

"What's your name?" I repeat.

He looks at me, and I see a flicker of something in his good eye. Regret, maybe? Or more wishful thinking? He slumps onto the ground then, maybe seeing the futility. Maybe giving up. I don't know, but the look of resignation on his face will stay with me forever.

"Shawn." It's Aiden who speaks, but Bennett turns automatically, so that must be it. Shawn. Not Bennett.

"His name is Shawn," Aiden repeats. "He's here because of me."

"You sent him?" Hope asks, aghast.

"I saw you push him," Aiden says to me instead. His voice is broken. *He* is broken. "I was on the bridge. I was high, but I know what I saw. You were arguing, and you pushed him."

"It was more than an argument," I say.

"He wasn't trying to kill you," he says, but he flinches in the middle of the word. Like he can't quite make himself believe it.

"He was strangling me," I say. "Another thirty seconds, and I would have died."

He shakes his head. "You pushed him in. And I couldn't do anything. I was wasted—just—gone. I saw him go under the bridge, I watched him. There was nothing I could do. And then Hope was there on the other side, right at the water's edge."

Aiden turns to her.

"You could have grabbed him. You could have helped."

Hope doesn't answer. Her face is schooled to blankness, her eyes flat and unmoving. I think of her cold fury in the car outside of Madison's. And I know in this moment that none of us will ever know how close Hope was to the water or whether or not she could have saved Declan. My gut tells me she will take that secret to the grave.

"Why didn't you just tell?" I ask.

"Valerie wouldn't let me. Probation. My word against yours." Aiden shrugs and then looks at Connor. "I didn't remember recording you. I found it later and then I got Shawn's number from a group text Declan sent us."

"Aiden sent you the video?" I look at Bennett. He doesn't look up at me now. His head is between his legs like he's trying not to pass out. Or maybe about to get sick. "When? When did this happen?"

"Three weeks before I moved," Bennett says. Except I guess it isn't Bennett. It's Shawn. He still doesn't look up; his confession is aimed at the tiled floor between his legs. "I knew the cops wouldn't do shit. There was no crime. It was the word of one drunk kid on probation against all of you. So, I moved to Columbus. I made a plan."

"Just like that. You moved."

"We have family here," he says. "Our grandma. Our uncle."

I shake my head, feeling foggy. "Declan said he had no one here."

"Because they hated him too. Just like you. He was supposed to live here, but Grandma was afraid she couldn't handle him. They didn't get along."

Something in Shawn's face tells me that there's more to that grandma story. Something more violent, I'd bet. But I'm too weak to ask.

"What about your uncle?" I try.

"He sometimes let Declan come by his place for a night or two, but he didn't want to deal with him either. But he'd leave stuff there sometimes. And my uncle got the box of things from your mom. That's where I got all that shit."

But not everything was in that box. "You had my nail file."

"At my uncle's. In the guest room. And I knew what it was the second I saw it, because Declan told me what you did with that file, Cleo. He called me and laughed about what a spitfire you were."

My mouth goes sour with saliva. I hear footsteps outside. A muted commotion.

"He told me everything," Shawn says, seeming lost in himself. "Every date, every little fight, every bitchy thing you did. The names you called. What you did to his hand. And he loved you anyway."

He looks at me like it revolts him to admit this and I feel numb with shock. I can't sort the ways his truth is twisted. To Shawn, I am the monster in the corner, not the girl bleeding on the floor. All those phone calls with Declan gave him the stories, the places—had had all of the pieces to this mystery. But he put the puzzle together upside down and inside out.

A voice calls from the hallway. "Police!"

"We're in here," Aiden calls out.

"You did all of this," I whisper. "Moved to another state. Pieced together these clues. Planned all of this. This was four months of your life for what? For revenge?"

Shawn looks right at me, and I can see the despair in his eyes. "What would you do for your brother?"

The police burst through the pool doors seconds later, and I tense, searching for Connor. Hope is already there, squeezing his hand, making it clear Connor isn't a threat. There is a whirlwind of shouts and movement, but my mind is a clear and quiet place. When they place the handcuffs on Shawn's hands, I hear his words again.

What would you do for your brother?

She's been really worried about the police interacting with Connor up to this point, but this action does seem a bit calm. Would she be more worried? Would Connor?

OK if no, just noting that I did notice in this scene that her worries for him didn't come out as much as they have in other spots with police.

I lean into his side and think of the picture in the hallway, his arms around my baby self. I think of him putting Pop-Tarts on a plate. Helping me draw my sevens the right way.

And the answer is simple: anything.

I would do anything.

THIRTY-ONE

31 HOURS LATER

THESE ARE OUR SEVEN DIRTY SECRETS.

I caused Declan to fall.

Hope saw him in the water and did nothing.

Aiden saw it all from above on the bridge.

Jack didn't hate Declan, but he didn't like him enough to care.

Valerie used her head to save her brother.

Connor played the hero to save me.

And Declan wound up dead.

I have to live with my part in that. I pushed Declan into the water. He drowned because of my choice. A choice I'm finally ready to talk about and should have talked about long ago.

Connor shifts beside me, looking up the limestone building with the lions on either side. Steps lead to the police station's double doors, and To Protect and Serve is etched over the entrance. On my other side, Hope stands calm and still.

"You literally got your scholarship acceptance this morning," he asks. "And you want to celebrate by...giving your statement to the police?"

"Well we don't exactly have a choice," I say. The police made it clear we'd all need to come in to talk after getting medical treatment and a bit of rest. They made it easy for all of us. Shawn didn't say much more at the pool, and I get the impression he didn't say much after he got to the station, because the police haven't called to move up our appointments.

But it wouldn't matter if they asked. I need to do this anyway. I can't keep on like this, with the past lurking just behind me, a shadow waiting to tug me back.

"Nothing is going to happen to you," Hope says. She's dressed in a blazer and khakis and looks determined to get through this. I think she's saying it to comfort herself as much as me, because I'm not the only one who has to give a statement.

I squeeze her hand, because I can't agree that nothing is going to happen. We don't know that for sure, but we can hope. Maybe they'll hear our stories and take the reports and send us on our way, but it could be different than that.

I could lose my scholarship.

There could be charges brought against me.

I could go to jail.

The truth is, I'll have to live with my choices. I have no idea if I'll live happily ever after. But I know I'll live.

A car door slams behind us and I turn, shocked to see Valerie behind the wheel parking. Aiden has stepped out of the passenger seat. He's cut his hair and shaved. He still looks tired, but he manages to look me in the eye.

"Hi," Hope says, sounding surprised.

"Hey," I say, and then, because there's literally nowhere else to go with a conversation outside of a police station, I continue. "What are you doing here?"

"Valerie knew you were coming down here," he says. "I tried to call, but your phone went straight to voicemail."

"I have it in Do Not Disturb other than the police," I admit.

"Well, I wanted you to know that I talked to the police yesterday. I thought you should hear what I said."

"Oh." I swallow hard and try to keep my knees from going rubbery. He saw me push Declan, and I don't know how he framed that. But it doesn't matter. No more secrets, no more lies; if I'm telling the truth, I have to support Aiden doing it too.

"Did you ever tell her all of what happened that day?" Aiden asks Hope.

Hope shakes her head, looking a little ashamed.

"We confronted Declan that day," he tells me. "We all decided an intervention was a good idea. Everyone except Jack, that is. He wasn't too happy to be dragged into it."

Hope swallows hard, and seems to make up her mind. "When Valerie took you off for that walk, that was planned. We did it so we could talk to Declan."

"Why didn't you tell me?" I ask.

"I was focused on not killing Declan with my bare hands when we were there," Connor said. "But later, it felt pointless."

Hope nods. "It felt like a thing that would just upset you more."

I shake my head. "I don't understand. Why would it upset me?"

"Because we confronted him for hurting you," Aiden says, looking down. "We said we all thought you were both better off apart. He was furious with us and took off into the woods, and I couldn't find him. None of us could, and everyone was out there. Hope wanted to find you. Connor went after her. Valerie came after me because I was maybe even more messed up than Declan. Even Jack was out wandering around, but none of us found him."

"He found me instead," I say softly.

"I saw him choking you," Aiden says, and he forces his eyes up. Looks right at me. "I know I played it off as just a fight, because I didn't want to admit the truth. But they needed to know that too. They needed to know that I saw what he did to you."

"Why didn't you ever say this before?" I ask.

"It didn't feel real. You looked so small, like a doll he was throwing around. I thought he was playing at first or that I was dreaming it up. I was so messed up. I don't know. But I knew you were in trouble and I just froze. When you pushed him in. When he floated right underneath me. I just stood there, watching, knowing it was partly my fault too. It took me forever to even pull out my phone and start taping and by then it was just empty ground. And then Connor, obviously."

"It wasn't your fault," I say. "You didn't do anything."

Aiden laughs. "Yes, I did. That's why I didn't talk. It wasn't Valerie or the probation shit. It was because I knew it wasn't just your push that put Declan into that water. It was a hundred little pushes, and I was one of them."

"Why did you call Bennett—I mean, Shawn? Why him instead of the police?"

"The police weren't going to bring Declan back. But I thought someone in his family should know what really happened. I felt like I had to confess. Shawn was on a group text with me and Declan. Nothing regular—just a place he'd send funny shit sometimes, you know? Anyway, a while after Declan died, Shawn started texting the chat. He kept asking me questions about the two of you. He got me to send that video. I swear, he never said he wanted to do anything. I just thought he wanted to know because it was his brother."

"You never even told us that Declan had a brother," Connor says.

"I had no reason to think you didn't know," Aiden says. "Anyway, I didn't know what he'd do. And I had no idea Shawn was Bennett then."

"How'd you figure that out?"

"I didn't," he says. "Valerie did. After we had pizza, I told Valerie about the video, because it was pretty obvious that either Declan was alive or Shawn was messing with you two. I tried to text him, to tell him to be cool or I'd go to the police, but he reminded me that the police would have some questions for me about why I kept this video from them for so long. And then Hope called, thinking I'd planned it. And I just froze because she was right about a lot of it. It was my video. I did see you push him. But I didn't know how to explain."

"I helped him start tracking back before Hope even called," Valerie says. "It took a while to find him, but I eventually found the connection on an old social media account—someone that was friends with a friend of Declan. There was a picture from a few years back where a much younger Bennett was tagged as Shawn. Shawn Bennett, to be precise. That's when we both started realizing that Bennett had spent months planning this. Coordinating every little thing." She shudders and looks down.

"Thank God you came," I say to Aiden. "But how did you know? It was the middle of the night."

"When Hope called to accuse me she said she knew I was at the pool and she was coming to talk to me. She was absolutely sure it was me."

"I was," Hope says, cheeks flushed. "I'm sorry."

"It wasn't that hard to figure out what pool," Aiden says, "and I don't know... I just had a bad feeling. I didn't even know Shawn would be there."

"You said you found a picture?" I ask Valerie.

She turns her phone to show me. And there they are, Bennett and Declan. It's the picture of Declan that was printed in his room. Left on the corkboard. Only now I can see the other half of the photo, where Bennett is grinning beside him, a sliver of beach to his left. Florida probably, but it's the faces I'm looking at. Two boys I loved once. Same chins. Same shoulders. Brothers.

"I still can't believe he went so far," Hope said. "Who would do that? Who would throw away their life to get back at someone?"

"A brother," Connor says. And he looks at me. "When your whole life you only have each other…"

Valerie lifts her chin. "You'd do anything to keep them safe."

Hope nods, her cheeks faintly pink. But she'll say no more. As an only child, she knows this is beyond the world she understands.

I take a bracing breath and square my shoulders, looking at the door.

"You ready?" Connor asks.

I think of Declan's voice in the video, the words an echo of a past that feels far too close.

I close my eyes in the shade and when I open them again, the sun is bright. I guess the past is always with me, but that's not where I am. It's where I was. I take a breath and nod at my brother, because whatever happens next, we'll face it together.

And, yes, I am ready.

ACKNOWLEDGMENTS

EACH BOOK IS A BIT OF A MIRACLE, BUT WRITING THROUGH a pandemic was difficult in ways I won't soon forget. It's always hard to not make this section its own chapter, to fill long pages with the many people who contribute to my writing. With this book that is especially true.

Thank you to my editor, Eliza Swift, who understood this book and my writing in a way that I can only describe as editorial magic. I am so lucky to be working with this brilliant woman. And speaking of brilliant women, I would be utterly lost in the publishing universe without my outstanding agent super duo, Suzie Townsend and Dani Segelbaum, who always have the best questions and the wisest answers. Thank you also to my talented Sourcebooks dream team. Cassie, Beth, Jackie, Caitlin, and so many others—you are all stars, and I am lucky.

There are friends and family that kept me going on long, tough days. To Edie, Margaret, and Lisa, for a distant lawn lunch that turned my whole week around. I am grateful to call you my friends. To Robin and Sheri, who are always up for a night of laughs and a kick in the pants when needed. To Leigh Anne, Tiff, Sharon, Sheila, Angela, and Debi: thank you for making it easy to fall right into step even when time and distance keep us apart more than we'd like. And a very special thank-you to Ben, Ben, Vic, and Lacey. Sometimes a bonfire and good conversation is enough to keep a writer writing. (Artichokes and tacos don't hurt either.) And to Jody. Every book, every morning call, every ranty text. You are the Hope to my Cleo forever and ever.

A special note to Shaina Berry. Your friendship and laughter saved my bacon on those cold, dark MCNA mornings. You bring a lot of goodness and light into everyone's world—lean into all that goodness in you, lady. You were born amazing for a reason.

And finally to God, who I assume planted all these seeds of stories in my soul for a reason, and to my lovely family who handles my bonkers deadline hours and coffee requests with admirable grace and good humor. And a small note to my giant dog Wookiee, who cannot read but makes every writing day a little bit easier by always being there to warm my feet and steal my bagels.

ABOUT THE AUTHOR

Lifelong Ohioan Natalie D. Richards writes books that will keep you up way past your bedtime. A champion of literacy and aspiring authors, Richards is a frequent speaker at schools, libraries, and writing groups. In addition to writing, she spends her days working at a local public library. Richards lives with her wonderful family in Columbus, Ohio. When she's not writing or reading, you can probably find her wrangling Wookiee, her enormous dust mop of a dog.

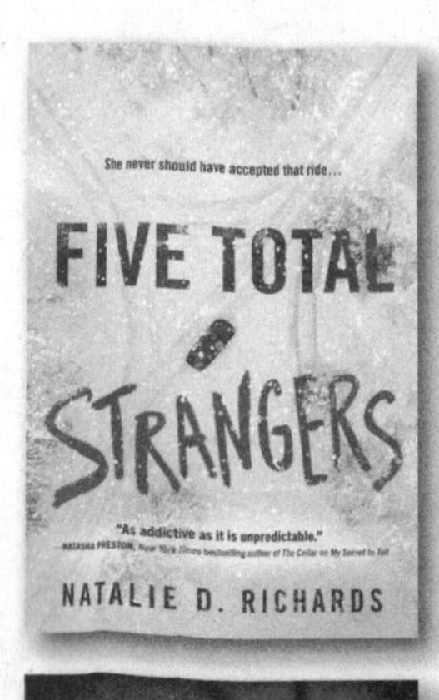

She never should have accepted that ride...
FIVE TOTAL STRANGERS
"As addictive as it is unpredictable."
NATALIE D. RICHARDS

"Brimming with suspense and intrigue."
ONE WAS LOST
NATALIE D. RICHARDS
AUTHOR OF SIX MONTHS LATER AND GONE TOO FAR

"As addictive as it is unpredictable."
GONE TOO FAR
NATALIE D. RICHARDS

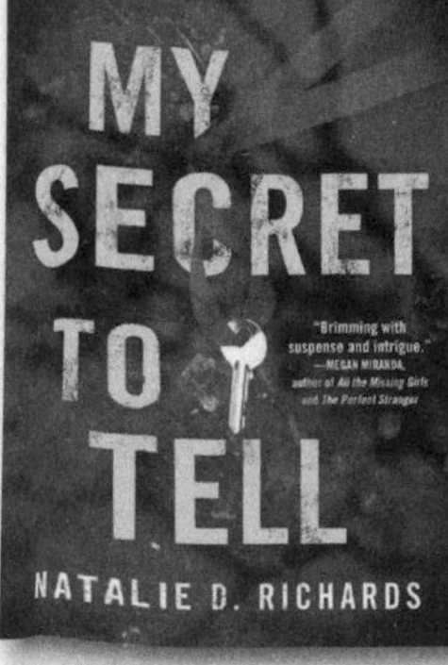

MY SECRET TO TELL
"Brimming with suspense and intrigue."
NATALIE D. RICHARDS

"A haunted love story about a couple who bring out the best—and worst—in each other."
—MINDY McGINNIS, author of The Female of the Species
WE ALL FALL DOWN
NATALIE D. RICHARDS
AUTHOR OF ONE WAS LOST AND SIX MONTHS LATER

WHAT YOU HIDE
NATALIE D. RICHARDS
AUTHOR OF ONE WAS LOST AND SIX MONTHS LATER